THE WISDOM OF THE SAND

Philosophy and Frank Herbert's *Dune*

Critical Bodies
Joseph J. Pilotta, *series editor*

The Body in Human Inquiry: Interdisciplinary Explorations of Embodiment
Vincente Berdayes, Luigi Esposito, and John W. Murphy (eds.)

Knowledge and the Production of Non-knowledge: An Exploration of Alien
Mythology in Post-War America
Mark Featherstone

The New Age Ethic and the Spirit of Postmodernity
Carmen Kuhling

Abjection and Corrections in Ethnographic Studies: Communication Issues in the
Cultural Tourism of Isla Mujeres, Mexico
Jill Adair McCaughan

Seductive Aesthetics of Postcolonialism
Rekha Menon

The Divine Complex and Free Thinking
Algis Mickunas

Plato's Cave: Television and its Discontents (rev. ed.)
John O'Neill

The Sensuous Difference: From Marx to This ... and More
Joseph J. Pilotta and Jill Adair McCaughan

The Fate of Philosophy
Arvydas Sliogeris

Why I Still Want My MTV
Kevin C. Williams

The Wisdom of the Sand: Philosophy and Frank Herbert's *Dune*
Kevin C. Williams

forthcoming

Phenomenology, Body Politics, and the Future of Communication Theory
Hwa Kol Jung (ed.)

Hispanic Tele-visions
Elizabeth Lozano

The Logic of Cultural Studies
Algis Mickunas and Joseph J. Pilotta

Body Works: Essays on Modernity and Morality
John O'Neill

An Introduction to Niklas Luhmann
Wei-San Sun

THE WISDOM OF THE SAND

Philosophy and Frank Herbert's *Dune*

Kevin C. Williams

Shepherd University

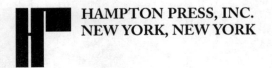

HAMPTON PRESS, INC.
NEW YORK, NEW YORK

Printed in the United States of America

Library of Congress Cataloging-in-Publication Data

Williams, Kevin C.
   Wisdom of the sand : philosophy and Frank Herbert's Dune / Kevin C. Williams.
      p. cm. — (Hampton Press communication series. Critical bodies)
   Includes bibliographical references and indexes.
   ISBN 978-1-61289-008-1 (hardbound) — ISBN 978-1-61289-009-8 (paperbound)
   1. Herbert, Frank. Dune series.   2. Science fiction, American—History and criticism.   3. Dune (Imaginary place)   I. Title.
   PS3558.E63Z95 2011
   813'.54—dc22   2011005788

Hampton Press, Inc.
307 Seventh Ave.
New York, NY 10001

For TC and Pooh Dog, and for my family, friends and students

Contents

List of Illustrations/Figures

List of Illustrations

List of Figures

Acknowledgments

Special thanks go to series editor Joe Pilotta for selecting this text for publication; he is responsible for the publication of many outstanding books on the phenomena of communication. Barbara Bernstein and everybody at Hampton Press have been extremely helpful.

Assistant editor Casey Forbes has spent many hours reviewing this manuscript. He was especially helpful when cutting the seven hundred pages of the original monograph down to a more manageable three or four hundred. His insights and labors have been invaluable.

Danielle Corsetto has provided beautiful artwork. Additional art credit goes to Nick Dachris who donated some excellent pictures to this book. Unfortunately, due to spatial limits, these had to be removed from the final version. They can be seen at: <http://www.starcry.gr/nddesign.htm>. Both Danielle and Nick have created visual renderings of the later *Dune* books that are rarely pictured and thus contribute greatly to the visualization of *The Chronicles*.

Research for this manuscript was made possible in part by grants from the Shepherd University Committee for Faculty Development and the office of the Vice President of Academic Affairs. Shepherd University is very supportive of research that is equally creative and reflective.

My wife, TC Williams, has been right beside me through the writing and editing of this book and indeed every aspect of my everyday life. She, along with my parents and in-laws, foster an atmosphere of love in which the daily task of writing is a pleasure.

My thought is but an extension of the insights of my teachers and their teachers before them. Roger Johnson, Imafadon Olaye, Jenny Nelson, David Descutner, Algis Mickunas, Elizabeth Lozano (who contributed greatly to the original essay of which this book is an extension), dug cooper, Linda Tate, John Bardy and Bradley Sanders, as well as others, form a background or context of which this text speaks. Much of the present text is inspired by their words. It is no longer possible to tell where they end and I begin. Please allow me to cite them here as contributing to every phrase in this book.

Some material was previously published or presented: Imperialism & Globalization: Lessons from Frank Herbert's *Dune*, *Reconstruction*, Summer 2003, 3(3), <http://www.reconstruction.ws>; Politics & Power: Communicative Action in Frank Herbert's *Dune*, *Integrative Investigations*, 2001, 7(1); Communicative Action in Frank Herbert's *Dune*, presented at the XXIII meeting of the Jean Gebser Society for the Study of Culture & Consciousness, Athens, OH; The Communication of History in Frank Herbert's Dune, presented at the 1993 meeting of the International Communication Association, Washington, DC; The Dimensions of History & Historical Consciousness in Frank Herbert's Dune, presented at the XI meeting of the Jean Gebser Society for the Study of Culture & Consciousness, Shippensburg, PA. All material has been substantially modified and reprinted with permission.

Finally, I owe a great debt to the inspirational work of Frank Herbert. The only words necessary are "thank you."

Abbreviations

To conserve space, the titles of *The Dune Chronicles* (*Dune, Dune Messiah, Children of Dune, God Emperor of Dune, Heretics of Dune* and *Chapterhouse: Dune*) will be abbreviated in footnote citations as: *Dune, Messiah, Children, God Emperor, Heretics* and *Chapterhouse*. Also, because footnotes are used throughout, books that are referenced many times are cited first in the text; following the first citation, the name and title is given and the full citation is referenced to the bibliography.

Foreword

The more I find out, the more I realize that I don't know what's going on.
How fortunate that you have discovered the way to wisdom.[1]

This book originated from a single essay written while I was taking a history course. The essay used Herbert's fictional accounts of history and historians to reflect on nonfictional history and to challenge the naïve notion that history was a true representation of the past—as it "really" was. The primary text for the course was Jacques Barzun and Henry Graff's *The Modern Researcher*.[2] The central thesis of their book concerns the integration of researching and reporting with a strong emphasis on good writing and is very sound. However, its notions of pragmatic history and its assumptions about the nature of research were, in my estimation, shot through with unexamined and too easily accepted metaphysics.

The college course celebrated the historian as the master of technique, the finder of facts, and the revealer of the (absolute) truth about the (singular) past. The idea that finding and employing the right method (that is, technique) would lead to certain and infallible knowledge, coupled with the idea that facts were absolute and simply waiting to be uncovered by the right method, and tied to the belief that facts uncovered by such a method would lead to The Truth, seemed to me presumptuous (especially as I was reading Gadamer's *Truth and Method* at that time). If one studies communication and discourse (i.e., the limits imposed on what statements can be made on a given subject), it becomes apparent that human knowledge and understanding appear through the phenomena of communication, which include other phenomena such as interests, values, and so on. The academic study of the past is oriented toward an unexplicated future project—the project of education itself. Although it is most common to think of communication as a transmission of information, communication both disseminates knowledge and is the appearance of that knowledge. The phenomena of that appearance cannot be taken for granted.

The course text book was aptly titled *The Modern Researcher*. Its guiding stars—the assumptions that facts lead to truth, that method (as technique) leads to facts, that history unfolds in linear time, and that history is teleological (i.e., goal oriented)—are *modern* assumptions. In order to explore these assumptions, I began looking for insights not in communication theory (I wanted to stay clear of esoteric work), but in popular literature. I found critiques of modern thought in general and history in specific—a postmodern philosophy of history—in Frank Herbert's *Dune Chronicles*. Although Barzun and Graff are correct when they say that "fiction is not history,"[3] it is also the case that documents have a historical dimension. They speak to us, in our current language, of a past as perceived in the present. Moreover, as Herbert turned his percipient gaze toward the myopia of modern civilization, *The Chronicles* are a historical document that reflect on that status of knowledge in a world informed by Jungian psychoanalysis, quantum physics, postmodern art, and general semantics. *The Dune Chronicles* present a historicity (a living and authentic expression of history) of historiography (a study of historical writing) and open a way for cultural studies. Herbert's work can be read as an examination of cultural presuppositions and values concerning taken-for-granted phenomena such as history.[4]

Over a period of several years, the term paper I wrote for this history class became several research papers. These were presented for peer review at various national and international communication and philosophy conferences. Two essays derived from these presentations were published.[5] For the most part, however, my files sat in digital oblivion from about 1992 until 1999.

In 1999, Brian Herbert and Kevin J. Anderson began publishing the *Dune* preludes. By 2001, I knew that it was time to open the old files and begin writing again. I found that the *Duniverse* had vastly expanded during my time away from it; I stepped back into Heraclitus' river to find a much swifter current. The Internet and World Wide Web made it possible for numerous listservs, usenet groups, and web pages to emerge. Discussing minute details of *The Dune Chronicles* has become, to a notable extent, fashionable. Semidormant texts such as Herbert's wonderful *Listening to the Left Hand*, out-of-print books such as the *Dune Encyclopedia* and O'Reilly's *Frank Herbert*, as well as production notes on the *Dune* movies (those realized as well as those that fell by the wayside) were put online (at least in part) or made available for the first time; these precious materials are all now widely and freely disseminated.

The *Dune* universe is indeed alive and growing. With such a wealth of material available, it is a good time for those inspired by Herbert's contribution to humanity. *The Wisdom of the Sand: Philosophy of Frank Herbert's Dune* emerges from this fertile context.

Notes

1. Dialogue between Duncan Idaho and Leto Atreides. *God Emperor of Dune*, 223.

2. Jacques Barzun and Henry Graff, *The Modern Researcher* (San Diego: Harcourt Brace Jovanovich, 1975).

3. Barzun, ibid., 250.

4. For a simple example of the inclusive and exclusive nature of discourse consider that it is possible to talk about the earth as being a flat disk (inclusion), even in the face of evidence (e.g., the appearance of a ship's sail as it sets against the horizon), until one sees the earth from space. Although one can still discuss the geometry and flatness of our experience of land, the idea that the planet is a flat disc is now excluded from discourse. You would find great difficulty publishing a paper, within the current discourse, claiming that the planet was a flat disk. See Michel Foucault's *Archeology of Knowledge* and *The Order of Things* for continued study.

5. "Imperialism & Globalization: Lessons from Frank Herbert's Dune," *Reconstruction* (Summer 2003: 3(3) <http://www.reconstruction.ws>). "Politics & Power: Communicative Action in Frank Herbert's Dune," *Integrative Investigations*, 7(1), 2001.

Preface
A Mentat's Handbook v2.0

Thou shalt not make a machine in the likeness of the human mind.[1]

The Mentat

The Butlerian Jihad, or Great Revolt as it is sometimes called, was a war waged by humans against the intelligent machines that dominated and enslaved humans. After the war, all thinking machines (computers) were outlawed, and the Mentat school was developed to train humans to perform the complex calculations that computers performed so well. As "human computers" the Mentats had powerful cognitive and analytical ability. However, Mentats are not simply human calculators. Mentats draw on human intuition, perception, and ingenuity, and thus, they transcend mere hyper-logical hypothesizing or calculating. Mentats are supreme interpreters. They engage problems with as few preconceptions as possible. They think along multiple thought-ways, integrate several ways of knowing, and propose prime computations in their problem-solving capacity.[2]

The Mentats served the Great and Minor Houses of the Empire until the reign of Leto II, The God Emperor. In a monumental effort to steer the course of humanity along what Leto called The Golden Path, the Mentats were destroyed. However, some survived and the tradition was maintained underground by the Bene Gesserit Sisterhood.

The Handbook v2.0

Philosophy is always dangerous because it promotes the creation of new ideas.[3]

Illustration 1. Frank Herbert

Frank Herbert wrote six novels now called *The Dune Chronicles*. They include: *Dune, Dune Messiah, Children of Dune, God Emperor of Dune, Heretics of Dune* and *Chapterhouse: Dune*. They were published between 1963 and 1985. He was working on a seventh *Dune* novel when he died in 1986.[4] *The Chronicles* provide an overview of the ebb and flood of the Atreides, descendants of the ancient Greek House Atreus of Mycenae.[5]

Each book of *The Chronicles* contains a narrative and fragments from other texts such as *The Manual of Muad'Dib* and *The Stolen Journals*.[6] Each text within the text provides commentary on the story from a particular point of view. The reader is positioned in a manifold hermeneutic.[7] She is able to see the events of the novel from various points of view, each with its cultural, social and political biases brought to bear on the text.

One of the texts is *The Mentat Handbook*. *The Mentat Handbook v2.0* culls from the pages of *The Chronicles* and the remaining fragments of the old *Mentat Handbook's* theories and methods used in Mentat training—and more, as this book draws on all of *The Chronicles*. Like any work built on fragments of another, the text you now hold in your hands is not a reproduction or representation of the older material. It is a new book with all the advantages and disadvantages that writing has to offer the reader.

The French philosopher Maurice Merleau-Ponty noted that reading, interpreting and writing are not objective acts; the author is not an absolute authority.[8] We never simply appropriate a writer's thoughts (indeed, we never fully possess our own), and our interpretations are never truly disinterested. When we comment on any text, we come toward an understanding of the author's thoughts only through the world that he or she opens.

Moreover, a commentary on a text cannot reveal the author's intent because it is not a true dialogue; after all, the interpreter both asks and answers the questions. Thus, this book claims to be neither "objective" nor "disinterested." Rather, the objectives and interests of this work can easily be spelled out in advance. (1) We seek to learn from *Dune's* uncommon wisdom the Mentat's way of perception. (2) We seek to interpret these *Chronicles* in the terms of these times and within the purview of contemporary communicology and cultural studies. Thus, this book, *The Wisdom of the Sand*, or *Handbook v2.0* does not reiterate the original, but is a new text that draws on the wisdom found in the books of *Dune* as apprehended in this light. It is a noncanonical, perhaps heretical attempt to relearn how to think and act. Think of it as a *Dune companion*.

Palimpsest

The Wisdom of the Sand is a palimpsest and companion book to *The Dune Chronicles*.

> Flesh . . . a palimpsest upon which the Tleilaxu could write almost anything.[9]

> A . . . surface upon which the Tleilaxu had written . . . what?[10]

A palimpsest is simply a manuscript page or scroll that is written on, scratched off, and written over. Like Freud's mystical writing pad, traces of the earlier work remain visible. Likewise, *The Wisdom of the Sand* was composed by reading and typing excerpts from *The Chronicles* into a word processor. Written above, below, and next to these words were my reflections on those passages. Passages were added and subtracted over more than a ten-year period, until the present text remains. This method is not very far removed from Herbert's paradigmatic style of writing.[11]

This palimpsest of *Dune* is not a "pure" text, but it is a "flesh," a meeting or *chiasm* in which the integration of two texts produces a third, which is related to, but different from, both.[12] Thus, the present volume makes no claim to suggest what *The Chronicles* "really" mean. Such a meaning is reserved for each of us in the pleasure of reading. This is a new book, more an act of creation or recreation than official interpretation.

In fact, we may go further and suggest that all writing has a palimpsestual dimension. Ideas are written on top of other ideas. In a sense, science fiction, for Herbert, was less a genre of fiction and more a vocabulary for expressing that ancient form of fire-circle speech—the *fantastic tale*.[13] Herbert's writing is not a development of previous science fiction as found in H.G. Wells or Jules Verne, for example. Indeed, Herbert's literary pedigree is not two hundred years old, but at least three thousand.[14] The Chronicles draw on *The Bible*, *The Bhagavad Gita*, *The Mahabarata*, *The Iliad* and *The Odyssey*, *Gilgamesh*, *Le Morte de Arthur*, and *Beowulf*, as well as Shakespeare, Sophocles, Dostoevsky, The Tao Te Ching, and modern sources.[15] This is to say that Herbert's writing is profoundly *original*, not in the sense that original means unique or somehow "freaky," but that he speaks from textual, and hence human, origins—an archeology of sorts. His work relates to a field of human expression and mutual intersignification. Thus, *Dune* draws upon classic themes in a contemporary epic.

Like *Oedipus Tyrannous*, *Dune* is a tragedy, of oracle and fate, of the blind prophet and the flawed man, who walks into the wasteland to die.[16] Like Alexander the Great, the protagonist has the greatest teachers, and his victories blur the boundaries between mortality and divinity. Like *Henry V*, Paul learns the mood of his people by walking among them. Like Christ in Dostoyevsky's *Brothers Karamazov*, Paul is taken down, even killed, by the Church established in his name.[17] Like Paul of Tarsus, Paul Atreides has a cosmic and mystical experience. Both undergo religious conversion. Both establish a Church that will grow far beyond any original intentions. These references are not examples of plagiarism. Rather, they reveal the depths into which Herbert's words descend as he taps the very origin of human perception through the classic works of human expression. This ability to use artistic creation and literary sources, more than any specific theory, is one of the lessons that psychoanalysis provides: we are myth-makers, and the myths we make are the myths we live by. Freud took up classic literature, such as the Oedipus cycle, and set a course toward understanding cultural pathology. Herbert does the same as he draws from ancient and modern sources to flesh out ill assumptions and common pathologies.

In the tradition of the great epic poets, Herbert narrates an account of persons in such a way as to reveal social and cultural beliefs, and more importantly cultural presuppositions that arise when interpretations are accepted as facts. Herbert's tales thus stand in relationship to the issues of today in the manner that the tragedies written by Aeschylus, Sophocles, and Euripides would have to the ancient Greeks—a living commentary. To locate the characters in this greater history and bring them to life, Herbert constructs his characters, concepts, and plot through the character's inner voices, dialogues, and texts-within-texts, such as historical interpretations of an event or person.[18]

Herbert's use of inner dialogue has been compared to Shakespeare's technique of asides, in which an actor will state his or her thoughts in direct address to the audience; Herbert augments this technique by placing significant inner thoughts in italics.[19] Duke Leto, for example, reveals his complex concern for his son:

> *The truth could be worse than he imagines, but even dangerous facts are valuable if you've been trained to deal with them..... This must be leavened, though; he is young.*[20]

The characters of *The Chronicles* may be interpreted in the same spirit as the ancient Greek gods and goddesses.[21] Those who study Herbert's work (e.g., O'Reilly, Touponce, Brentor, Palumbo, and McNelly) have noted that even the minor characters of the *Dune* universe appear to be superhuman or godlike by common standards. The Greek gods can be seen as the incarnation of physical and psychic phenomena: Poseidon is the raging sea; Aphrodite is the wiles of love. In a similar fashion, the characters of *The Chronicles* are the phenomena of *Dune* personified. Characters, situations, even entire planets illuminate the workings of mind, body, and world as analogs of the situations we face today—crises, terrorism, the scarcity of precious resources.[22]

For example, tradition tells us that prophets and messiahs are good; they lead the way; they save us; they deliver us from evil. But *what if a messiah or savior was dangerous to humanity?* What analog can Herbert draw? What "god" can he conjure that would provide an adequate image of and for our world? That is a goal of myth-making; to draw from life an image that explains through metaphor and analogy the workings of the spiritual and cultural world. We are given both the Prophet Paul Muad'Dib Atreides, and his son Leto II, the God Emperor.

Paul's plight has an all-too-real parallel in recent history (one obviously not intentionally planned but perhaps foreseen by Herbert). Today, the figure of Muad'Dib looms ever more darkly, not only in imagination but in reality.[23] Consider: The young Paul Atreides is betrayed by the Empire of which his family is a Major House and flees into the desert. There, he joins forces with a nomadic tribe of rebels who are downtrodden and already alienated from the "civilized" world. Together they form a religious-based, terrorist army of desert warriors (their language and custom based upon Earth's present Arab cultures). In a terrorist attack using forbidden weapons, this small band of warriors harness the powers of spirit, religion, revenge and justice and wage a war against the superpower—the Emperor of the Known Universe.

Commenting on Herbert's writing, Touponce suggests that *Dune* "does not merely represent. It always includes in itself the process of coming to knowledge whose process is also represented in the novel."[24] The author loses himself in a myriad of writings about writings, books about books. When Herbert writes about "plans within plans," he is at the same time literally showing the reader what multiplicity looks like.[25]

The Chronicles, through this pastiche and play, are a prime example of postmodern literature. As Touponce continues:

> *Dune* was not an aesthetic object to be contemplated, but rather each, reader and text, formed an ever-changing environment for the other during the act of reading.[26]

These prosaic inventions are themselves augmented by poetic devices.[27] Following Shakespeare and A.E. Van Vogt, and perhaps Tolkien, Herbert at times disguises standard, nonmetered prose via blank verse, unrhymed pentameter, sonnet, and even haiku.[28]

> Much of the prose in *Dune* started out as Haiku and then it was given minimal additional word padding to make it conform to English sentence structure.[29]

Perhaps even more significantly, given visual culture's eclipse of literacy in the late twentieth century, Herbert writes in a profoundly visual style.

> For *Dune*, I also used what I call a camera position method—playing back and forth (and in varied orders depending on the required pace) between long-shot, medium, close-up and so on.[30]

Color figures prominently (e.g., yellow signifies danger), and Herbert goes so far as to incorporate the visual meditation of a Jungian mandala.

> I often use a Jungian mandala in squaring off characters of a yarn against each other, assigning a dominant psychological role to each.[31]

The use of visual layering, of writing upon writing, of palimpsest, allows me to remain *true* to the text, to turn to "the text itself," as it were. The palimpsest is simply a means of checks and balances, a test of my humanity. It is the *gom jabbar* at my back:

> I hold at your back the gom jabbar. . . . It's a needle with a drop of poison on its tip. . . . It kills only animals. . . . Let us say I suggest that you may be human.[32]

The palimpsest is, then, "true" not because it is the "correct" interpretation, but because Herbert's words are next to mine. You can read both. You can judge for yourself.

Endnote: Hermeneutics

Schools of hermeneutics:[33]

1. Natural hermeneutics is the spontaneous, everyday, unreflective interpretation necessary when intersubjective understanding breaks down. Because natural—also called naïve—hermeneutics remains within the natural attitude, it remains uncritical.

2. Normative hermeneutics is the deliberate art of text interpretation by specialists. When a society is dominated by an organized religion or constitution, a high premium accrues when dogma or intent are challenged. The priest and the judge have a special authority they bring to bear on a text. As priest and judge act to conserve the status quo, normative hermeneutics also remain uncritical. Normative hermeneutics is practiced by the priests who corrupt Muad'Dib's teachings by turning his vision into a religion.

3. Scientific hermeneutics is the foundational discipline of the human sciences. It seeks a solid methodology of historical inquiry and verification.

> Historians exercise great power and some of them know it. They recreate the past, changing it to fit their own interpretations. Thus, they change the future as well.[34]

By presenting many histories, often revealing paradoxes and alternative interpretations, *The Chronicles* show us a fallacy of scientific hermeneutics.

4. Philosophical hermeneutics is a general philosophy of human existence. It claims that interpreting is less something that people do and more what people are—interpreters. Philosophical hermeneutics seeks to fill the void left by overcoming positivism and, in the absence of ultimate truths and absolutes, find "the conversation that we ourselves are" (Gadamer, drawing upon the German poet Holderlin). The Reverend Mother Taraza speaks to this condition when she says;

> We have long known that the objects of our palpable sense experiences can be influenced by choice. . . . I address a pragmatic relationship between belief and what we identify as 'real.'[35]

5. Depth hermeneutics is part of the effort to liberate people from dogma, error, and the superstitions; the "depths" include critical approaches to interpreting human activity such as power (Nietzsche and Foucault), political economy (Marx and Althusser), metaphysics (Derrida), the unconscious (Freud and Lacan) and the ways consciousness is structured (Husserl and Merleau-Ponty). Regarding power, The Princess Irulan says;

> A governed populace must be conditioned to accept power-words as actual things, to confuse the symbolized system with the tangible universe. In the

maintenance of such a power structure, certain symbols are kept out of the reach of common understanding.[36]

Notes

1. Orange Catholic Bible. *Dune*, 11–12. The Reverend Mother Gaius Helen Mohiam adds a qualifying statement: "Thou shalt not make a machine to counterfeit a human mind."

2. A prime computation should not be confused with a singular answer. The Mentat is prepared to respond and take responsibility for her response. If an answer to a problem appears to go wrong, accept responsibility and make corrections. For a description of the Mentat's overlay-integration-imagination methodology, follow a wormhole to Appendix B.

3. Taraza. *Heretics*, 449.

4. For reviews of the *Dune* series see William Touponce, *Frank Herbert* (Boston: Twayne Publishers, 1988); Daniel J. Levack and Mark Willard, *Dune Master: A Frank Herbert Bibliography* (Westport, CT: Meckler Press, 1988); Timothy O'Reilly, *Frank Herbert* (New York: Frederick Ungar Publishing Company, 1981, 12); O'Reilly, ibid., <http://tim.oreilly.com/herbert/ch07.html> 2/1/06. The June 2006 Wikipedia posts are excellent.

5. "I, Agamemnon, your ancestor, demand audience!" With these words, uttered by Alia Atreides' Other Memory, we learn without doubt that the Atreides of Caladan are the descendants of the Ancient Greek House of Atreus. Atreides in ancient Greek would mean son or descendant of Atreus. According to the *Iliad*, Agamemnon, son of Atreus, led the Greeks in the Trojan war. The *Iliad* is an epic poem derived from oral tradition. *Dune* is written in this tradition of epic poetry and oral literature. As Herbert lends his voice to the chorus and picks up the *Iliad*'s narrative thousands of years in the future, he becomes one of the Homeric poets.

6. New texts in the canon that document the years before and after the events in the *The Chronicles* are being authored by Brian Herbert (son of Frank) and Kevin J. Anderson.

7. Hermeneutics is the art and science of interpretation. It provides both an explanation of the interpretation of texts and the observation that humans are "interpretive" beings. There are several schools of hermeneutic thought (see endnote).

8. See Maurice Merleau-Ponty, *Husserl at the Limits of Phenomenology Including Texts by Edmund Husserl* (Leonard Lawlor with Bettina Bergo, eds. Evanston: Northwestern University Press, 2002, xi, 5–10).

9. *God Emperor*, 53.

10. *Messiah*, 63.

11. *Dune* was written, as a thought experiment, in a cinematographic and vertically layered style. Readers could enter at different levels with each reading and find something new. Frank Herbert, in Brian Herbert and Kevin J. Anderson, *The Road to Dune* (New York: Tor, 2005, 283).

12. The terms *flesh* and *chiasm* are taken from Merleau-Ponty's *The Visible and Invisible* to refer to the phenomena of perception and embodiment through which the eye *touches* what it sees, the finger *feels* itself as it feels an object; flesh is the mutual

communion and interpenetration of ourselves and world (translated by Alphonso Lingis. Evanston: Northwestern University Press, 1968, 130–155).

13. Kristen Brennan (feral mythologist), "Star Wars Origins: Dune" (Jitterbug Fantasia <http://www.jitterbug.com/origins/dune.html>) 2/1/06

14. It is worthy of note that Leto, The God Emperor of Dune, lived for three thousand standard years.

15. Kristen Brennan, "Star Wars Origins: Dune" (Jitterbug Fantasia <http://www.jitterbug.com/origins/dune.html>) 2/1/06

16. The blind prophet is a common theme in Greek mythology. The Preacher speaks out against the blasphemies and hypocrisies committed in the name of Muad'Dib. Paul, like the blind prophet of ancient Greek mythology, Tiresias, tells the truth about the past, present, and future. And like Tiresias, Paul's voice is not heard, as the rabble are too caught up in their daily concerns to hear the wisdom of his message. (See Gebser, *The Ever Present Origin*, N. Barstad with A. Mikunas, Trans., Athens: Ohio University Press, 1991, 271).

17. Kristen Brennan, "Star Wars Origins: Dune" (Jitterbug Fantasia <http://www.jitterbug.com/origins/dune.html>) 2/1/06.

18. See W.F. Touponce, *Frank Herbert* (Boston: Twayne, 1988, 14). For an example of this text-within-text structure, each chapter begins with a fragment from a fictional text that speaks of events in the stories or makes philosophical observations as told by another person, thus providing another perspective and interpretation of the unfolding events.

19. Kristen Brennan, "Star Wars Origins: Dune" (Jitterbug Fantasia <http://www.jitterbug.com/origins/dune.html>) 2/1/06.

20. *Dune*, 42.

21. Philosopher Algis Mickunas has lectured widely on the relationship between the gods and phenomena (personal communication).

22. It is important to distinguish between natural and precious resources. The earth has no shortage of natural resources. What's at risk are the resources a species determines precious. The Baron Harkonnen goes so far as to point out that "air" is such a resource; if withheld, the person dies. Oil and spices are also precious because economic and transportation systems function because of them. But alternatives usually exist.

23. Reality is a difficult idea. After all, whose version of reality do we accept? Mine? Yours? Religious? Scientific? Ideological? It is wise to consider the power structure behind any mere conception of reality and ask ourselves who is speaking? It is also wise to view "reality" as discursive. For example, we can speak of a conservative reality or a feminist reality. Our attempts to grasp a singular reality tend to fail. The advantage of nominalism over realism is intellectual flexibility. Even if we agree that physical reality is always real (a moving car is always a moving car), our spiritual reality is always caught up in webs of meaning. Herbert seems to agree with this nominalist vantage when he notes that reality is consensual. In other words, the real is whatever we happen to agree upon as being real. Thus, reality is historical, cultural, discursive, contingent, and conventional. Herbert sites, for example, the "local" definition of sanity as time-space specific and not applicable to all persons in all cultures in all times.

24. Touponce, op. cit., ii.

25. *Dune*, 18.

26. Touponce, op. cit., 3.

27. Kristen Brennan, "Star Wars Origins: Dune" (Jitterbug Fantasia <http://www.jitterbug.com/origins/dune.html>) 2/1/06.

28. Brian Herbert and Kevin J. Anderson, *The Road to Dune* (New York: tor, 2005, 282). Brian Herbert, *Dreamer of Dune* (New York: Tor, 2003).

29. Frank Herbert, in Brian Herbert and Kevin J. Anderson, *The Road to Dune*, ibid., 282.

30. Frank Herbert, in Brian Herbert and Kevin J. Anderson, *The Road to Dune*, ibid., 282.

31. Frank Herbert, in Brian Herbert and Kevin J. Anderson, *The Road to Dune*, ibid., 282.

32. *Dune*, 8.

33. See Timothy W. Crusius, *A Teacher's Introduction to Philosophical Hermeneutics* (Urbana: NCTE, 1991, 5–6).

34. Leto II, His Voice, from Dar-es-Balat. *Heretics*, 371.

35. Arguments in Council. *Heretics*, 272.

36. Lecture to the Arrakeen War College. *Children*, 201.

Chapter One

Learning How to Learn

A beginning is the time for taking the most delicate care that the balances are correct.[1]

Palimpsestual Context

The Dune Chronicles can be read as a palimpsest—a literary ghola—and critical appropriation of Einstein's theories of relativity, Heisenberg's uncertainty principle, Gödel's realization of the limits of mathematical systems, Korzibsky's general semantics, Piaget's developmental psychology, Jaspers' and Heidegger's existentialism, Jung's theories of archetypes and the collective unconscious, and more.[2] The thread that binds together this highly theoretical, cultural, and historical subject matter is a critique of absolute knowledge and power.[3] As The God Emperor of Dune, Leto II, puts it:

> Every judgment teeters on the brink of error. To claim absolute knowledge is to become monstrous.[4]

The dream of many politicians and military leaders, *absolute power* attracts the corruptible and fascist elements of a society.

> All governments suffer a recurring problem: Power attracts pathological personalities. It is not that power corrupts but that it is magnetic to the corruptible. Such people have a tendency to become drunk on violence, a condition to which they are quickly addicted.[5]

The bane of many scientists and philosophers, *absolute knowledge* is an elusive quest for stasis in a dynamic world.

Dune offers its readers a critical reflection on the workings of culture and society, one in which knowledge is revealed less as absolute, certain, and positive and more as contingent, questionable, and contextual. As Leto puts it:

> Knowledge is an unending adventure at the edge of uncertainty.[6]

1

Illustration 2. Paul and His Teachers

Knowledge and uncertainty walk hand in hand. Mentat education is, then, a matter of both learning and unlearning. We learn from *The Chronicles* how to *think* and *act* as Mentats.[7] But we also unlearn the rules and rotes that restrict growth and channel thought into narrow crevasses; distrust anything that dampens creativity.

> *Creativity*! Always dangerous to entrenched power. Always coming up with something new. New things could destroy the grip of authority.[8]

Thus, we look to a critical pedagogy, a teaching that tears apart the social fabric to see its warp and woof, a pedagogy for the person un-oppressed by his social mores. The mentat must be open both to whatever passes for knowledge in a given time and place and to the possibility that this same knowledge can be not only misleading but wrong in another time and at another place.[9] Like a flu shot, the narrative flow of *The Chronicles* gives us an injection of a weakened form of the virus—our own thought systems—that spread faster than the rate at which they are understood. As the flu shot prepares the body to fight off an infection and dis-ease, so too *The Chronicles* prepare us to live well in an ambiguous and uncertain world.[10] In this way, *The Chronicles* can be seen as a work of critical and cultural philosophy and Mentat education as a pedagogy of the un-oppressed.

Pedagogy of the Un-Oppressed

> We never completely escape the teachers of our childhood nor any of the patterns they formed in us.[11]

To learn mathematics we often start with simple patterns such as multiplication tables—mathematical patterns. When we study an instrument, our teacher introduces us to scales—musical patterns. History, archeology, and the fine arts are presented to us in terms of patterns—Renaissance history, Aztec archeology, and impressionistic music are defined by a return to original texts, ritual performances, and the use of whole-tone scales, respectively. These patterns and the images associated with them are defined by human activity; that is to say, history, archeology, and musicology are possible because humans categorize texts, conduct ritual practices, and differentiate harmonic progressions. However, these patterns may also inform a horizon of assumptions, expectations, and associations that become institutionalized and hegemonic.[12]

The Mentat's overlay integration method of seeing and learning rejects the uncritical acceptance of previous patterns. Sometimes these educational patterns are paradoxical or even hypocritical. Consider the simple fact that some adherents of the monotheistic religions often preach peace and practice violence. Underneath the rhetoric of love lies fear and hostility.

> Much that was called religion has carried an unconscious attitude of hostility toward life.[13]

Instead, Mentat education seeks to understand the assumptions on which patterns are made and to learn how to put knowledge into practice through a working knowledge of formal and material domains of practice.[14]

> Knowledge without action is empty.[15]

The pragmatic position, *knowledge without action is empty*, is realized in part through great attention paid to the phenomena of teaching and learning; both teaching and learning are activities.

> All men must see that the teaching of religion by rules and rote is largely a hoax. The proper teaching is recognized with ease. You can know it without fail because it awakens within you that sensation which tells you this is something you've always known.[16]

And yet the activity of teaching-learning is often lopsided. Teaching is often perceived as something somebody does to somebody else. Learning is often perceived as difficult. Seen this way, education appears as a rather violent activity with both its form and content dictated by some over-arching authority. In such an environment, children are often reluctant to learn and teachers are often alienated from their art. This is a sad state of affairs, especially for a postindustrial society in which the primary commodity—information—only has meaning for those educated in a particular discourse; formal education may be more important in a postindustrial society than in an industrial or agricultural society.

Mentat education takes another tack. The basic insights of this approach have been summarized by Stewart and Mickunas, who note that education is temporally oriented. It appears in a context of given values and goals that constitute a tradition. This tradition can be considered at many levels—capitalism, the sciences and humanities, the specific requirements of knowledge at a given moment (e.g., the requisite possession of computer skills in the contemporary lifeworld). The intentionality and purpose of the traditional education is constituted by the academic institution for the sake of the future; viable graduates must be produced.

If we consider this wider context of temporality, locality, and intentionality, education cannot be reduced to teaching and learning; such a reduction is mere conditioning, and the Mentat must always see beyond such conditioning.[17]

The Mentat must become aware of the values on which the educational institution is based. If we do not understand the tradition, radical reflection and action is not possible, and any genuine thought or practice is curtailed at the outset; this is antithetical to the presupposed goals of education, but the message is clear—don't rock the boat. Moreover, if we merely train technicians, those people will be incapable of evaluating the tradition in light of the social movement into the very future that they are purportedly being educated for nonentity. The material conditions of Mentat education are thus floated by consciousness and values located in tradition.[18]

The Chronicles, most notably *Chapterhouse*, address both the politics of education and the phenomenology of learning. They treat both teaching and learning as an art that the learner must embrace wholeheartedly, accept responsibly for, and attend to carefully. As if to answer the critique of modern education raised by Paulo Freire's *Pedagogy of the Oppressed*, *The Dune Chronicles* can be read as a *pedagogy for the emancipated*.

Critical Pedagogy

The Pedagogy of the Oppressed is one of the most influential books on the politics of modern education.[19] This book, along with the work of John Dewey and

the Cultural Studies movement in general, has spawned a social transformation in education known as *critical pedagogy*. Critical pedagogy is a response to
a perceived crisis in institutionalized education. This crisis is characterized in
part by (1) the failure of the public to participate in politics (the very negation
of democracy itself), (2) the growing rates of illiteracy and poverty (the failure of education and economy), (3) the increasing separation of the rich from
the poor (the loss of the middle class), and (4) the prevalent view that social
criticism and social change are irrelevant to democracy (the very negation of
politics).[20] The critical pedagogy movement is also a response to social crises
brought about through Eurocentrism, racism, and sexism and a radical politics
of difference.[21]

Critical pedagogy is, as well, a response to structural changes in the
economy and family: Industrial society has given way to a technological age
of communication whose principle capital exchange consists more of information and services than materials and goods. Critical pedagogy emerges from a
growing self-awareness of educators (set into motion by writers such as Paulo
Freire, Carl Jaspers, Michele Foucault, Ivan Illich, and Louis Althusser) that
education is itself a social institution that engages teachers and students in the
cultural production of knowledge, networks of power relationships, and viable
graduates.

The Dune Chronicles offer their own critique of institutional education.
Mentat education constitutes a critical pedagogy that is geared away from limitation and oppression and toward political participation and emancipation from
power structures and oppression. Author Frank Herbert (who taught at the
university level) was concerned with the institutional structure of education:
"Academe is far gone down this long road of 'education can be done with
power.' "[22] While Herbert credits the dedication and hard labor of many of the
actual teachers, he also considers the corporate impulse of organized education.
"A school is a 'person' who has information which works. He can demonstrate
that it works and it is people who want to do what this person does. They
want to learn how to make things work that way."[23]

Seen this way, the academy is not the Socratic paradise of the mind
in which questions are as important as answers and wisdom is more highly
regarded than mere knowledge. The modern system is homogeneous (despite
the oddly not-so-obvious recognition that people are not) and productive (it
creates graduates with all the limitations of those who control the flow of what
is considered useful information).

Frank Herbert's *Dune* addresses these issues and adds to them a particular
insight: If it is generally recognized that learning is not something one does
only in school, but is a lifelong activity that goes on as much informally as it
does formally, then why is learning so often perceived as difficult? For the true
student, every experience carries a lesson:

> Many have marked the speed with which Muad'Dib learned. . . . [W]e can
> say that Muad'Dib learned rapidly because his first training was in how to
> learn. And the first lesson of all was the basic trust that he could learn. It
> is shocking to find how many people do not believe they can learn, and
> how many more believe learning to be difficult. Muad'Dib knew that every
> experience carries a lesson.[24]

If we truly recognize that "every experience carries a lesson," then learning
could become not only a continual and inevitable activity, but a joyous and
continuous adventure.

However, many people do find learning hard. Conventional wisdom even
suggests that learning gets harder as you get older; "you can't teach an old dog
new tricks." This remains the case despite recent findings in neuroscience showing that age-associated declines are neither universal nor inevitable. There are
aspects of our bodies that do not retard as we grow old. "Neuron loss with age
is not found in all regions of the nervous system; not all neurons atrophy; not
all transmitter systems decline; some neurological measures do not show decre-
ments; and some degrees of neuronal plasticity is retained in the aged nervous
system."[25] If this is the case, then not only are our notions of aging outdated,
but belief in these models is debilitating. Likewise, many people believe that
learning a language or mathematics is difficult. At the same time, people become
experts on sports, wine, or the music they appreciate. A general tendency and
paradox appears. On the one hand, people appear to learn without effort those
things they perceive as fun. On the other hand, people appear to resist learning
about those subjects that are aspects of our formalized schooling and that are
coded as difficult.[26]

Why do we *believe* that learning is difficult? Consider that our initial
experience with formal education is largely compulsory. From kindergarten to
college, a formal education is seen as necessary, and not optional, for those
wishing to compete in the job market. Compulsory means that one is required
by law and caused by force to learn. Choice, the ability to act of one's own
accord, is already greatly diminished. In such a context, the person is positioned
below the authority of academy, and we live in an age (as McLuhan suggested)
in which our teachers are lesser role models than our athletes and rock stars.

In *Dune*, compulsory education is revealed as inevitable, even important,
but not the true path to wisdom and emancipation. "The oppressors," says Freire
in Herbertian harmonics, "are the ones who act upon men to indoctrinate them
into a reality which must remain untouched."[27] In the final book of *The Chronicles*, *Chapterhouse*, the Bene Gesserit have accepted the only Honored Matre ever
captured as a novice. They are training her in the Bene Gesserit ways despite the
knowledge that she plans to escape, stealing their most valuable secrets—including immunity from disease. The Reverend Mother Darwi Odrade teaches the

Honored Matre Murbella using a variety of sources, including instruction and "word weapons," in a successful attempt to overcome Murbella's Honored Matre conditioning and training. The interaction between these characters presents a clear meditation on the politics, power, and institutional nature of education and shows us a path that transcends traditional guidelines. It outlines for us both a pedagogy of the oppressed and a pedagogy of the un-oppressed.

Beyond False Limits

> The hardest thing for an acolyte to learn is that she must always go the limit. Your abilities will take you farther than you imagine. Don't imagine, then. Extend yourself![28]

Much of what passes for education today installs false limits on a person. The great violin teacher, Suzuki, reminds us that to educate means to *educe*—to make something latent appear. In contrast, much education is largely a matter of *instruction*—the second of the two concepts interwoven in the word "education." Note that whereas *instruction* is implied in the suffix and *educe* in the root, it is the suffix that is favored in the modern world. If we can reverse this and valorize the root over the suffix, the educative over the instructive, then the purpose of education becomes the cultivation of one's inner wisdom; we would strive to "bring out." We would first trust in the knowledge we already have, and then we would cultivate that knowledge into wisdom. Wisdom is applied knowledge (and the withholding of judgment). Wisdom, coupled with knowledge, provides one with the ability to act consciously, to use skills wisely, and to make one's way in the world purposely.

> When you think to take determination of your fate into your hands, that is the moment you can be crushed. Be cautious. Allow for surprises. When we create, there are always other forces at work.[29]

Our goal, as knowing participants in Mentat education, is the overcoming of false and self-imposed limits and the striving to reach the true limits of our abilities.

The Emulation of Adults by Children

> Religion (emulation of adults by children) encysts past mythologies: guesses, hidden assumptions of trust in the universe, pronouncements made in search of personal power, all mingled with shreds of enlightenment. And

always an unspoken commandment: Thou shall not question! We break that commandment daily in the harnessing of human imagination to our deepest creativity.[30]

It is quite interesting, even revelatory, that the Bene Gesserit define religion as "emulation of adults by children."[31] It is even more interesting that the Bene Gesserit use religion as a tool of control for the masses and their engineering, techno-science techniques (which might be better nominated tech-no-science) combine education and religion.[32] However, within their own ranks, they critique conventional teaching for imposing false limits on human beings.

Illustration 3. Odrade and Murbella

There is a meditation in *Chapterhouse* that follows Reverend Mother Odrade's teaching of Murbella (the only Honored Matre captured by the Bene Gesserit) in the Bene Gesserit way. Odrade's teaching consists of deprogramming and reprogramming Murbella's talents via "word weapons:" Power words, phrases, and ideas are implanted in Murbella like seeds sown in rich soil; with care and fertilizer, they germinate and sprout, sending out roots to gather water and branches to gather sun. In this way, Odrade does not ask for Murbella to repeat or imitate, but to absorb and integrate. The student co-creates a new understanding through her previous knowledge—she develops talents she already possesses.

Murbella's Honored Matre education (the antithesis of Bene Gesserit and Mentat education) is emblematic of conventional education. Such education teaches students how to lie and cheat—to repeat knowledge that is not theirs, but the knowledge of their masters. More specifically, conventional education is based on bad faith—actions do not equal intentions or words.

> If you convince yourself, sincerely, you can speak utter balderdash (marvelous word; look it up), absolutely poppy larky in every word and you will be believed. But not by one of our Truthsayers.[33]

The conventional education is predicated on meaningless drivel. One learns a variety of facts and figures that are easily forgotten because they are not relevant to everyday life; or the relevance is not revealed or intuited by the student and so they go unused. Such teaching begins and ends with definitions, "what is's" and "how to's." It proceeds by method of emulation of adults by children; and it is easy to see, though difficult to realize, that even one generation of this sort of practice has its perils. Recall the childhood game of telephone. A small group of people sit in a circle. Only the first participant knows a phrase—"it looks like rain," for example. The phrase is whispered into the ear of the person next to him or her, and so on. By the time the message moves around the group, it reappears as a distorted phrase, "the teacher's in pain." This exercise, taught to most young children as a game, reveals that so-called "messages" are not messages as such. A message would be an utterance that had a singular meaning. In other words, what we call a message is actually a "text."[34] A text is an object or utterance that is read or interpreted, and interpretation is not a simple matter of message reception, but a complex matter of sensation, sense, and sensitivity.

If teachers are to cultivate freedom and liberation from restrictive thought patterns (and to a very real degree the student must ultimately do this herself), then we have to assume that the emancipation resides within the learner from the outset; emancipation is an ever-present potential, a latent phenomenon. We cannot assume that others, especially our own teachers, have had such radical freedom in mind! To see the truth in this statement just look at the state of the world today. Ethnic, religious, and tribal wars have been waged for centuries with little reprieve; great empires conquer lesser countries, ignoring the perils and lessons of imperialism and colonialism that are so very blatant.

Just as Rome is no longer an empire, so today's empires, the United States chief among them, will eventually fall (this is the lesson of history, but few seem to be reading the books); although the preceding proposition is not *necessarily* true, we see in today's empires a similar pattern to the old. And yet, when faced with an observation we don't like, we act as proverbial ostriches with our heads in the sand.

> We will misread and/or misunderstand almost anything that challenges our favorite illusions.[35]

It is as if nothing has been learned.

No less a man than Einstein (that figure held as the icon of genius in the Western world) has said that insanity is nothing more than doing the same thing and expecting different results.[36] We live in a world that is not better off now than previously, and yet we show a tendency to think that the people who have created and perpetuated the world in which we live are somehow in a position to teach the young. In fact, current programs in the United States are pushing toward more state control, more regurgitation, in the "no child left behind" program—a program that leaves no child behind in terms of conventional teaching; children will be taught the conventional way, to repeat the mistakes of their elders. The temporal project, which is supposed to look forward, often looks backward. The state then plays the game of religion—the emulation of adults by children that encysts past mythologies.

> Educational bureaucracies dull a child's sensitivity. . . . The young must be damped down. Never let them know how good they can be. That brings change. . . . Don't spend any time dealing with how the conventional teacher feels threatened by emerging talents and squelches them because of a deep-seated desire to feel superior and safe in a safe environment.[37]

When teaching is designed solely to instruct, and not to educe, it is destined to impose. One imposes a convention on a student. The teacher says, "This is what it is" and "this is how it is done." The student who thinks for him or herself is lost in and to such a world. Such conventional education must be abandoned or turned on its head.

To turn the conventional system on its head means that students would be taught to recognize the conventions, the social contracts, by which knowledge, truth, and understanding are communicated. Students would look to see what people and what interests create and are served by a particular way of seeing the world; they would be taught to recognize conventions. This is the way of the Mentat's education in communicology. Learn to recognize the patterns by which a field of production, such as economics (which is a field of production with its proponents and dissidents, subjects and objects, products and services), is communicated. Then, you will be able to see the system for what it is—a discourse (a way of talking about things with specific rules of what can and cannot be said).

If we turn the educational system on its head, we do see moments of beauty, but exceptional students (and their exceptional works) are just that— exceptions! Needed is an educational system in which the exceptions are the "unexceptional." Instead, we see all too often that the conventional education system, typical of power-hungry, fear-based societies, teaches people to pro- crastinate and diddle around. It leaves people practically incapable of making decisions.

> The worst products of what I'm describing are almost basket cases—can't make decisions about anything, or leave them until the last possible second and then leap at them like desperate animals.[38]

Regurgitation & Repetition

When Murbella is indoctrinated into the Bene Gesserit, she recites an oath. At first she merely regurgitates the oath. Later, when she has converted to the Bene Gesserit way, the words come back to her. She realizes not only that her original cynicism was recognized by the Bene Gesserit proctor, but that her own cynicism was allowed; *her acts of criticism and resistance were critical acts*—she was beginning to act on her own accord. As the words flood her awareness, a tear falls down her cheek.

> I stand in the sacred human presence. As I do now, so should you stand some day. I pray to your presence that this be so. Let the future remain uncertain for that is the canvas to receive our desires. Thus the human con- dition faces its perpetual *tabla rasa*. We possess no more than this moment where we dedicate ourselves continuously to the sacred presence we share and create.[39]

By bending like the willow, rather than standing tall like an oak, Odrade brings Murbella to a critical consciousness.[40]

> Most civilization is based on cowardice. It's so easy to civilize by teaching cowardice. You water down the standards which would lead to bravery. You

restrain the will. You regulate the appetites. You fence in the horizons. You make a law for every moment. You deny the existence of chaos. You teach even the children to breathe slowly. You tame.[41]

The model for learning, in a culture of enforced education and the taming of the masses, is not repetition but *regurgitation*. Repetition is practice with attention paid to detail and nuance. It is practicing scales over and over until the musician not only gets the notes right, but also makes beautiful tones. Regurgitation implies that the student repeats what has been taught in a purely mechanical manner, with no evidence of personal talent, thought or understanding. As Herbert suggests, there is a tendency for the teacher to say: "Here's how I do it." "This might not be the only way to do it." "It may not be the best way." "We may develop far more effective ways of doing these things. But, under a power-oriented society, power adheres to people who have knowledge of how a thing works, no matter how temporary that 'working' may be."[42]

The passing down of *messages*, or the already known, rather than *questions*, so we might learn what we don't know, is still the most popular form of a formal education. The teacher speaks, the students repeat. In this context it is the job of the teacher to check the quality of the regurgitation—to make certain that the student is able to repeat the teacher correctly. But this method of ingestion and regurgitation, when coupled with the authority-based, top-down method of instruction, produces a *bulimic culture*.

Calling a culture or institution bulimic is justified; the metaphor may fit better than we like, and finding the right metaphor may be the highest form of literary criticism.[43] The archetypal psychologist James Hillman suggests that the psyche resides neither "in here," in some subjective mind, nor "out there," in some objective matter, but rather in between, in the relationship people bring to the world.[44] When one sees a rise in the occurrence of bulimia, depression, schizophrenia, manic-depression, heart disease, or the hardening of the arteries, one might do well to look at the society. Our institutions have no heart; people are but tools for the purpose of doing business; health and retirement plans atrophy. Our education system is increasingly narrowed, clogged by the cholesterol of a common curriculum (as if all people needed to learn the same skills). Our workdays are full of hurry-up-and-wait, manic-depressive commutes and meetings. Our civilization splits men and women into Martians and Venusians. The buildings, cubicles, and factories in which we work are depressed. Our educational system promotes regurgitation.

I learned cheating as an infant. How to simulate a need and gain attention. Many "how to's" in the cheating pattern. The older she got, the easier the cheating. She had learned what the big people around her were demanding. I regurgitated on demand. That was called "education."[45]

Reverend Mother Darwi Odrade critiques this method of "education." In fact, she suggests that the dampening of imagination brought about by the practice of regurgitation is not education, but convention and custom—in a word, religion. Religion, like education, promises transcendence, or at least both hold that potential. In practice, however, they are largely an institutionalization of systems of beliefs and practices. These are often arranged in a hierarchy by an orthodoxy that often forbids questioning and promotes mindless repetition. This conventional vision imposes false limits on a person; it stunts one's growth and maturation. It is possible, however, to seek the limits, to test the limits of the possible. Our next step is to critique the very grounds of what passes for knowledge—the *data* itself.

Data, Capta, & Acta

Richard Lanigan notes that we, especially those who take up the traditional scientific method, have inherited an approach to knowledge founded primarily on *data*.[46] However, the Mentat recognizes that the seemingly obvious, that which is *given* (or *data*, Q.E.D., *quod erat demonstrandum*), is actually not at all given, obvious, or factual but is that which is literally *taken* (or *capta*, Q.E.I., *quod erat inveniendum*); in other words, *capta* represents that which is interpreted—captured. The Mentat is able to recognize the political intentions and historical conventions of the *capta-data* continuum and thus enters into analysis (or *acta*, that which is done) in a systematic and methodological approach that sets aside prejudice and presuppositions, the naive acceptance of *capta* for *data*, and focuses on the interpretation of conscious experience.

Instead of moving deductively from that which is given to the analysis of the given (as is the way of most science), the Mentat begins analysis (*acta*) with what is *taken* (interpreted) by consciousness (Q.E.I.). Only after reducing this information to its intentional and essential configurations does the Mentat accept the remainder as *data* (Q.E.D).[47]

Mentat analysis thus focuses on conscious experience (*capta*, Q.E.I.) rather than hypothetical constructs (*data*, Q.E.D). The mentat refuses to stand on the proverbial shoulders of giants and thinks as freely and as completely as possible; the mentat institutes an emancipatory, radical reflection.

Fanaticism and Radicalization

Muad'Dib's imperial reign generated more historians than any other era in human history. Most of them argue a particular viewpoint, jealous and sectarian.[48]

We live at a time of unprecedented educational opportunities. And yet, too many of our students are not, in a general sense, positioned in a manner conducive to learning. We live in a time when fanaticism, fueled by instrumental reason, is pushing our educational system into deeper and darker recesses of oppressive structures and the statistical drive for all students to learn the same things.[49] Partisan politics and sectarian beliefs limit potential. Just as the fanatic worshipers of Muad'Dib, such as Korba, are ultimately perverted by their own beliefs, so too our fanatics are like racehorses wearing blinders: They move very quickly in one direction and cannot see alternatives. What happens when the needs of the state are placed above the lives of the children?

> Sectarianism, fed by fanaticism, is always castrating. Radicalization, nourished by a critical spirit, is always creative. Sectarianism mythicizes and thereby alienates; radicalization criticizes and thereby liberates. Radicalization involves increased commitment to the position one has chosen, and thus ever greater engagement in the effort to transform concrete, objective reality. Conversely, sectarianism, because it is mythicizing and irrational, turns reality into a false (and therefore unchangeable) "reality."[50]

Active modes of teaching are needed over the lecture form.[51] Students do best when involved, and student involvement may well be the most important reform needed in undergraduate education.[52] We cannot ignore the students' themes, languages, conditions, and diverse cultures, so as to favor those of the orthodoxy and establishment. Student participation and action over traditional reception and regurgitation is the Mentat way. Mandatory and uniform testing has become more prevalent even in the face of the recognition that "unilateral teacher authority in a passive curriculum arouses in many students a variety of negative emotions: self-doubt, hostility, resentment, boredom, indignation, cynicism, disrespect, frustration, the desire to escape."[53] Many will recognize these emotions as pervasive in today's society.

> To teach skills and information without relating them to society and to the students' contexts turns education into an authoritarian transfer of official words, a process that severely limits student's development as democratic citizens.[54]

Nobody likes to be told what to do or even what to learn.

> What you really want is to conjoin our experiences, make me sufficiently like you that we can create trust between us. That's what all education does.[55]

Students see this inequity, but they are in no position to challenge the teacher's authority except, perhaps, through bad behavior. The power relationship is spelled out in advance and rewards those who accept that structure. Between the extremes of fanaticism and radicalism are millions of real people caught in a system that favors its own perpetuation over personal growth.

Transformation of Consciousness

Writer, critic, and educator bell hooks tells us that a "critical pedagogy seeks to transform consciousness, to provide students with ways of knowing that enable them to know themselves better and live in the world more fully."[56] To accomplish this transformation of consciousness, from oppressed to emancipated, the *The Chronicles* suggest: (1) Encourage the basic trust and belief that learning is possible; (2) Educator-educated relationship is dialogical and mutually reciprocal; (3) Education is consciousness transforming rather than consciousness instituting; (4) Education can reveal the political workings of conventions rather than merely indoctrinating people into them; (5) Education is educive as well as instructive; (6) Candor and honesty as the basis of all learning; and (7) Emulation of adults by children is problematic.

The Chronicles provide a context in which these thoughts are nurtured, obtain purpose, and (hopefully) inspire human growth—maturity. Mentat thought that we must take learning into our own hands, learn how to learn, and direct our vision toward latent possibilities:

> Education is no substitute for intelligence. The elusive quality is defined only in part by puzzle-solving ability. It is the creation of new puzzles reflecting what your senses report that you round out the definition.[57]

The Mentat thus sees culture as a cipher. Mentat education starts with deciphering and decoding and, then, becoming aware of the codes that create for a society a local definition of sanity or regional understanding of marriage. The "transformation" of consciousness is a radical reflection "on" consciousness—an apprehension of apperception as well as perception. We call Mentat thinking "Mentat Overlay Integration" because the Mentat must integrate and see through the layers of thought as so many strata of sediment built historically and politically. The Mentat cannot be satisfied with the given (always argue with the data) until she sees "how" it is given: With what values, interests, presuppositions, and purposes? What codes and discourses are being enacted? What myths are masquerading as rational statements? What magical incantations are undetected? Note here, then, that consciousness is not "transformed" from one state to another ("all states are abstractions"[58]), nor is it "raised" to another level (a spatial metaphor). What we seek is a radical reflection. That is, a reflection on the thought-lines themselves.

To grasp these thought-lines, the Mentat must learn to be receptive. The wisest characters in *The Chronicles* all reveal a deep learning of receptivity: Leto notes many times that the Fremen live in a world of sounds; "[he] felt himself caught up in the Fremen agrapha: The ear-minded night."[59] Paul is differentiated from other children because "at the age of fifteen, he had already learned silence."[60] Farad'n learns patience under Jessica's tutelage.

> You've begun to learn patience, too. You've just crept over the lip of this learning. . . . Before . . . you were only a potential. . . . You will practice this thing you've learned. . . . I want you able to do this at will, easily. Later you'll find a new place in your awareness which this has opened. It will be filled by the ability to test any reality against your own demands.[61]

The listener is in many ways as adept, if not more, than the seer. When rendered blind, Paul still sees because of his insight and foresight. *The Chronicles* appear to be wary of the visual and expressive bias in Western philosophy. Vision reaches out and touches. The ear takes in and apprehends.[62] Do not be mislead: The ear can be fooled. But rely on receptivity as well as expressivity.

> Paul nodded. He saw how Chani had been fooled. The timbre of voice, everything reproduced with exactitude. Had it not been for his own Bene Gesserit training in voice, and for the web of dao in which oracular vision enfolded him, this Face-Dancer disguise might have gulled even him.[63]

The true lesson, the true mastery of Bene Gesserit Voice, is to become receptive and recognize its use on us in the sphere of everyday life and the natural attitude. Then, and only then, will you be free from the Witch's incantation.[64]

Today it is the radical, the one who actively seeks change, and looks to a dynamic future, who has the potential for growth. It is the heretic who learns how to learn and finds a lesson in every experience.

> In ten-centimeter letters along one wall, written by her [Alia's] own hand in mnemonic paint, stood the key reminder from the Bene Gesserit Creed: 'Before us, all methods of learning were tainted by instinct. We learned how to learn.'[65]

Notes

1. From the "Manual of Muad'Dib" by the Princess Irulan. *Dune*, 3.
2. A ghola is a being regrown from a cadaver's cells that retains the memories of the original. The Bene Tleilax grow these gholas and tinker with their psychological makeup for political purposes. See Frank Herbert, "Science Fiction and a World in

Crisis," in Reginald Brentor, Editor, *Science Fiction, Today and Tomorrow* (New York: Harper & Row, 1974, 69–97). See also Kristen Brennan, "Star Wars Origins: Dune" (Jitterbug Fantasia <http://www.jitterbug.com/origins/dune.html>) 2/1/06.

3. Herbert biographer Timothy O'Reilly sees Herbert's work as a response to the changing nature of science. Einstein, Heisenberg, and Gödel represent the end of the scientist's dream of finding natural laws from which the total technological control of nature could be made; they mark the end of the search for absolute, positive knowledge (O'Reilly, *Frank Herbert*. New York: Frederick Ungar Publishing Company, 1981, 7).

4. Leto II, the God Emperor of Dune, in Brian Herbert, *Notebooks of Frank Herbert's Dune* (New York: Peregree, 1988, 18).

5. *Missionaria Protectiva*, Text QIV (decto). *Chapterhouse: Dune*, 68.

6. Leto II, the God Emperor of Dune, in Brian Herbert, *Notebooks of Frank Herbert's Dune* (New York: Peregree, 1988, 18).

7. See Maurice Merleau-Ponty, "Preface" to *Phenomenology of Perception*, in which he outlines the practice of Husserlian Phenomenology along with his insights into the further workings of phenomenology as philosophy and science (Colin Smith translation, New York: Routledge, 1989, vii–xxi).

8. Reverend Mother Darwi Odrade to Taraza. *Chapterhouse*, 259.

9. For more information, follow a wormhole to Chapter Two, "The Unclouded Eye." See also Edmund Husserl, *Ideas Pertaining to a Pure Phenomenology and to a Phenomenological Philosophy: First Book* (translated by Fred Kersten. Dordrecht: Kluwer, 1982).

10. See Tim O'Reilly, *Frank Herbert*, Chapter One: Dancing on the Edge. (<http://tim.oreilly.com/herbert/ch01.html>) 6/25/06.

11. Reverend Mother Belladona. *Heretics*, 349.

12. Hegemony is the dominance of one group over another without the recourse of force so that the dominant party dictates the structure (patterning) of society to its advantage. Culture itself favors the dominant group and its beliefs. Hegemony, then, controls the ways that ideas become naturalized in a process that informs notions of *common sense*. See R. Williams, *Keywords: A Vocabulary of Culture and Society* (New York: Oxford University Press, 1983, 144–146); Jennifer Bothamley, *Dictionary of Theories* (Detroit: Visible, 1993, 248).

13. C.E.T.'s conclusion during an attempt to unify religion. *Dune*, 504.

14. Formal domains are those whose existence is purely immanent, such as mathematics. To practice a formal system one must learn the rules of the system before one can correctly put that knowledge to work. Material domains are transcendent and empirical and, thus, fall into the domain of the sensuous. Do not make the mistake of thinking these two domains do not intersect diaphanously in some fields of practice (music, for example). See David Stewart and Algis Mickunas, *Exploring Phenomenology: A Guide to the Field and its Literature* (Athens: Ohio University Press, 1974).

15. C.E.T.'s conclusion during an attempt to unify religion, *Dune*, 504.

16. C.E.T.'s conclusion during an attempt to unify religion. *Dune*, 504.

17. In book one, *Dune*, we see an inherent problem of conditioning. Dr. Yueh, the Suk doctor, has received Imperial conditioning and must uphold life at all costs. However, he is but a man, and his conditioning is broken by Baron Harkonnen. He betrays the Atreides and murders the Duke. The Atreides knew they had a traitor

in their midst, but because they naively believed in the power of conditioning, they considered Dr. Yueh safe. A well-educated Mentat would not make that mistake. The operant conditioning of B.F. Skinner is treated with skepticism.

18. David Stewart and Algis Mickunas, ibid., 128. Education for nonentity is the title of a lecture by Alan Watts. For more information on the presuppositions that constitute academic traditions, follow a wormhole to Chapter Two, "The Unclouded Eye."

19. Paulo Freire, *Pedagogy of the Oppressed*. Translated by Myra Bergman Ramos. (New York: Herder and Herder, 1970).

20. Henry Giroux, *Border Crossings: Cultural Workers and the Politics of Education* (New York: London: Routledge, 1992, 199). See also the collective works of Patti Lather.

21. For more information on the radical politics of difference see bell hooks, *Yearning: Race, Gender, and Cultural Politics* (Boston, MA: South End Press, 1990); Cornel West, *The New Cultural Politics of Difference. Race, Identity and Representation in Education* (Ed. Cameron McCarthy and Warren Crichlow. New York: Routledge, 1993).

22. Frank Herbert interview, *Vertex Magazine* (Volume 1, Number 4, October 1973).

23. Frank Herbert, *Vertex Magazine*, ibid.

24. From "The Humanity of Muad'Dib" by the Princess Irulan. *Dune*, 65–66.

25. James A. Mortimer, Francis J. Pirozzolo, and Gabe J. Matetta, *The Aging Motor System* (New York: Praeger, 1982, 9).

26. The recognition of codification is here quite significant. Some things, such as languages and particular musical instruments, are coded as difficult. These codes have an existential basis, but when taken for granted easily become self-fulfilling prophesies. The Mentat brackets such codes as presuppositions so to enter into the education of any subject with an open and joyous attitude.

27. Freire, *Pedagogy of the Oppressed*. Translated by Myra Bergman Ramos. (New York: Herder and Herder, 1970, 83).

28. The Reverend Mother Darwi Odrade. *Chapterhouse*, 126.

29. The Reverend Mother Darwi Odrade. *Chapterhouse*, 423.

30. Bene Gesserit Credo. *Chapterhouse*, 115.

31. *Chapterhouse*, 115.

32. *Children*, 171.

33. Odrade, *Chapterhouse*, 128. Freire notes that an emancipatory pedagogy is dialogical and thus grounded on words. "Dialogue cannot exist . . . in the absence of a profound love for the world and for men. The naming of the world [words], which is an act of creation and re-creation, is not possible if it is not infused with love" (*Pedagogy of the Oppressed*, 1970, 77).

34. Umberto Eco, *A Theory of Semiotics* (Bloomington: Indiana University Press, 1979).

35. Frank Herbert, *Listening with the Left Hand*, ibid.

36. Albert Einstein, *Out of My Later Years* (New York, Random House, 2000).

37. Odrade, discussing the Honored Maters. *Chapterhouse*, 127.

38. The Reverend Mother Odrade. *Chapterhouse*, 129.

39. Murbella's oath to the Bene Gesserit. *Chapterhouse*, 130.

40. The bending of the willow is a major theme in *Dune*. For example, Paul overcomes Feyd-Rautha in a knife fight by bending, giving, and flexing; he overcomes Feyd's force with a gentle power.

41. The Stolen Journals. *God Emperor*, 366.

42. Frank Herbert, interview in *Vertex* magazine (Vol. 1, No. 4, October 1973).

43. Friedrich Nietzsche, as well as Herbert, supports the power of the metaphor as a high form of critical analysis, for the metaphor is the word-idea that can teach us something new about what we thought we already knew in a simple and elegant manner.

44. James Hillman, *The Thought of the Heart and the Soul of the World* (Dallas: Spring Publications, 1981).

45. The Honored Matre Murbella, while held captive by the Bene Gesserit. *Chapterhouse*, 126.

46. Richard Lanigan, *Phenomenology of Communication* (Pittsburgh: Duquesne University Press, 1988).

47. For more information, follow a wormhole to Chapter Seven.

48. *Messiah*, 9.

49. For more information about instrumental reason, follow a wormhole to Chapter Four.

50. Freire, *Pedagogy of the Oppressed*, 21–22. It is significant that Freire is a proponent of dialogue, and Herbert's novels are written in a dialogical style. Both celebrate the naming of the world in the creative activity of using words. Furthermore, both Freire and Herbert ultimately find love, as opposed to fear, at the heart of freedom.

51. Shor, 1992, commenting on statements made by the National Institute of Education, 1984. Ira Shor, *Empowering Education* (Chicago: University of Chicago Press, 3rd printing, 1992).

52. Shor, 1992, 21.

53. Shor, 1992, 23.

54. Shor, 1992, 18.

55. The Honored Mater Murbella. *Chapterhouse*, 301.

56. bell hooks, "Eros, Eroticism, and the Pedagogical Process," in H. Giroux and P. McLaren (Eds.) *Between Borders: Pedagogy and the Politics of Cultural Studies* (New York: Routledge, 1994, 113–118).

57. Mentat Text One (decto). *Chapterhouse*, 94.

58. Octurn Politicus, BG Archives. *Chapterhouse*, 162.

59. *Children*, 245.

60. From "A Child's History of Muad'Dib" by the Princess Irulan. *Dune*, 241.

61. Jessica to Farad'n. *Children*, 279–280.

62. We are given speech classes in college. How little time we spend listening and learning to listen (even in music appreciation classes). How much less time we spend learning how to listen well.

63. *Messiah*, 136.

64. For more information, follow a wormhole to Chapter Six.

65. Excerpt from the Bene Gesserit Creed. *Messiah*, 78. For a description of the Mentat's overlay-integration-imagination methodology, follow a wormhole to Appendix B.

Chapter Two

The Unclouded Eye

The unclouded eye was better, no matter what it saw.[1]

Observation and Assumption

How do we learn to learn? Mentat education challenges some of the basic precepts of modern education: (1) Paul finds that consensual beliefs such as "seeing is believing," that "reality is something that lies outside of us," that "mathematics is the best way to uncover the mysteries of this physical reality," limit perception. But the equation of vision and knowledge, the separation of mind and matter, and the idea that things are best known through mathematical reduction are cultural assumptions at best and presuppositions at worst. Vision—even with insight, foresight, and hindsight—is not equated with absolute and certain knowledge, (2) The Bene Gesserit and Mentats have abolished mind-body dualism in *prana-bindu* and other training methods, and (3) The mathematical reduction—especially as performed by computers—has been replaced by a Mentat meditation that integrates communication methods (mathematics being one of many).

Paul's training, for example, includes the study of many philosophical issues that emerge at the modern/postmodern nexus. Paul's meditations reveal that consciousness can be in-formed, literally directed and channeled, into patterns. His considerations of these patterns expose the historical conditions in which certain questions and answers appear:

> Our questions and answers are determined in part by the historical tradition
> in which we find ourselves. . . . The content of our truth depends upon our
> appropriating the historical foundation.[2]

The Chronicles seek to expose these foundations and propose that:

1. Consciousness is structured:[3]

The human requires a background grid through which to see his universe . . . focused consciousness by choice, this forms your grid.[4]

2. These structures are often followed uncritically:

Emulation of adults by children . . . [A]n unspoken commandment: Thou shall not question![5]

3. We can become conscious of consciousness, break free of ideological imperatives, and form new patterns as creative persons:

We break that commandment daily in the harnessing of human imagination to our deepest creativity.[6]

This background grid (or channeling and structuring of consciousness) reveals cultural assumptions about the nature of reality. Unquestioned, these assumptions lock us into predetermined grooves and limit human potential and consciousness. Such limitation is studied via the phenomena of ideology, hegemony, and reification. But we also break free from these limits via critical thinking and radical reflection. Seeking freedom and creating new patterns is a clearing of the way—an unclouding of the eye.

Assumptions and Telos

Science is so obviously man-made.[7]

Mentat thought can be read as a response to the changing nature of science. When the first Mentat Handbook was written, the dream for total technological control of nature and absolute scientific optimism was challenged: Einstein, Heisenberg, and Gödel's theorems unbalanced scientific absolutism and signaled the end of positive knowledge. Science fiction sheds light on the changing structure of scientific thought. As Touponce noted, Herbert believed that science fiction did its greatest, most enduring work in exposing the unexamined assumptions of our society and that an alien setting gives us a chance to look at and evaluate those assumptions from a different perspective.[8] Perhaps the most important observation about observation: (1) Observation is driven by assumptions (many of which are unarticulated), and (2) People who observe the same phenomena may perceive differently (call this the Rashomon effect).

The Chronicles raise at least two fundamental questions about observation: (1) What do we presuppose when observing? and (2) What is the purpose of observing? That is, what are the goals? Whose power is served?

The assumptions that underly these questions can be further broken down into several fundamental philosophical debates:[9] (1) What is the nature of reality? (2) How do we know what we claim to know? (3) What is a human being? (4) Is truth discoverable through scientific method? (5) How do values shape observation? (6) Do we observe to understand the status quo? (7) Do we observe to make changes for the betterment of society?

Each of these philosophical questions is traditionally polarized by objective and subjective schools of thought.[10] That is, persons will often argue that reality, for example, is either (1) Objective (that is, it exists physically "out there" in the physical world and is transcendent of human experience). Or, it is (2) Subjective (that is, it exists mentally or "in here," in the psychological world, as immanent) (see Figure 1).

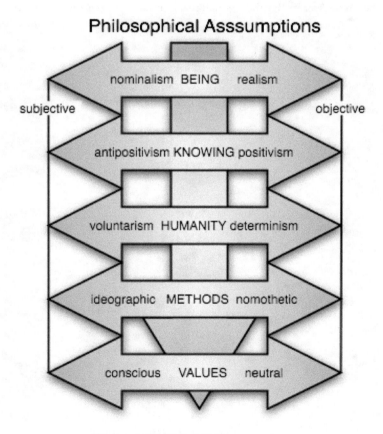

Figure 1. Philosophical assumptions

The Chronicles articulate both a science of the subjective and more. However, Mentat training will here take up both sides of the coin so that modern presuppositions can be seen in any text. Then we will be prepared to move into more radical territory.

What Do We Presuppose When We Observe?

At least since the time of Aristotle, philosophy has sought to grasp the principles, origins, or wellsprings of thought. Philosophers have sought to understand the fascinating faculty of intelligence itself, but they tread on soft ground.

> Deep in the human unconscious is a pervasive need for a logical universe that makes sense. But the real universe is always one step beyond logic.[11]

Illustration 4. Honored Matre and Futars

Today we live in a world so theoretically rich, so full of ideas, that we run the risk of forgetting that our thoughts are built on the thoughts of others. It seems that many have largely forgotten how to take the world at face value. *Physiognomy* is a potentially lost art practiced by fringe psychology, phenomenology, and some postmodern thinkers. Instead, many stand on the shoulders of giants, building theory on top of theory. Rarely do we go back to the wellsprings from which an idea sprang. And even if we did, we would find that the springs themselves are not the beginning of anything. A spring is but a momentary densification of intensities—a locus at which the watercourse way of the cosmos turns from less tangible phenomena such as vapor into the more easily traced water itself. They are both integral and interpenetrated aspects of a larger system—the hydraulic system of the earth.

But wisdom may be found by returning to the wellsprings. For ideas today have their origin, their *arche*. And when we return to the spring, even if it has since dried, we can dig through the layers of sand and strata of dried clay, and see traces of the ancient formations. We can uncover, to some degree, the springs from which now taken-for-granted assumptions first flowed.

Ontology: What is Being or Reality?

> We have long known that the objects of our palpable sense experiences
> can be influenced by choice. . . . I address a pragmatic relationship between
> belief and what we identify as 'real.'[12]

With a storehouse of memories going back thousands of years, the Bene Gesserit recognize that what passes for "reality" is historical, discursive, and contextual. We pass ideas about the nature of reality down from generation to generation, and these ideas form for us a cultural inheritance—often independent of what our senses report.

> Education is no substitute for intelligence. The elusive quality is defined
> only in part by puzzle-solving ability. It is the creation of new puzzles
> reflecting what your senses report that you round out the definition.[13]

Assumptions about the nature of reality, or the nature of *being*, are formally known as *ontology*. Ontology is the branch of philosophy that asks, what is the nature of reality? What is the nature of a thing's being? Or what is the nature of the subject matter at hand? A great tension between the two dominant schools of thought—realism and nominalism—echoes throughout *The Chronicles*.[14]

ONTOLOGY OBJECTIFIED—REALISM

> The universe is just there; that's the only way a Fedaykin can view it and
> remain the master of his senses. . . . You cannot fend off such realities with
> words.[15]

For the realist, there is a hard reality "out there," independent of human perception and expression. This implies, for the thinker, that the world is ready-made
and is either waiting to be understood by science or lies beyond the limits of
human understanding. Likewise, for the realist, the social world is considered as tangible, just like the natural world. A government, for example, is an
aggregate to be studied mechanically; consciousness can be reduced to chemical
relationships. This is Galileo's world and the world as generally understood at
the end of the twentieth century.[16] However, we see at the same time how the
Bene Gesserit sow myths that become the reality that real people believe. This
indicates that another, more subtle position is possible and even desirable.

ONTOLOGY SUBJECTIFIED—NOMINALISM

> There is no reality. Only our own order imposed on everything.[17]

Whereas realism is the main current of modern thought, it is a way of thinking both acknowledged and challenged by *The Chronicles*. Few will deny the
reality of the world (in the sense that a sandstorm is deadly), but its real-*ism*
or appearance is questionable. The critical thinker may find good reason to
question the authority of the tribe and the sets of beliefs passed down from
generation to generation—especially if those beliefs appear to be designed by
persons of power who sought control and domination. The appearance of the
world, in its manifold verisimilitude, and for all its solidity, is woven together
by webs of ideas and articulated in speech—words. The "real," therefore, can
be seen as a product of human action. That is, the things we consider real are
culturally manifest. Things appear to consciousness as they are observed and
named. This naming of objects of consciousness is *nominalism*.

> If you believe certain words, you believe their hidden arguments. . . . [Y]ou
> believe the assumptions in the words which express the arguments. Such
> assumptions are often full of holes, but remain most precious to the
> convinced.[18]

Nominalism, from the Greek *nomos*, to name, is the doctrine that considers the world in terms of the words we use to describe it. In other words,
language may serve to lock its speakers into a realist world; take the realism
discussed above as a manifestation of Fremen speech, for example.

> Fremen speech . . . is immersed in the illusion of absolutes. Its assumptions
> are a fertile ground for absolutist religions. . . . They confront the terrifying
> instability of all things with institutionalized statements.[19]

Language cuts grooves into perception. These grooves just as easily contain as liberate. Consider labels, for example; when someone is called a terrorist, the label conjures a field of meanings that reveal more about the culture that produced the field of associations that the word connotes than it truly describes the person to whom the label is applied; there is no Terrorist or Woman or Politician, but fools substitute these labels for experience.[20]

> Humans have this deep desire to classify, to apply labels to everything . . . that
> way we lay claim to what we name. We assume an ownership that can be
> misleading and dangerous.[21]

Nominalism, it must be noted, is not a rejection of the physical world. Rather, nominalism raises questions concerning the relationship between language and the world. Nominalism asks, "to what extent do our labels, terms, classifications, categories, and languages shape our perception of physical and ideal experience?" Consider, for example, how many observations called "laws" are now more modestly considered "theories." Physicist Max Planck has said "We have no right to assume that any physical laws exist, or if they have existed up to now, that they will continue to exist in a similar manner in the future." The word "law" implies enforcement and the notion that nothing exceeds a set boundary—the speed of light, or the pull of gravity, for example. Theory, on the other hand, is a word that allows for future modification; it acknowledges that any observation may not hold true at all levels of human understanding.

For the nominalist, the social fabric is seen as softer, more internal, more subjective, and is considered as socially informed through language and human action. This tradition derives from German idealism. For the idealist, the social structure is seen as changing all the time. The world is seen as a kaleidoscope continuum. We create and are mutually created by the world through the mediation of language and other human interventions.

Epistemology—What do we know?

> Climb the mountain just a little bit to test that it's a mountain. From the
> top of the mountain, you cannot see the mountain.[22]

The branch of philosophy that questions the basis of knowledge is called *epistemology* (from the Greek *episteme*—to know). It asks: What do we know? What can we know? How do we know what we claim to know? The common approaches to answering these questions polarize along objective and subjective lines and produce the schools of thought known as *positivism* and *antipositivism* (or *postpositivism*).[23]

EPISTEMOLOGY OBJECTIFIED—POSITIVISM

Positivism assumes that knowledge is objective.[24] The goal of positivism is to gain certain and absolute knowledge in order to explain and predict. This comes about generally by examining regularities and causal relationships. The positivist thus believes in: (1) apodictic knowledge—this we call "absolute" or "positive knowledge" and (2) apophantic knowledge—this is the belief that we know *what* things are; it deals with a thing's *being*. Such knowledge has been achieved in some respects by the physical sciences, and one should be able to see the worth of positivist thought, especially when considering fields of human inquiry such as medicine.

However, there are limits to positive knowledge. As Vico notes in his monumental *New Science*, the ability to predict outcomes based on Newton's laws of motion and gravitation does not immediately cultivate prudence, eloquence, or ultimately wisdom enabling us to deal with physical knowledge; consider the dangers inherent in nuclear technology, for example.[25]

> People generally prefer the *predictable*. Few recognize how destructive this can be, how it imposes severe limits on variability and thus makes whole populations fatally vulnerable to the shocking ways our universe can throw the dice."[26]

EPISTEMOLOGY SUBJECTIFIED—ANTI-POSITIVISM

Although positivism is the dominant epistemological position of modern science, a question remains: What are these limits? *The Dune Chronicles* present a simple, quiet, and effective criticism of positivism and objectivism in accordance with a postmodern and quantum-mechanical worldview.[27] This critique of positive knowledge, which flies in the face of conventional, common wisdom and consensus reality, produces a position taken up by many in the humanities and quantum sciences today; it is called postpositivism or antipositivism. This is the way of the Mentat.

> The great revolt took away a crutch. . . . It forced *human* minds to develop. Schools started to train *human* talents.[28]

The subjectivist position regarding epistemology known as antipositivism is firmly set against establishing a set of rules, laws, hypotheses, or any kind of underlying theses of *regularity* when observing the world; one is constantly on the lookout for the inexplicable and unpredictable. This does not mean that there are no patterns in nature or behavior. It means that patterns are a result of human observation using specific tools at an historical moment. Thus, patterns can only be understood from the perspective of those doing the observing. As such, what counts as knowledge is never certain or "positive" and includes all possible foreseen and unforeseen potentials.

> Ready comprehension is often a knee-jerk response and the most dangerous form of understanding. It blinks an opaque screen over your ability to learn. . . . Be warned. Understand nothing. All comprehension is temporary.[29]

Postpositivist questions include: Who is the thinker who does the thinking?

> Who is it that thinks?[30]

When is knowledge certain or final?

> Uproot your questions from their ground and the dangling roots will be seen. More questions![31]

Knowledge is couched in language and thus limited to what words can express:[32]

> Knowledge, the Duncans [Mentats to the House Atreides] believe, resides only in particulars. I try to tell them that all words are plastic. Word images begin to distort in the instant of utterance. Ideas imbedded in a language require that particular language for expression.[33]

The Mentat adopts a theory of knowledge that is open-ended:

> A Mentat's skills lay in that mental *construct* they called "the great synthesis." It required a patience that non-Mentats did not even imagine possible. Mentat school defined it as perseverance. . . . At the same time, you remained open to broad motions all around and within. This produced naiveté, the basic Mentat posture.[34]

For the Mentat, knowledge is never positive, absolute, or fixed.

Method and Methodology

> You will learn the integrated communication methods as you complete the next step in your mental education. This is a gestalten function which will

> overlay data paths in your awareness, resolving complexities and masses of input from the mentat index-catalogue techniques which you have already mastered. Your initial problem will be the breaking tensions arising from the divergent assembly of minutiae/data on specialized subjects. Be warned. Without mentat overlay integration, you can become immersed in the Babel Problem, which is the label we give to the omnipresent dangers of achieving wrong combinations from accurate information.[35]

If thought proceeds according to a background grid of assumptions and follows lines along this grid, we can raise questions concerning the tools or methods we might use to bring about clear observation; we can ask, "how should we travel along these lines and navigate this grid?" "Is there a method that will allow us to see beyond this grid and discover something new?" Or, "are we trapped by our cultural assumptions?" Such questions of procedure are questions of both method, the steps one takes when thinking and observing, and methodology, that is, the underlying philosophy that guides one's steps. Philosophical assumptions about methodology are based largely on the first two sets of assumptions outlined in this chapter (i.e., on the questions of ontology and epistemology) and again can be easily seen as polarized according to whether one takes an objectivist (*nomothetic*) or subjectivist (*ideographic*) approach to the matter.[36]

A philosophy of method may seem esoteric, or not important for everyday thought, but we do approach problems with a specific tack, from a specific angle, and in so doing give silent credence to our presuppositions. The debate concerning methodology is the debate over *order*; do we proceed by steps that prescribe our observations and, thus, can be repeated in order to verify our findings for all persons at all times? Or, do we seek to peer beyond steps that might themselves be predetermined and, thus, predispose us to think in one way and not another?

> But there was nothing humans hated more than unpredictability. 'We want it natural!' Whatever that means.[37]

METHODOLOGY OBJECTIFIED—NOMOTHETIC METHODS

Objectivist methodologies are known as *nomothetic*. These methodologies are based on systematic inquiry or step-by-step methods. This process, known in general as the *scientific method*, includes formulating research questions and hypotheses and testing these to find the outcome of experiments.[38] The goal is to find an answer (generally a cause). Nomothetic inquiry, formalized historically by Bacon, Galileo, and Newton, claims to be objective and absolute. It claims to explore what is general, universal, and thus natural.

Just as *The Chronicles* critique realism, positivism, and other objectivist notions, so too they critique rules that predetermine thought patterns. The reason for this critique is not based on the ideals of nomothetic inquiry (which are quite admirable and produce spectacular results). Rather the critique raised via the machinations of the Major Houses and Primary Schools concerns the possibility that such methods may actually be self-limiting. Although we can apply objective methods to the physical world with a high degree of accuracy, this in no way implies that such methods will work when concerning questions of human understanding itself.

METHODOLOGY SUBJECTIFIED—IDEOGRAPHIC METHODS

> It was a typical Mentat approach: concentrate on the questions. Mentats accumulated questions the way others accumulated answers. Questions created their own patterns and systems. This produced the most important *shapes*. You looked at your universe through self-created patterns—all composed of images, words, and labels (everything temporary), all mingled in sensory impulses that reflected off his internal constructs the way light bounced from bright surfaces.[39]

The corollary subjective pole for methodological procedure is known as *ideographic*. Here is a vantage for which multiple answers for a single question are possible. Paradox is acceptable. This represents the approaches and methods of the arts and humanities. It favors multiple perspectives. It claims to explore what is unique, personal, and relativistic. Its methods are largely interpretive. It is the way of the Mentat.

Values and Observation

The philosophical study of values is called *axiology*. An axiom is a type of statement taken to be self-evident or true and is thus a statement of value. The first axiological question that underlies formal observation is: Can observation be value-free? Common responses to this question:[40] Value-Neutral: The position of classical science maintains that observation may be value-neutral, and the observer should not apply values to observing and theorizing things as they really are. Value-Positive: A second position counters the classical point of view by suggesting that substantive values are built into the very fabric of research. The pursuit of fact, truth, objectivity, the importance of ideas, and even science itself are values. So, values are a benign, but unavoidable, presence for the observer.

A second axiological question raises the issue of responsibility: Are scientists responsible for what is done with their work?[41] The classical, or *pure-*

science, answer to this question is simply "no." According to this perspective, the scientist is only responsible for observing and describing the natural flow of events. A more modern response to the same question is the opposite—"yes." Because scientific research favors a set of values and may unleash powers hitherto unknown, such as the use of atomic energy to produce an atomic bomb, the scientist is a political participant. Merely denying political participation is not a substantial or responsible claim.

A third pervasive axiological question also concerns the impact that science has on its object of observation: To what extent does the practice of social inquiry influence that which is being studied?[42] On one hand lies the notion that scientists observe without disturbing anything. However, quantum mechanics in physics and ethnography in the humanities suggest that the act of observing influences the observed. This second position is that of the participant-observer—the scientist who understands that he or she is an active participant in the activity of research.

The manner of response to the three questions posed above can be configured, again, into a set of binary oppositions based on one's underlying assumption of an objective or subjective metaphysics; these poles are value-neutrality and value-consciousness.[43]

VALUES OBJECTIFIED—VALUE-NEUTRALITY

On the objective side of the axiological equation is the position that science is aloof and value-neutral. Ideally, science does not interfere in any way with observation. Good scholars, it is presumed, control the effects values might have on research.[44] *The Chronicles* challenge these notions.

> If they were only observers, they were doomed.[45]

In *Dune*, we find that the Mentats and other thinking beings are not interested in pure knowledge, but in pragmatic knowledge, and that pure knowledge may be unobtainable in a human world. Indeed, the quest for knowledge is a human value. By the conclusion of *Chapterhouse*, we find that mere observation is not enough. Observation is a form of creativity. In other words, thought and observation *are* values and purposes.

VALUES SUBJECTIFIED—VALUE-CONSCIOUSNESS

On the subjective side of the equation is the position that scientists must be conscious of the ways that values necessarily impinge on any act of observation. They recognize the importance and impact of values and human participation in any inquiry.[46]

Do We Observe to Conserve or Change?

> The assumption that humans exist within an essentially impermanent universe, taken as an operational precept, demands that the intellect become a totally aware balancing instrument. But the intellect cannot react thus without involving the entire organism. [But] societies move to the goading of ancient, reactive impulses. They demand permanence. Any attempt to display the universe of impermanence arouses rejection patterns, fear, anger, and despair.[47]

Coupled with the underlying assumptions concerning one's philosophy of observation (discussed above) are fundamental issues regarding the purpose of observation. Observations generally make at least a few simple, but significant and often unrecognized assumptions: (1) Do we seek to understand the status quo or propose change? If we assume to observe things as they are—as what we call reality or at least norms and, thus, explain the status quo—then we are participating in a sociology of regulation, and (2) If we seek to understand things so that we might propose change, then we are participating in a spirit of radical change.[48]

Observations in the Service of Regulation

The first position regarding the purpose of observation can be called a science of regulation. Its purpose is to provide an explanation of the status quo. Such a science when applied to physics seeks to describe natural events. When applied to sociology, it seeks to explain and understand the social forces that prevent chaos.

Donald Palumbo suggests that *The Chronicles* are composed in a fractal aesthetic; every theme appears at all scales of interpretation.[49] One of these fractal themes is Herbert's critique of the maintenance of the status quo. Although the masses may desire an unchanging and conservative universe—to live within the status quo—*Dune* rejects this idea as reactionary and ill-suited for a life lived in an ever-changing world.

> The person who takes the banal and ordinary and illuminates it in a new way can terrify. We do not want our ideas changed. We feel threatened by such demands.[50]

Dune may be read as a manifesto for radical change.

Observation in the Service of Radical Change

> Major flaws in government arise from a fear of making radical internal changes even though a need is clearly seen.[51]

The second position, with regard to the purpose of observation, deals with radical change. Observations are used to bring about new experiences, structures, and understandings. Observation is concerned with looking at deep-seated structural conflict and modes of domination that operate in society.[52] It is interested in people's emancipation from oppressive social structures, material and psychic deprivation.

Radical change is proposed at many levels in the saga of *Dune*. For example: Paul Muad'Dib Atreides, The Preacher:

> This is the fallacy of power: ultimately it is effective only in an absolute, a limited universe. But the basic lesson of our relativistic universe is that things change.[53]

The Bene Gesserit:

> A major concept guides the Missionaria Protectiva: Purposeful instruction of the masses. This is firmly seated in our belief that the aim of argument should be to change the nature of truth. In such matters, we prefer the use of power rather than force.[54]

The Bene Tleilaxu (who speak of a paradoxical conservative change):

> What do Holy Accidents teach? Be resilient. Be strong. Be ready to change, for the new. Gather many experiences and judge them by the steadfast nature of our faith.[55]

Frank Herbert:

> There may be a quiet spot in my mind where nothing moves and the places of my childhood remain unchanged, but everything else moves and changes. . . . We should salvage what we can, but even salvaging changes things.[56]

These quotes, and others, suggest that radical change is more than an idea or ideal, but rather, *radical change is the status quo*! Mentats transcend the given binary formation and take a third path that is deeply philosophical. Wisdom suggests that one's observations always be ready to perceive change. And, observations provide the necessary fuel to propose change.

> Remember your philosopher's doubts. . . . The mind of the believer stagnates.[57]

Matrix of Four Paradigms

Burrell and Morgan's detailed study of sociological paradigms and organizational analysis take the assumptions discussed above and set them into a set of relationships (see Figure 2).[58] This set is established by playing the assumptions about the philosophy of observation (polarized by considering things as objective or subjective) against the presupposed purpose of observation (polarized by explaining the status quo or proposing radical change). Once familiar with these polarities, it becomes important to look beyond these binaries at the matrix or *grid* formed by placing these two axes in relationship to each other.

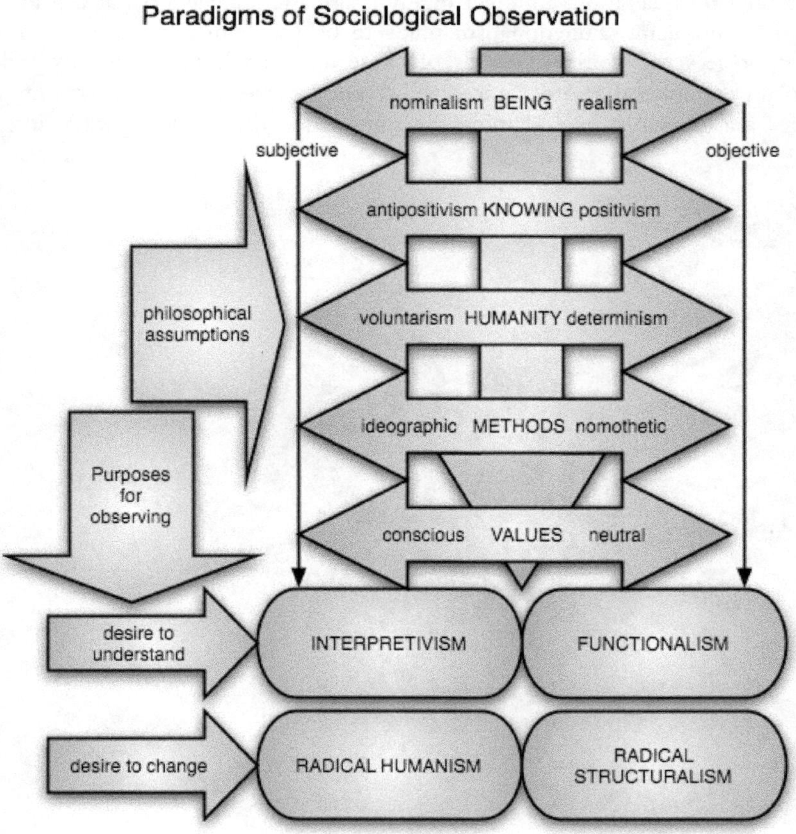

Paradigms of Sociological Observation

Figure 2. Paradigms

These two axes, set into such an interrelationship, form a matrix of four paradigms: (1) Functionalism, (2) Interpretivism, (3) Radical Humanism, and (4) Radical Structuralism. Four major paradigms (or discourses with rules of inclusion and exclusion) characterize the majority of social and cultural observation and purpose and contain the various schools of sociocultural study. But take heed, these paradigms should be read as points of departure for further understanding and discussions, not as the ends of sociological or organizational thought or absolute categories.

Fremen Functionalism

Functionalism, sometimes called positivism or experimentalism, seeks rational and logical explanations to affect highly pragmatic knowledge that can be used to solve problems. Functionalism tends to be problem/solution oriented and, thus, it sees the world in terms of cause and effect. Functionalists seek to explain the ways that order and stability are achieved and can be maintained. They are interested in explaining the status quo, social order, cultural integra-

Illustration 5. Muad'Dib and Stilgar

tion, political solidarity, and need satisfaction. For the functionalist (who seeks absolute and certain knowledge), the social world and the physical world are seen as tangible, objective, and factual.

It is tempting to call the Mentat a positivist. But the Mentat rejects singularities and simple causal logics (although she will include these in the analysis of another person's statements; it is important to know when somebody has made these assumptions). Functionalism is the dominant power today; it is the dominion of the radically successful physical sciences. Functionalism is powerful because it works at both the crude physical level of materials and supports the logic structure of English and the scientific mythos. It fails to find what it seeks (absolute and certain knowledge), however, because for all its explanatory power, the universe appears to be always one step ahead of our present knowledge—its explanations always raise more questions. The ever-changing nature of knowledge is addressed by Leto:

> In all of my universe I have seen no law of nature, unchanging and inexorable. The universe presents only changing relationships which are sometimes seen as laws by short-lived awareness. These fleshy sensoria which we call self are ephemera withering in the blaze of infinity, fleetingly aware of temporary conditions which confine our activities and change as our activities change. If you must label the absolute, use its proper name: Temporary.[59]

Often confused with science itself, functionalism is so pervasive that it often appears as the obvious and only correct method of thinking. As such, its values have the force that Church dogma would have had in the dark ages. Also, because the functionalist's language is the language of mathematics, the primal and qualitative consideration of the world is reduced to a secondary, quantitative measurement of that experience.

Although the task at hand is not a matter of pigeonholing, the Fremen appear most closely aligned with the ideals of functionalism. This is because the Fremen's faith is fundamentalist and absolutist. They have absolute values based on groundless mythos and superstition. Indeed, because of their belief in an objective world they are manipulated by the Bene Gesserit and Paul Atreides. By following the Word, they eventually follow others who lead them to their own destruction.

The Chronicles may be read as a critique of functionalist thought.[60] Pragmatic knowledge is sought and highly valued (as the training of Mentats attests), but the ideals of absolute knowledge are debunked even by those characters with prescience and Other Memory. While Mentats seek "prime computation," the closest possible prediction, they realize that they are interpreters and are thus subject to limits. We begin to see that all computations and projections are, in the final analysis, interpretations; this leads us to the second paradigm, interpretivism, and the science of the subjective.[61]

Mentat Interpretivism

> Deep within the human unconscious is a pervasive need for a logical universe that makes sense. But the real universe is always one step beyond logic.[62]

The interpretive paradigm (sometimes called ethnographic) maintains an interest in explaining the status quo, but abandons objective assumptions about the nature of observation and reality. Ethnographers see themselves as thinking within a situation rather than as neutral observers outside looking in. Interpretive observers see the world as an emergent process and are interested in the practices of daily life. They seek to understand the subjective relationship between persons and world and the social construction of reality. Interpretivism is widely practiced in the humanities and more recently in postpositivist social sciences. *The Chronicles* reflect and illuminate this postpositivist (antifunctionalist), interpretive thinking. This can be seen in the interpretive dimension of Mentat computation and attention to the ways that language shapes reality. Words (as discussed throughout this chapter), when accepted uncritically, trap people in the power of those who made them. And words are not fixed, physical entities, but fluid, malleable, and changeable:

> Words are plastic. Word images begin to distort in the instant of utterance.[63]

By recognizing the interpretive dimension of all human thought, the Mentat stands on the cutting edge of scientific and postmodern thought. However, Mentats traditionally worked for the Great and Lesser Houses of the Landsraad. In a post-Imperial, post-God-Emperor world, we must take care to look to ways that change can be enacted.[64]

The Preacher's Radical Humanism

Radical humanism (sometimes called conflict theory) takes a different position. Although it embraces the same (subjective) assumptions regarding the nature of observation and reality as does the interpretive paradigm, there is an emphasis on promoting change rather than on explaining the status quo. For the radical humanist, there is an underlying interest in how ideology and hegemony split consciousness.[65] In other words, the consciousness of socialized humans is seen in relationship to and as informed by oppressive social structures. The purpose of radical humanism is to critique the status quo and provide citizens with way-out options. Radical humanists seek release from dominating social structures, and thus they have a profound commitment to social change.

Radical humanism appears today in the work of people like Paulo Freire and Ivan Illich (in educational theory) and movements such as feminism. Radical humanists write about the ways that humans become systematically oppressed by both physical and ideological force. They promote ideas and practices in hopes of affecting a change of consciousness that will open heretofore unforeseen opportunities.[66]

The Preacher asks for a change of consciousness—a radical shift in the way of life.

> The only business of the Fremen should be that of opening his soul to the inner teachings. The worlds of the Imperium, the Landsraad and the CHOAM Confederacy have no message to give him. They will only rob him of his soul.[67]

He speaks to the Fremen whose activist participation is becoming clouded by ideology:

> I will not argue with the Fremen claims that they are divinely inspired to transmit a religious revelation. It is their concurrent claim to ideological revelation which inspires me to shower them with derision. Of course, they make the dual claim in the hope that it will strengthen their mandate and help them to endure in a universe which finds them increasingly oppressive. It is in the name of all those oppressed people that I warn the Fremen: short-term expediency always fails in the long-term.[68]

He denounces those who uncritically adopted Muad'Dib's religion (and he *is* Muad'Dib), and he preaches that self-deception and dysfunctional thoughts be exposed:

> Holiness has replaced love in your religion.[69]

He warns the Bene Gesserit:

> I come here to combat the fraud and illusion of your conventional, institutionalized religion. As with all such religions, your institution moves toward cowardice, it moves toward mediocrity, inertia, and self-satisfaction.[70]

The Preacher desires that the oppressive religious domination established in the name of Muad'Dib be overthrown not by war or invoking deep-seated structural changes to the society (although these might follow), but by a change of consciousness. His sermons reveal a clear critique of functionalist, positivist thinking and propose a cosmic consciousness:

> If you would possess your humanity, let go of the universe. . . . I realize that humans cannot bear very much reality. . . . Most lives are a flight from selfhood. Most prefer the truths of the stable. You stick your heads into the stanchions and munch contentedly until you die. Others use you for their purposes. . . . Is your religion real when it costs you nothing and carries no risks? Is your religion real when you fatten upon it? Is your religion real when you commit atrocities in its name? . . . Muad'Dib . . . showed us that men must do this always, choosing the uncertain instead of the certain. . . . Abandon certainty! That's life's deepest command. That's what life's all about. . . . To exist is to stand out, away from the background.[71]

The God Emperor's Radical Structuralism

Whereas the radical humanist seeks to promote change of consciousness, the radical structuralist seeks to promote institutional and material change. The radical structuralist has a deep-seated concern with economic and political structures. Radical structuralism is interested in the hard, tangible, "out-there" structures of society and reality. Thus, the radical structuralist shares the drive for change with the radical humanist, but takes an objective stance toward observation and reality; and in this, the radical structuralist is more akin to the functionalist than the interpreter.

Radical structuralism is not a dominant force in social theory today. Some of the theories of Karl Marx, the global exportation of democracy and contemporary power-politics, can be put forth as examples. Techno-science may also be seen as a radical structuralist endeavor. Techno-sciences, such as genetics and medicine, are predicated on making radical changes to the structures of our foods and bodies.

Examples of radical structuralism can be found in Paul's conquest of the Imperium in the first book of *The Chronicles*. It appears in the Bene Gesserit's selective breeding program. And it appears most vividly in Leto's Golden Path; the path that Paul, who speaks as a radical humanist (in the form of The Preacher) in *Children of Dune*, could not take. Paul, however, had seen that path, and as The Preacher, set it into motion, even as he left it to his son to complete. The Golden Path is itself a structural oppression so great that it promises to teach people to never again allow themselves to be caught in such a trap.

> When I set out to lead humankind along my Golden Path, I promised them a lesson their bones would remember.[72]

Leto takes control over the structure of the world:

> What did I take from them? The right to participate in history.[73]

But the radical structuralism is not completely objective in its assumptions or goals: Consequent with the rejection of positivism, Leto II is a Janus-faced god. Whereas the Golden Path is a form of radical structuralism, in the end the result is a change of consciousness—a humanist change.

> Odd as it may seem, great struggles such as the one you can see emerging from my journals are not always visible to the participants. Much depends on what people dream in the secrecy of their hearts. I have always been as concerned with the shaping of dreams as with the shaping of actions.[74]

Hope Clouds Observation

> We live in a universe dominated by relativity and change, but our intellects keep demanding fixed absolutes. We make our most strident demands for absolutes that contain comforting reassurance. We will misread and/or misunderstand almost anything that challenges our favorite illusions.[75]

Although it is said that Muad'Dib taught a balanced way of life, Leto tipped the scales. Leto rearranged the signs. By oppressing civilization, his rule was so one-sided as to render binary oppositions transparent. On the one hand, binaries such as subject and object make sense; one experiences immanence and transcendence differently. On the other hand, however, both immanence and transcendence, objectivity and subjectivity, go together and are unified by embodiment and world. Their meaning is localized by expression and perception. Therefore, at the end of the protracted discussion above, three findings appear.

Three Observations

1. The Mentat's "science of the subjective" (as O'Reilly suggests that *The Chronicles* establish) is based more on a postmodern, quantum mechanical and human studies understanding than a classical, modern physics or social science model. For the Mentat, the world is an ever-changing kaleidoscope flux. Any attempt to know "*what* that flux *is*" is limited by language, historical forces, and the fallibilities of simply being human. Paul's prescient vision is not absolute. A Mentat's prime computations are not always accurate. The Bene Gesserit, with their storehouse of past memories, are unable to project an absolute future based on past experiences.

2. We all make assumptions about the nature of the world whether we are aware of these or not. Realizing these assumptions, especially if they are based on another person's reason handed down uncritically, is a path to clearing

the eye and a way to avoiding being duped. The idea here is to shift presuppositions into the light of consciousness. Awareness of the ways one's thought moves literally lightens the load; one is able to see more clearly why one thinks as one does and why certain conclusions are drawn. For the Mentat, who often think in the service of others, the ability to detect the silent assumptions in the argument of another is a valuable, convivial tool.

3. Do not allow the neat and tidy paradigms to fool you into complacency. These paradigms are the thought grids of twentieth-century sociology. Although they account for the presence of modern and postmodern science and philosophy, they are but a momentary territorialization of the desert of the real. The Mentat does not "think outside the box"; the Mentat thinks all boxes simultaneously, transparently. Each may be seen through the other and all at once. Whereas Kuhn has observed that Western science moves by paradigmatic ruptures, the Mentat must *jump these tracks* and use the thought guides above to grasp the whole.

The Bene Gesserit's Razor

A Bene Gesserit axiom serves to keep thought clear:

> Hope clouds observation.[76]

This chapter opened by stating that the unclouded eye was better—no matter what it saw. We see, to a great extent, what we expect to see. Unclouding the eye, setting aside our hopes and dealing with the matters at hand (no matter how unpleasant), is largely a matter of making the subconscious conceptual grids by which we think available to consciousness, by interrogating the historical, linguistic, and political constitution of common sense and consensus reality. This can be achieved by understanding what phenomenologists call the *intentionality* of perception. Herbert noted in his famous essay, *Listening to the Left Hand,* that students learning to read X-ray plates

> [a]lmost universally . . . demonstrate an inability to distinguish between what is shown on the plate and what they believe will be shown. They see things that are not there.[77]

Perception, this suggests, is an active process in which human beings choose from a vast array of sensory and intellectual *capta* and organize it into recognizable forms—*data*. Most often this is an unconscious process. Past training, experience, and values establish a horizon of expectations that dictate that only certain information will be seen. Things that do not match a preconceived model are rejected by all but the most critical thinker.[78]

Be forewarned: There are fads and fashions in philosophy. In many ways, the scientific and philosophical endeavor is less a pure search for truth than it is a political response to a social environment; scientists are people who can get jobs as a scientists, and these job opportunities will open around issues to which money has been diverted. In short, philosophy and science appear within, and not separate from, politics. Thus, the *Mentat Fixe* reminds us that:

> Ready comprehension is often a knee-jerk response and the most danger-ous form of understanding. It blinks an opaque screen over your ability to learn. The judgmental precedents of law function that way, littering your path with dead ends. Be warned. Understand nothing. All comprehension is temporary.[79]

Mentats know well their limits, limits in general, and are constantly open to the possibilities implied by an indefinite universe.

> Most deadly errors arise from absolute assumptions.[80]

"Thinking outside the box" is easy to say, but difficult to do, because we run out of thought grids.[81] But we can see all available boxes because we know the rules of the discourses and language games. At that point, at that limit, we are in the best possible place to see through tradition. Even if we cannot grasp the "new," we can grasp the whole. This is important because, even when the basic presuppositions of "objective" methods are rendered problematic and the limits of mathematical systems are well demonstrated, these approaches toward under-standing continue to appear in the most unfruitful of places (e.g., corporate and ratings media research and audience analysis). This is why understanding assump-tions and presuppositions and the informed nature of intentionality is so vital.

> Holders of power wish to suppress 'wild' research. Unrestricted questing after knowledge has a long history of producing unwanted competition. The powerful want a "safe line of investigations," which will develop only those products and ideas that can be controlled and, most important, that will allow the larger part of the benefits to be captured by inside investors. Unfortunately, a random universe full of relative variables does not insure such a "safe line of investigations."[82]

The Mentat knows that hope and expectation cloud observation, and the unclouded eye is better—no matter what it sees.

Endnote: Journalistic Objectivity

Herbert was a journalist before a novelist, and journalism works on its own sets of assumptions that may have inspired him to take such a significant twist concerning both objectivity and subjectivity in his novels. Consider the specific case of "journalistic objectivity" as a form or style of objectivity. To note just a few points: An objective journalist reports the facts, considers both sides of the story, is fair, and writes in clear declarative prose (usually active voice).

Although these are certainly ethical values, they are values generated by human interests and not, as so often supposed, facts or truth in and of themselves. They are thus less objective than what we can call subjective. They are neither "purely" objective nor are they an access to The Truth: A "report" is already a rhetorical form. It is not inherently better at describing "reality" than poetry—in fact, it may be worse for its prosaic limits. A report is a form of rhetoric that often makes tacit use of narrative that imposes a form (a limitation) on how the news is presented and positions people as characters within a story.

"Facts" are generated by a discourse with its rules of inclusion and exclusion and thus are always interpretations. This does not mean that a fact is not a fact, but rather that its objectivity requires substantiation, and such substantiation is always tied to a discourse or communication constellation.

The idea that a story has "two sides" is a clear sign of the demand that the cosmos be fitted into a dualism and binary opposition indicative of rationality. And rationality is a powerful form of rhetoric. When ever did you know a story to have only two sides? Consider as well: What is "fair"? In other words, fair to whom? The press? The politician? The audience? Which audience? In still other words, from what position is fairness determined. The problem is not that the "objectivity" of journalism is ethical or unethical, but that it is a value system constituted by human desire; journalistic objectivity is an extreme form of idealism and subjectivity.

Take as another example the case in point, that beautiful means of expression, mathematics. I will not underestimate the beauty or the use-value of mathematics for describing certain phenomena. However, mathematics does not deserve the grand title of "objective language." The empirical, sensual world offers us no quantities that were not first qualities that have been reduced, for a purpose, to measurable quantities. There are no "values," no "numbers" out there in the material, objective world, waiting behind a tree to be "discovered." They are constructed, ideated, made in accordance with social requirements.

Whose requirements? What interests? These become key questions. Rather than take the world at face value, we seem to have chosen a course by which we make the world in accordance to human desires. The reality engine is geared, fueled, and driven by human interests. It is time to ask ourselves, "can we face the things as they present themselves to us and not as we want them to be?" The study of physiognomy (and the practice of phenomenology) begins by exploring the phenomenon of communication through which local definitions of phenomena, with their discursive formations, appear.

Notes

1. Reverend Mother Superior Darwi Odrade. *Chapterhouse*, 57.

2. Jaspers, "On My Philosophy," from *Existentialism from Dostoyevsky to Sartre* (W. Kaufman, Ed.). Herbert was reportedly inspired by Carl Jaspers' existentialism.

3. It is fashionable today to define consciousness in terms of neurochemistry because of the fantastic findings in this field of study. However, the study of consciousness as a biochemical process tends to overlook the flow of consciousness itself. Because our interest is the cultivation of a critical, analytical, synthetical, and integral understanding of the flow of awareness, we will take here a phenomenological approach in the style of Edmund Husserl.

4. Paul's meditation. *Dune*, 5.

5. Bene Gesserit Creed. *Chapterhouse*, 115.

6. Bene Gesserit Creed. *Chapterhouse*, 115.

7. Missionaria Protectiva, *Chapterhouse*, 263. This chapter owes its form and underlying content to the work of many scholars: Gibson Burrell and Gareth Morgan, *Sociological Paradigms and Organizational Analysis* (Exeter, NH: Heinemann, 1979); Richard Lanigan, *Phenomenology of Communication*; Steven Littlejohn and Karen Foss, *Theories of Human Communication* (Belmont, CA: Wadsworth, 2004); Ben Agger, *Socio(onto) ology, A Disciplinary Reading* (Urbana: University of Illinois Press, 1989). Additional material is taken from lectures by Imafadon Olye of William Paterson University, NJ, and Jenny Nelson, Joseph Rota, David Descutner, and Algis Mickunas of Ohio University. See also L. Kurt Engelhart, "The Golden Path: Frank Herbert's Universe," Phenomenological Study (<http://kengelhart.home.igc.org/goldenpa.htm>) 3/9/06.

8. Touponce, ibid., 11.

9. The issues of ontology, epistemology, inquiry, and others are discussed also in *The Golden Path: Frank Herbert's Universe, a Phenomenological Study*. L. Kurt Engelhart (http://kengelhart.home.igc.org/goldenpa.htm) 7/20/05.

10. These poles represent extreme positions and are the unfortunate remnants of Cartesian dualism. The dichotomies drawn here are meant to provide the reader with an introduction to complex issues, by starting with simple oppositions. Most people's assumptions about science fall somewhere in between and even beyond these structures of thought. The characters in *Dune* show both the extremes and the problems inherent in taking an extremist position on any issue.

11. From The Sayings of Muad'Dib by the Princess Irulan. *Dune*, 373.

12. Argument in Council, The Reverend Mother Superior Taraza. *Heretics*, 272.

13. Mentat Text One (decto). *Chapterhouse*, 94.

14. Gibson Burrell and Gareth Morgan, *Sociological Paradigms and Organizational Analysis* (Exeter, NH: Heinemann, 1979).

15. Muad'Dib to his Fedaykin. *Children*, 179.

16. Consider, for a moment, the power inherent in such a notion. The Fedaykin death-commando terrorists, for example, accept the world, including their death as objective, and therefore are able to suspend worries, doubts, and fears. If the world just is, then what use is worry? Why not die for your cause? The appearance of the Fedaykin in *Dune* is one of the more frightening and fascinating prescient visions found in Herbert's

writing. It has been historically noted that Herbert felt that the populace of the United States was dangerously ignorant of Arab culture. The Fedaykin—ﻦﻴﻴﺋﺍﺪﻓ—appear closely related to Feda'yin used for the Palestinian guerillas in the 1960s and for Saddam Hussein's guerilla forces. The United States has dealt directly with warriors ready to sacrifice themselves in World War II—the Kamakazi forces—but was largely unprepared for 9–11. See Arabic and Islamic themes in *Dune* (Submitted by Khalid on 2004/01/22 <http://baheyeldin.com/literature/arabic-and-islamic-themes-in-frank-herberts-dune.html). 4/11/06.

17. Bene Gesserit Dictum, Reverend Mother Darwi Odrade. *Chapterhouse*, 137. "There is no 'real' or 'unreal,' only what we create together." Frank Herbert in a note to his wife, in Brian Herbert, *Dreamer of Dune* (New York: TOR, 2003, 434).

18. The Open-Ended Proof from The Panoplia Prophetica. *Children*, 244. The Panoplia Prophetic, the watching of prophets, suggests that the naive realist can be overcome with words and their mythic import. Thus works the Missionaria Protectiva, which successfully sows purposeful "myths" so easily received by realists.

19. Bene Gesserit Private Reports/folio 800881. *Children*, 320.

20. The study of labels falls under the academic rubric of General Semantics. Herbert was most profoundly influenced by Korzibsky, who founded the contemporary General Semantics movement.

21. The Reverend Mother Odrade. *Chapterhouse*, 25.

22. From "Muad'Dib: Family Commentaries" by the Princes Irulan. *Dune*, 68.

23. Burell and Morgan, op. cit.

24. For more information, follow a wormhole to the Endnote, Journalistic Objectivity.

25. See Newton, *Principia Mathematica (1687)*; Vico, *New Science (1725)*; see also Hans Georg Gadamer, *Truth and Method* (New York: The Seabury Press, 1975, 20).

26. Assessment of Ix, Bene Gesserit Archives. *Heretics*, 84.

27. To write about science without writing about quantum theory is nearly impossible at this moment in history. However, the application of quantum theory to the humanities, no matter how interesting, is a risky venture for anybody who has not extensively studied both. This book, *The Wisdom of the Sand*, is a work of humanistic inquiry. Recourse is made to quantum theory as a matter of cultural significance, not as a matter of building scientific theory or using scientific methodology.

28. The Reverend Mother Gaius Helen Mohiam. *Dune*, 12.

29. Mentat Fixe (adacto). *Chapterhouse*, 178.

30. Terminology of the Imperium. *Dune*, x.

31. Mentat Zensufi. *Chapterhouse*, 220. See also Foucault, *Archeology of Knowledge*.

32. Knowledge may be limited by language, but there are realms of experience beyond knowledge. To claim to know can be seen as an ability to express the known object in words. The word (or phenomenon) *intuition* is used here to denote experience that includes and transcends knowledge and understanding.

33. The Stolen Journals. *God Emperor*, 342.

34. Duncan Idaho. *Chapterhouse*, 82.

35. The Mentat Handbook. *Children*, 253.

36. Burell and Morgan, op. cit.

37. The Reverend Mother Darwi Odrade. *Chapterhouse*, 64.

38. The scientific method is not quite so simple or closed in practice as it is in theory. The method can be reduced to a few basic ideas: Observation and description of phenomena. Formulation hypotheses to explain the phenomena observed. Use of the hypothesis to predict new observations. Experimentation based on the hypothesis to confirm or reject hypotheses.

39. The Mentat, Duncan Idaho. *Chapterhouse*, 81.

40. Littlejohn and Foss, ibid., 28.

41. Littlejohn and Foss, ibid., 28.

42. Littlejohn and Foss, ibid., 29.

43. Burell and Morgan, op. cit.

44. Littlejohn, op. cit., 29.

45. The Reverend Mother Darwi Odrade. *Chapterhouse*, 316.

46. Littlejohn, op. cit., 29.

47. The Book of Leto, After Harq al-Ada. *Children*, 137. Note as well in this passage the subtle overcoming of mind-body dualism.

48. Burell and Morgan's work concerns sociological analysis. However, their work may easily be extended to consider scientific investigation in general. This is the case especially in the age of techno-science; techno-science is largely concerned with producing new things such as room temperature super conductivity. Classical science, on the other hand, is more concerned with describing the ways the universe works, as in Newton's classic studies of gravitation and planetary motion.

49. Donald Palumbo's work is scholarly, insightful, disciplined, and creative. Donald Palumbo, *Chaos Theory, Asimov's Foundations and Robots, and Herbert's Dune* (Westport: Greenwood Press, 2002).

50. The Zensufi Master. *Chapterhouse*, 12.

51. The Reverend Mother Darwi Odrade. *Chapterhouse*, 182.

52. Burell and Morgan. op. cit.

53. The Preacher at Arrakeen. *Children*, 154.

54. The Coda. *Chapterhouse*, 196.

55. Tleilaxu Doctrine. *Chapterhouse*, 413.

56. Frank Herbert, *Listening with the Left Hand.*

57. (From *Heretics*) in Brian Herbert, *The Notebooks of Frank Herbert's Dune*, 45.

58. Burell and Morgan, op. cit.

59. The Stolen Journals. *God Emperor*, 408.

60. See Timothy O'Reilly, *Frank Herbert* (New York: Frederick Ungar).

61. O'Reilly, ibid.

62. *Dune*, 273.

63. The Stolen Journals. *God Emperor*, 342.

64. For a description of the Mentat's overlay-integration-imagination methodology, follow a wormhole to Appendix B.

65. For more information, follow a wormhole to the Appendix, Ideology and Hegemony.

66. In this respect, it is easy to consider Frank Herbert an example of a radical humanist.

67. The Preacher at Arrakeen. *Children*, 20.

68. The Preacher at Arrakeen. *Children*, 110.

69. From "a sermon of the desert" by The Preacher. *Children*, 112.

70. The Preacher at Arrakeen. *Children*, 224.

71. The Preacher. *Children*, 228–233.

72. Leto II, God Emperor. *Chapterhouse*, 9.

73. The Stolen Journals. *God Emperor*, 373

74. The Stolen Journals. God Emperor, 79. The hypothesis, the hybrid is stronger than the purebred, is a major theme of *Chapterhouse* in which one story line culminates in the cross-fertilization of Bene Gesserit and Honored Matre.

75. Frank Herbert, *Listening to the Left Hand*.

76. Reverend Mother Gaius Mohiam. *Dune*, 10.

77. Frank Herbert, *Listening to the Left Hand.*

78. See O'Reilly, op. cit, chapter Four.

79. Mentat Fixe (adacto). *Chapterhouse*, 178.

80. Ghanima. *Children*, 81.

81. Indeed, an ongoing debate in the Human Science of Communication, Postmodernism and Cultural Studies is namely, "Can we see from an Other vantage?" "Can we see past our own tradition?"

82. Assessment of Ix, Bene Gesserit Archives. *Heretics*, 210.

Chapter Three

Past, Presence, and Prescience

The universe is timeless at its roots and contains therefore all times and all futures.[1]

The Kwisatz Haderach can go where others cannot; he can see the future.[2] His descendants, like the Bene Gesserit Reverend Mothers, have direct awareness of their ancestral memories; they thus draw upon the experiences of many lives. For those of us who think that we're locked into the present, are trailed by the past, and project our desires (often in vain) into the future, these are clearly superhuman feats. But are they? Modern conceptions of time are not the only ways time is experienced. Alternate experiences, existential perceptions, and cultural expressions of time do exist. What we call *real time* is a relatively recent invention.

All of our judgments carry a heavy burden of ancestral beliefs. . . . It is not enough that we are aware of this and guard against it. Alternative interpretations must always receive our attention.[3]

When we say that real time is clock time, there are "old patterns of thinking" at work, "patched together out of primitive communications attempts" that "continue to hamstring us" so long as we fail to see them *as* communication attempts.[4] This is to say that what we call time is a phenomenon—an appearance to consciousness. The understanding of this phenomenon is subject to the relationship between body and world and cultural inflection through mythos and the limitations of language.[5]

Contemporary communication attempts (such as *The Mentat Handbook v2.0*) may, ultimately, appear equally primitive. But primitive is a word with many meanings, and not all are derogatory. Philosophy, Aristotle suggested, is a quest for origin, a pursuit for the *primal*.[6]

A sophisticated human can become primitive. What this really means is that the human's way of life changes. Old values change. . . . This new existence requires a working knowledge of those multiplex and cross-linked events usually referred to as nature [what we are calling the world]. . . . When a human gains his working knowledge and respect, that is called "being primitive."[7]

Here we return to the world's primitive flow, to the origin of our conceptions, and ask: "What could time possibly mean before the church bell, the alarm clock and the wrist watch marked the time, inscribed time in numbers, located it in space or gave it direction"?[8] In order to make alternate interpretations (as Taraza suggests), the framework or cultural grid of our consensus reality must be exposed;[9] to paraphrase the French philosopher Maurice Merleau-Ponty we must seek to know the desert before the planetologist maps it, time before the watch marks the minute.[10] With our common sense held at bay, time as it is presented in *The Dune Chronicles* can be discussed. Correlations between Muad'Dib's experience and our own can be drawn through what Jean Gebser calls the "at-once" experience of time.[11]

Illustration 6. The Water of Life

The Kwisatz Haderach's Picasso Vision

The Kwisatz Haderach is the world's super-being, a man who can be "many places at once."

> And it came to pass in the third year of the Desert War that Paul-Muad'Dib lay alone in the Cave of Birds beneath the kiswa hangings of an inner cell. And as he lay as one dead, caught up in the revelation of the Water of Life, his being translated beyond the boundaries of time by the poison that gives life. Thus was the prophecy made true that the Lisan al-Gaib might be both dead and alive.[12]

Paul has at least two experiences with the Water of Life. After his mother has transformed the Water of Life for the Fremen seitch orgy, he partakes of these watered-down waters. As the liquid touches his lips, he enters an experience of pure time, folding future and past into the present in a transparent trinocular focus.[13] Paul recognizes that the Fremen, and perhaps by extension all of us, have this wild talent as a latent potential:

> But they suppress it because it terrifies.[14]

As Paul and Chani drink the changed Water and enter the orgy, Chani pulls Paul aside. She tells Paul that under the influence of the drug they share consciousness, can sense others within themselves.

As the drug takes him, Paul enters a Picasso time.

> He felt anew the hyper-illumination with its high-relief imagery of time, sensed his future becoming memories.[15]

Later, he takes one drop of the unchanged Water. He wakes after a three-week coma to note that he has been many places in time. Reborn, he downs a fist-full of water, takes his mother's hand and establishes a sense-sharing *telepathic communion* and asks Jessica to take him to the place Reverend Mothers cannot enter.[16] Paul can enter this no-place. As they realize that he is the Kwisatz Haderach, he speaks:

> There is in each of us an ancient force that takes and an ancient force that gives. A man finds little difficulty facing that place within himself where the taking force dwells, but it's almost impossible for him to see into the giving force without changing into something other than man. For a woman, the situation is reversed. . . . These things are so ancient within us . . . that they're ground into each separate cell of our bodies. We're shaped by such forces. . . . The greatest peril to the Giver is the

force that takes. The greatest peril to the Taker is the force that gives. It's as easy to be overwhelmed by giving as taking.[17]

As a man who confronts and transcends this awareness, Paul is Nietzsche's *Übermensch* incarnate; man is something that must be overcome. Paul overcomes man.

I'm at the fulcrum. . . . I cannot give without taking and I cannot take without giving.[18]

Paul reconciles masculine and feminine energies, yin and yang. Rational duality and mythical polarity are brought together in magical unity.[19]

The Appearance of Time

The Chronicles suggest that time is not merely what it appears to be, or we do not truly attend to time's appearances. Although they do not discount the valid cultural experiences of linear and cyclical time, for surely each demonstrates an aspect of human experience, the six books of *Dune* also introduce characters who lift time's veil, expose our conceptions and inscriptions as historical, and reveal the cultural nuances of time's language. For Leto, time appears as multiple and aperspectival.

Leto held the multi-thread reigns, balanced in his own vision-lighted view of time as multilinear and multilooped.[20]

The Chronicles present a universe in which people are awakened to their ancestor's memories and can see deeply, and to some degree accurately, into the future. *The past is a presence in the present for Other Memory. The future is a presence in the present for prescience.* Read through each other, an integral presence of many time phases, all available at once, becomes a plausible perception for a postmodern rendition of time.

Other Memory: The Past as a Presence in the Present

Muad'Dib . . . saw the subliminal reservoir of each individual as an unconscious bank of memories going back to the primal cell of our common genesis. Each of us, he said, can measure out his distance from that common origin. . . . Muad'Dib set himself the task of integrating genetic memory into ongoing evaluation. Thus did he break through Time's veils, making a single thing of the future and the past.[21]

Muad'Dib, like the Reverend Mothers of the Bene Gesserit, had an awareness called Other Memory. Other Memory is a conscious awareness of a person's genetic history passed down in the *spice-tau*, or awakened in some other manner.[22] Imagine what the past would mean to somebody who could recall every event lived by a member of her family or clan. Muad'Dib taught, however, that this ability is latent in us all. We can measure out our distance from a common origin and integrate genetic memory into ongoing evaluation.

The Archetypical Past in Other Memory

Other Memory has its conceptual origins in Jungian psychoanalysis and the collective unconscious.[23] Jung suggested that the unconscious is less a matter of repression, as it was for Freud, and more a collection of archetypes;[24] the collective unconscious is a genetic repository similar to biological and genetic inheritance. As a baby chick will recognize, without specific instruction from an adult, the shadow of a chicken hawk, so humans will recognize without specific instruction the images and patterns of humanity—the stuff of myths. The collective unconscious is the collective wisdom of humanity expressed in dreams, the arts, and myths.

Other Memory is, at the very least, the collective unconscious made conscious. For classical psychoanalysis, the unconscious is precisely those contents of consciousness of which one is not aware. They show up in dreams, works of art, and slips of the tongue, but these irruptions are not intended. To suggest that we can be conscious of something that is by definition unconscious is problematic.[25]

The unconscious has been rethought, however, by Maurice Merleau-Ponty as that *silent-consciousness*, that awareness of the world lived day-to-day prior to reflection. Understood this way, the unconscious is not an abstraction, conception, rationalization, or idealization. Rather, it is a recognition of a relationship between prereflective and reflective life. This prereflective—unconscious—life is our being in the world and our common origin; it is the life of an intersubjective body.[26] One becomes aware of the unconscious, then, through dreams, the arts, and so on, and also by reflecting on those aspects of life that are lived in seeming immediacy. Indeed, such a reflection seeks to understand the ways that immediacy is mediated (in ritual, language, culture, and communication).

The Mediated Immediacy

> Danger . . . is a precise memory.[27]

We are given what at first glance looks like an absolute and positivistic view of perfect memory and perfect recollection of the past:

> Oh, the landscapes I have seen! And the people. . . . Oh, the lessons in
> astronomy and intrigue, the migrations, the disheveled flights, the leg-ach-
> ing and lung-aching runs through so many nights on all of those cosmic
> specks where we have defended our transient possession. I tell you we are
> a marvel and my memories have no doubt of this.[28]

With his God's-eye view, Leto can live the past in the present. He, along
with the other Atreides pre-born and the Bene Gesserit Reverend Mothers who
have this power, sees more closely than anyone else what Leopold von Ranke
called the past as it really was in itself.[29] However, in spite of the implications,
positive knowledge (the "in itself") is still rejected (for the "thing itself," that
is, the memory as phenomenon and not numenon, the thing as known—tak-
en—and not as objective—given):

> The old unanswered question: Do we really have open access to every
> ancestor's total file of experiences?[30]

Leto and his sister Ghanima are keenly aware that these memories come with
their perspectives, their mythos, their egos. That which is true for us (the readers) and them (the characters) is true for all of the Other Memories as well.
Other Memory, then, may just as much make the past as reveal it:

> Too much knowledge never makes for simple decisions.[31]

When Leto writes his journals, he purposely writes a hermeneutic history
rather than an evolutionary one; he possesses the full knowledge that his intention will be scarcely discernible by the historians who unearth his journals.[32]

> You, the first person to encounter my chronicles for at least four thousand
> years, beware. . . . I am not sure what the events in my journals may signify
> to your times. I only know that my journals have suffered oblivion and that
> the events that I recount have undoubtedly been submitted to historical
> distortion for eons.[33]

Even Other Memory has its limits.[34]

A Genetic "Unconscious"

Starting with Merleau-Ponty's thought, both Herbert's and Jung's proclamation
of a genetic memory is not so farfetched (even if we set aside the theory of the
unconscious as a metaphysical postulate). The question may be less a matter of
Other Memory's existence and more a matter of its appearance; how is Other
Memory manifest? Although neither we nor Leto nor any of the others have

immediate access to the memories of other people, we do have *mediated* access to other memories in stories, myths and legends, in histories, and through inter-subjective life in general. Moreover, in a rational and technological lifeworld, the word *genetic* has come to signify the physical building blocks of life. Note, however, that the word also denotes origin, or coming into being—genesis. We can speak of a genetics of culture, language, symbol systems, and so on; we can seek the genesis, the origin, and creative activity of memory.

> Memory never recaptures reality. Memory reconstructs. All reconstructions change the original, becoming external frames of reference that inevitably fall short.[35]

Genetic phenomenology is the study of the ways that meanings are built up in the course of experience.[36] The study of meanings suggests that we do recuperate the past, but this recollection is neither absolute nor certain. In fact, we recuperate the past in the flow of consciousness. As The God Emperor Leto notes, we carry the hopes, fears, and desires of our ancestry:

> It continually astonishes me how people hide from their ancestral memories, shielding themselves behind a thick barrier of mythos. . . . I can understand that they might not want to be submerged in a mush of petty ancestral details. You have reason to fear that your living moments might be taken over by others.[37]

Digression: Alia's Schizophrenic Hell

The integration of Other Memory is not an experience without peril. There is risk taken by those who dive into the deep waters of the psyche—abomination. That is, one or more residual persons, the Other Memories themselves, may overthrow the host or the Self of the host.[38] Such is the problem faced by Alia and her demonic possession by the Baron Harkonnen. She literally looses her individuated self to an ego within the collective complex (i.e., the collective unconscious made conscious). The Self that is called upon to unify the collective relinquishes dominance and the horde within overwhelms. For Alia, this unifying self has lost its hold on the innumerable voices.[39] A lesson: We can become possessed by the Other. But this Other is a phenomenon and thus multivalent and manifold.

Although phenomena such as possession are easily dismissed as the stuff of horror movies, possession also nominates a profound human experience that is quite active in the human psyche and, perhaps, especially engaged in those who live within a capitalist mythos. After all, to possess is to have posses-sions—things. To be possessed is to be had by those things. Think of possession

Illustration 7. Alia's Hell

as an inverted subject-object relationship. Husserl's meditations on the flow of consciousness suggest that our awareness of objects moves from intersubjectivity to subjectivity to objectivity. The possessed person's objects have taken hold of their subjectivity and the flow is reversed. The object takes precedence over and possesses the subject. Intersubjectivity is either lost or relegated to the background. This is a real condition for those who are attached to their objects. Hell is not simply Other people, it is other people and objects possessing our attention. The Other is not an object but a phenomenon to experience in its manifold glory.[40]

The Past in the Present

> We carry all of our ancestry forward like a living wave, all of the hopes and joys and griefs, the agonies and exultations of our past. Nothing within those memories remains completely without meaning or influence, not as long as there is a humankind somewhere. We have that bright Infinity all around us, that Golden Path of forever to which we can continually pledge our puny but inspired allegiance.[41]

We not only remember. We not only relive. We live, in the present, the hopes, and fears, the dreams and nightmares of our selves, our families and our communities. Conscience is living the past—as a latent presence made manifest—in the present. We encounter the presence of those who came before us, and our own past, not in some abstract past, but in the living present.[42] Memory does not appear in the past (time is not a container into which the past is poured). More likely, memory is a renewal, integration, and realization of experience. What we call the past is a presence of past in the present. As such, Other Memory is the recuperation of the family, the society, and the civilization as an intersubjective and interpretive presence.

Memories do not, after all, mean anything by themselves. They derive their significance from their relationships to other encounters and endeavors. Their meaning appears in a field of relationships. Within this field, we select, read, and interpret as we participate in the creation of cultural memory:

> The life of a single human, as the life of a family or an entire people, persists as memory. My people must come to see this as part of their maturing process. They are people as organism, and in this persistent memory they store more and more experiences in a subliminal reservoir. Humankind hopes to call upon this material if it is needed for a changing universe. But much that is stored can be lost in that chance play of accident which we call "fate." Much may not be integrated into evolutionary relationships, and thus many may not be evaluated and keyed into activity by those ongoing environmental changes which inflict themselves upon flesh. The species can forget! This is the special value of the Kwisatz Haderach which the Bene Gesserit never suspected: the Kwisatz Haderach cannot forget.[43]

The Chronicles ask for our active, political, and heightened participation in the world: The Mentat should not forget!

This presence of past-in-the-present should bring us some comfort. After all, our dearly departed cannot be truly "gone" unless we forget. There is, in fact, no-where for something to go in time; time is less a some-where and more a some-when (that is, we are discussing time and not space; it is not necessary to discuss time in terms of space). Behind the veil of time, one only truly dies when the last memory is forgotten. Even the caveman lives today, not only in Lascaux, Niaux, and Gagarino, but also in Chicago, Shepherdstown, and Santa Fe. The caveman lives in Leto II:

> In the cradle of our past, I lay upon my back in a cave so shallow I could penetrate it only by squirming, not by crawling. There, by the dancing light of a resin torch, I drew upon walls and ceiling the creatures of the hunt and the souls of my people. How illuminating it is to peer backward through a perfect circle at that ancient struggle for the visible moment of the soul. All time vibrates to that call: "Here I am!" With a mind informed by artist-giants who came afterward, I peer at handprints and flowing muscles drawn upon the rock with charcoal and vegetable dyes. How much more we are than mere mechanical events![44]

In a society prone not only to judgment but prejudice, what benefit it is to recuperate the past rather than to consider it as gone. What knowledge and understanding are lost because we study history as a linear succession of events tied to an often misleading notion of progress rather than as a living presence that unifies all persons and civilizations as appearances in a world far greater than any meager now-point of some ego bent on self-aggrandizement? Leto suggests that we take grand safaris:

> Sometimes I indulge myself in safaris. . . . I strike inward along the axis of my memories. Like a schoolchild reporting on a vacation trip. I take up my subject. Let it be . . . female intellectuals! I course backward into the ocean which is my ancestors. I am a great winged fish in the depths. The mouth of my awareness opens and I scoop them up![45]

Finding the Other in ourselves, would we continue to infuse politics with suicide bombs, genocide massacres, or war? To recuperate these memories is to live not fifteen or fifty or one hundred years, from birth to death, but in depth, three hundred, three thousand years or more. Leto says of this past as presence in the present:

> As wine retains the perfume of its cask, I retain the essence of my most ancient genesis, and that is the seed of conscience. That is what makes me holy. I am God because I am the only one who really knows his heredity![46]

Would we act so quickly, with such brutality, television-cowboy romanticism, and cinematic-jihad realism, if we truly recalled and retained the pains of those who came before us?

You must remember that I have at my internal demand every expertise known to our history. This is the fund of energy I draw upon when I address the mentality of war. If you have not heard the moaning cries of the wounded and dying, you do not know about war. I have heard those cries in such numbers that they haunt me. I have cried out myself in the aftermath of battle. I have suffered wounds from fist and club and rock, from shell-studded limb and bronze sword, from the mace and the cannon, from arrows and lasguns and the silent working of slow poisons . . . and more I will not recount! I have seen and felt them all.[47]

Murbella's Agony and Grail

This is the lesson learned by Murbella when she undergoes the spice agony. She realizes that our descendants may be brutes. If we keep this vividly in mind we may jump the tracks and reconstitute society.

The psychic possibility of Other Memory creates a novel condition for the exploration of consciousness, as the Bene Gesserit Reverend Mothers have immanent access to innumerable lives and thus innumerable experiences.[48]

> We carry our grail in our heads. . . . Carry this grail gently. . . . Avoid excesses. Overcorrect and you always have a fine mess on your hands. . . . Fanatics are marvelous creators of oscillation.[49]

Odrade delivers this lesson to Murbella before Belladonna pours the bitter liquid into her mouth and she enters the acid-state of the agony.[50] As the drug overtakes her, Murbella's body awareness melts away, and she is reduced to consciousness—"a wispy adherence . . . constructed out of fog."[51] She is confronted with countless memories of the lives that came before her and has a *terrible realization*. Those lives, those people, were brutal barbarians beyond description and comprehension. Why? *"Because the victors bred."*[52] And the victors were those who put away all sense of morality so they might win—an ugly lot of terrible people.

She also meets a spirit guide—the guide of the *mohalata*. She communicates with this guide *telepathically*; after all, she and the guide are one. The guide is the one who steers Murbella clear of these horrible people—the destroyers. She asks that Murbella not become a destroyer herself. Murbella comes to the understanding that the Bene Gesserit's grail is not a thing to have but a question to answer: *How do we set the balances of those atrocities right?* In *Chapterhouse* we see empathy at the heart of Bene Gesserit's manipulative practices.

Murbella's grail, then, is much like the grail of modern Christian mythology. The grail is presented often as a question to answer or a call to experience as well as a physical thing, a cup. The solid thing, a cup, holds liquid, and the grail holds mystery. There is little need to find the grail, if seeking the grail brings us insight and illumination.[53] We hold the grail in our libraries, information systems, and ourselves. What we do with it is up to us. Just as Paul discovered that the Atreides shared the blood of their archenemy, the Harkonnen, Other Memory teaches us that we share our adversary's blood:

> I know the evil of my ancestors because I am those people. . . . I know that few of you who read my words have ever thought about your ancestors this way. It has not occurred to you that your ancestors were survivors and that survival itself sometimes involved savage decisions, a kind of wanton brutality which civilized humankind works very hard to suppress. What price will you pay for that suppression? Will you accept your own extinction?[54]

This living present, with its presence of past, combined with the personal and political implications of Other Memory, allows us a glimpse into time that is neither abstract nor conceptual, nor imagistic and cyclical, but transparent and existential.

> Oh the landscapes I have seen! And the people! . . . Even back through the myths of Terra. Oh, the lessons in astronomy and intrigue, the migrations, the disheveled flights, the leg-aching and lung-aching runs through so many nights on all those cosmic specks where we have defended our transient possession. I tell you we are a marvel and my memories leave no doubt of this.[55]

By recuperating our past and integrating Other Memory, the past appears as a presence in the present. The implications are personal and political.

> There is no escape—we pay for the violence of our ancestors.[56]

But these are debts that can be paid in full. Integrate Other Memory. Integrate the Memory of Others. Do not forget!

Prescience: The Future as a Presence in the Present

> It's a subtle and powerful thing, prescience. The future becomes now.[57]

When Muad'Dib and Leto II drank *The Water of Life*, their awareness of time irrupted into a multifaceted time consciousness. Temporality spread out beyond direction; they entered a Picasso time. Countless experiences engulfed them. Past, present, and future integrated into a manifold presence. They could see not only their personal future but potential and possible courses of humanity's *yet-to-be*.

Descriptions of prescient experience in *The Chronicles* suggest several things: (1) Prescience is a presence of future in the present; (2) Prescience is indeterminate; (3) Mathematical reductions fail to describe it; (4) Everyone is prescient; and (5) Creative interpretations of prescience serve pragmatic purposes.

Presence

The Chronicles provide several descriptions of intense prescient experience.[58] Paul, Leto, and Siona, for examples, are indoctrinated into heightened prescient awareness in the ritual ingestion of the spice-essence drug. During Leto's spice trance he notes:

> The vision . . . evolved into a stereologic memory which separated past and present, future and present, future and past. Each separation mingled into a trinocular focus which he sensed as the multidimensional relief map of his own future existence.[59]

Leto finds that the cultural categories of time collapse into a manifold presence:

> Past-present-now. There was no true separation.[60] [He was] able to see the past in the future, present in the past, the now in both past and future.[61]

As the traditional categories of time collapse, it is important to note that they collapse into a transparent and diaphanous presence of prescient experience. As it was for Other Memory, the future never appears *in* the future, but rather as a presence within the present. While Leto is within the grasp of the spice essence, his father speaks to him through Other Memory; he suggests a metaphor for this manifold time-consciousness—the *stroboscope*. Stroboscopic awareness is a momentary glimpse of past, present, or future as seen from the vantage of an ever-deferring now.[62] Paul speaks to a pragmatic significance; one remains within a *living present*.

Indeterminacy

The experience of prescience has its limits. For example, prescience shows itself as indeterminate, neither certain nor absolute. Paul notes:

> For every instant of reality there existed countless projections, things fated never to be.[63]

However, it is said that Muad'Dib had absolute knowledge of the future. This was best demonstrated when he was physically blinded in an assassination attempt. He used his prescient vision to see without eyes:

> He summoned up his oracular vision . . . turned and strode along the track that Time had carved for him, fitting himself into the vision so tightly that it could not escape. He felt himself grow aware of this place as a multitudinous possession, reality welded to prediction.[64]

How do we reconcile this ability with indeterminacy? Paul's "vision" remains an awareness of the future as a presence in the present. It can, therefore, be suggested that it is not Paul's vision that is problematic, but rather the contemporary consensual codification of time. The idea that time is a line dotted by a succession of now-points is itself a cultural construct. If all times are actually only available in the present (as diaphanous dimensions), then one's awareness may be sharp or dull, but the future is always already at hand. It is not the potential that is problematic, but the fidelity. And that fidelity has limits:

> Muad'Dib could . . . see the Future, but you must understand the limits of this power. Think of sight. You have eyes, yet cannot see without light. If you are on the floor of a valley, you cannot see beyond your valley. Just so, Muad'Dib could not always choose to look across the mysterious terrain. . . . He tells us "The vision of time is broad, but when you pass through it, time becomes a narrow door."[65]

Leto rejects absolute foreknowledge not only because of its implausibility, but also because such vision denies and spoils one of the joys of human being—the ability to be surprised.[66]

> Leave absolute knowledge of the future to those moments of déjà vu. . . . To know the future absolutely is to be trapped into that future absolutely. It collapses time. Present becomes future. I require more freedom than that.[67]

To see it all, every last detail with absolute fidelity, right down to your own death, would be absolute terror and boredom.[68] Likewise, those who seek prescience to win a bet find themselves in a trap.

> Those who sought the future hoped to gain the winning gamble on tomorrow's race. Instead they found themselves trapped into a lifetime whose every heartbeat and anguish was known. . . . I speak of the popular myth of prescience. To know the future absolutely! . . . What fortunes could be made—and lost—on such absolute knowledge? . . . The rabble believes this. . . . [I]f you handed one of them the complete scenario of his life, the unvarying dialogue up to his moment of death—what a hellish gift

that'd be. . . . Every living instant he'd be replaying what he absolutely knew absolutely. No deviation. He could anticipate every response, every utterance—over and over and over and. . . . Ignorance has its advantages. A universe of surprises is what I pray for![69]

The Chronicles suggest that one may choose to peer wisely into this presence, allowing for ambiguity and indeterminacy, or one may demand absolutes. But the future is a hydra-headed time sense that is best met with care and humility. When we open our awareness to the presence of the future in the present, not as dream, desire, or projection, but as a person situated in a cultural context, an organ of the world, we have an opportunity to overcome the shortsightedness and mental trap of absolutist thought.

We know this moment of supreme power contained failure. There can be only one answer, that completely accurate and total prediction is lethal.[70]

Mathematical Reductions

Mathematical explanations, *The Chronicles* suggest, fail to account for the qualitative experience of manifold time. Prescience must be grasped in its own terms:

Prescient future insists on its own rules. It will not conform to the ordering of the Zensunni nor to the ordering of science. . . . It demands the work of this instant.[71]

The Chronicles provide a very interesting case for the study of a fallacy inherent in mathematical reductions. Just as alternative histories are presented in such a manner as to provide several interpretations of the same event, so too the reader is given excerpts from a lecture on prescience only to find that same lecture critiqued at an earlier point in the book. In *Children of Dune*, Palimbasha insists on a mathematical reduction.[72]

However, the attentive reader will have noticed that earlier in the same book Ghanima had already reflected on Palimbasha's ignorance:

The man was a mathematical boor. He had attempted to explain Muad'Dib through mathematics. . . . He was a mindslaver and his enslaving process could be understood with extreme simplicity: he transfered technical knowledge without a transfer of values.[73]

In this way, *The Chronicles* maintain their critique of positive knowledge. By considering mathematics as a mythological institution (a way of sense-making), rather than as a method capable of breaking mythological barriers, the quantitative reduction is rejected for a qualitative account.

Everyone is Prescient

At once fantastic and marvelous, prescience is a phenomenon that is not beyond the boundaries of ordinary time-experience.[74] It is more likely a dimension of common experience. Leto, in fact, has this direct revelation: Every human is prescient!

> He saw Sabiha . . . as a vision-maker in her own right, and every other human carried the same power.[75]

Prescience is an integral part of human perception, its secrets withheld from us only by its lack of presence in contemporary cultural expressions.

Most people are aware of some degree of prescient experience. Premonition, foresight, and synchronicity are common examples of *petit prescience*.[76] We hum a song before we flip on the radio and discover that song is being broadcast; we think of a good friend and pick up the phone, without it ever ringing, only to find that he or she is on the other end waiting to speak to us; we hear numerous stories, their validity assured by the simple facts, of persons who escape their own death by not boarding a flight that crashes moments later;[77] we marvel at musicians who spontaneously improvise. These examples should suffice to demonstrate a certain style of the irruption of the future in the present.

Other forms of prescience are equally silent and pragmatic. We live in terms of our projections, the desires of ourselves, our communities, and our world. Noting the Fremen's reliance on myths, Jessica notes:

> They're in league with the future. . . . They have their mountains to climb. This is the scientist's dream . . . and these simple people, these peasants, are filled with it.[78]

If prescience is a latent potential, and if most people have had some form of prescient experience (no matter how small), then why deny it? *The Chronicles'* answer to this question lies in mythos and language. The mythos of classical physics, for example, with its bias for things linear and measurable, coupled with our language, directs us toward a word-oriented, single-pointed time:

> Because of the one-pointed Time awareness in which the conventional mind remains immersed, humans tend to think of everything in a sequential, word-oriented framework.[79]

Quantum physics, however, will not make the same assumptions. New myths, therefore, are possible. But within the realm of contemporary culture, people like Sabiha have learned to distrust their prescience:

> They've a little of the talent. . . . But they suppress it because it terrifies.[80]

> I've had visions . . . many times. They don't mean anything.[81]

Hearing these words, Leto realizes that:

> [Sabiha] was disdainful of her . . . visions. They caused disquiet and, therefore, must be put aside, forgotten deliberately.[82]

Sabiha's visions were tied to the myths of her time and place, and she held onto those myths because of the safety net they provided:

> She depended upon absolutes, sought finite limits, and all because she couldn't handle the rigors of terrible decisions. . . . She clung to her one-eyed vision of the universe, . . . time-freezing as it might be, because the alternatives terrified her.[83]

Leto, on the other hand, makes a choice similar to that proposed by Professor of Comparative Studies of Civilizations Jean Gebser. He opens himself to the whole and integrates his cultural mythos with an aperspectival consciousness:

> He was a membrane collecting infinite dimensions, and, because he saw those dimensions, he could make the terrible decisions.[84]

Leto accepts his experience of integral time and, in so doing, is able to act in concert and without obstruction to his atemporal vision.

Constructive Pragmatics

A creative (heuretic) and interpretive (hermeneutic) approach to understanding prescience both illuminates our experience of the future and shocks us out of complacency. When the veils of the future are pulled aside and the future appears as a presence within the present, what do we do with this newfound insight? The adept of *Dune* do not deny their prescience, but rather seek to live free from its enslaving potential. By the end of *The Chronicles*, the Bene Gesserit no longer seek a *scientific hermeneutics*, but an active *heuretics*, a creative and inventive response to life. This is because there is peril in prescience, and this peril is magnified by the reduction of ambiguity and the increase of want for absolute knowledge. If all becomes known, surely and absolutely, then, at that moment the perceiver is trapped—free-will disappears. The experience of prescience, even of premonition and foresight—seeing the plane's crash, hearing the radio's song, feeling the friend's presence—still leaves the perceiver with the ability to *choose*—to get on the plane, to turn on the radio, to pick up the phone, or in any case, to *believe* what has appeared to consciousness.

> My son didn't really see the future; he saw the process of creation and its relationship to the myths in which men sleep. . . . He saw the shapes which existing forces would create unless they were diverted.[85]

Those who are enlightened by Muad'Dib's experience look at social sense-making systems as mythologies—interpretations of experience. Prescience, in this context, was not used to win tomorrow's horse race, but to wake from the mythic slumber and look critically at the civilizations we create and the trajectories our culture travels.

Herbert noted that absolute thought produces short-term concepts of effectiveness and consequences, a condition of constant, unplanned response to crises.[86] Rather than submit to a knee-jerk response, it makes sense to live in a manifold presence of indeterminate futures, multiple projections, and possible pathways. Herbert argued directly for thinking in terms of such multiplicity: "It's a mistake to think about the future, one future. We ought to think more of planning for futures as an art form. . . . We have as many futures as we can invent."[87]

The At-Once

> He tried to focus . . . but past and future were merging into the present. . . . He saw . . . in countless ways and positions and settings.[88]

Muad'Dib became aware of integral time. Past, present, and future integrated into a pregnant whole. Time phases became transparent. The structures of cultural experience revealed to him latent possibilities and potentials. We can call this diaphanous, manifold, and integral time awareness the *at-once*.[89]

> I am a net in the sea of time, free to sweep future and past. I am a moving membrane from whom no possibility can escape.[90]

Paul's vision describes a way that time irrupts into consciousness; it reveals a way of understanding temporal awareness that is just as valid as clock or cyclical time. This is to say that the rational world, inaugurated in Greek antiquity and fully manifest by the Renaissance, has taken from time's potential a structure of understanding—measurable time. This structure is based on a pragmatic relationship between humanity and world. Clock time is rational, reasonable, and practical; it facilitates the kinds of human gathering that allows for the city, the factory, and the business meeting. Likewise, cyclical, mythical time describes the experience of the world's flow—day into night, waning to waxing moon, ebb and flood of tide, day into year.

Jean Gebser has argued that rational consciousness has reached its apex. As it falls, new potentials for consciousness emerge. The defining sign of this change, as seen in works by Einstein (in science), Picasso (in painting), and Herbert (in prose) is the awareness of time's concretion. Concretion is not reification but realization. To this facet of human evolution, *The Chronicles* are a contribution not only to science fiction, or the history of literature, but to the study of consciousness itself.

> I give you a new kind of time without parallels. . . . It will always diverge. There will be no concurrent points on its curves. . . . Never again will you have the kinds of concurrence that you once had.[91]

Although the at-once structure of awareness has been experienced for millennia, it can be shown as a relatively new time consciousness present in many domains of human expression. It can be seen in physics, psychology, poetry, prose, philosophy (including perennial philosophy), and painting. This implies that Herbert's *Chronicles* express a perception of time akin to the most forward thinkers in the sciences and the arts. Herbert, like Heisenberg and Picasso, Eddington and Klee, overcame reified time, saw through conceptual time, and presented us with an integral time capable of grasping the whole:

> One discovers the future in the past, and both are part of the whole. . . . You win back your consciousness of your inner being when you recognize the universe as a coherent whole.[92]

When we are aware of the *whole of time*, our perception becomes *integral*. We become aware of many times, each transparent to the others. All temporal dimensions and potentials appear in the now as a diaphanous presence—at-once.[93] This does not mean that we have achieved absolute or positive knowledge. Rather, it suggests that we have taken in the total intentionality of time's possible perceptions within the limits set by our embodiment, culture, and language.[94] The awareness that time is multidimensional is present also in some of the most recent science and philosophy, but still only just announced on the popular horizon.

Postmodernism has been described as the refutation of the "grand narratives" of modernity.[95] The all-encompassing story of time, we are taught, is the three-phase time—past, present, future. This three-phase syndrome is predicated on the sense that things are "in" time (and thus are located spatially by an "either/or" logic); events either occurred in the past (history), or are occurring in the present (now), or may occur in the future (yet to come). But we find, in these investigations, that time is not what it seems. Paul and Leto reject the rationalization of time as sequence and, as well, the notions of time as eternal or nonexperienced. For the perceiver, all temporal phases (linear, cyclical, prescient, etc.) are grasped as fields of overlapping significance and differentiation that are transparent to one another—thus one sees through time's veils. When lifting these veils, we find that the past is not then, the present is not now, and the future is not when. Rather, all are present in a cosmic depth—at-once. Such integral awareness is essentially emancipating; we are freed from the bonds of conceptual time.

> The prophet is not diverted by illusions of past, present and future. The fixity of language determines such linear distinctions. Prophets hold a key to the lock in a language. The mechanical image remains only an image to them. This is not a mechanical universe. The linear progression of events is imposed by the observer. Cause and effect? That's not it at all. The prophet utters fateful words. You glimpse a thing "destined to occur." But the prophetic instant releases something of infinite portent and power. The universe undergoes a ghostly shift. Thus, the wise prophet conceals actuality behind shimmering labels. The uninitiated then believe the prophetic language is ambiguous. The listener distrusts the prophetic messenger. Instinct tells you how the utterance blunts the power of such words. The best prophets lead you up to the curtain and let you peer through for yourself.[96]

Shakespeare wrote, "Our virtues lie in our interpretation of time."[97] And as we sift the dune sands for wisdom, we find interpretations of time, ordinary and fantastic. We can see, in a moment's reprise, that time can be conceived, apprehended by the rational mind, and, as such, produces an ideal, abstract, and homogeneous time. The arrow and the timeline represent this conceptualization; the clock and the watch measure its motion and formulate for us a consensual reality into which we are born, by which we age, and in terms of which we die. But if time's interpretation reveals a virtue, as the great playwright suggests, then alternatives must be available.

> Anyone can rip aside the veil of Time. You can discover the future in the past or in your own imagination. Doing this, you win back your consciousness in your inner being. You know then that the universe is a coherent whole and you are indivisible from it.[98]

Notes

1. Leto II, The God Emperor of Dune, in Brian Herbert (ed.), *The Notebooks of Frank Herbert's Dune* (New York: Perigee, 1988, 37). Few fields of perception have changed in the twentieth century as much as time. From Einstein to Picasso to Husserl to Herbert, time has been recast not as a line along which we travel but a field or dimension that we enact and that is an irreducible phenomenon of human experience; our accounts of human being assume time in their explanations.

2. *Dune*, xviii.

3. Argument in Council, by the Mother Superior Taraza. *Heretics*, 272.

4. Frank Herbert, *Listening to the Left Hand*.

5. For a description of the Mentat's overlay-integration-imagination methodology, follow a wormhole to Appendix B.

6. See Aristotle's *Metaphysics*. Trans. Joe Sachs. 2nd ed. (Santa Fe: NM: Green Lion, 2002).

7. The Leto Commentary, After Harq al-Ada. *Children*, 69.

8. For further discussion of the development of alphabetic literacy and clocks see Daniel Boorstein, *The Discoverers* (New York: Random House, 1985).

9. In order to hold presuppositions at bay, they should be articulated. The cultural conventions of time experience (i.e., consensual time) are discussed in the appendix, Consensual and Existential Time.

10. See Maurice Merleau-Ponty, *Phenomenology of Perception* (New York: Routledge, 1989).

11. Jean Gebser, *The Ever-present Origin* (Athens: Ohio University Press, 1985).

12. *Dune*, 255.

13. Paul's experience with the Water of Life marks the end of the second book of *Dune*, Muad'Dib, and prepares us for the final section, The Prophet. *Dune*, 354–356. As the signs of reality are rearranged, it is time to start a new book.

14. *Dune*, 355.

15. *Dune*, 356.

16. Telepathy is another sign of a magical structuring of consciousness. See Jean Gebser, op. cit.

17. Paul's awakening. *Dune*, 437–440.

18. Paul's awakening. *Dune*, 437–440.

19. Paul's awakening. *Dune*, 437–440.

20. *Children*, 348.

21. Testament of Arrakis by Harq al-Ada. *Children*, 82.

22. *Children*, 60.

23. Brian Herbert, *Dreamer of Dune*.

24. Archetype is derived from *arche* (origin) and *genre* (kind). According to Jung, an archetype is an inherited image or pattern of human intelligence.

25. See Gilles Deleuze and Felix Guattari, *Anti-Oedipus: Capitalism and Schizophrenia* (Minneapolis: University of Minnesota Press, 1987). Note also that Herbert was at least aware of the problematic of positing an unconscious without demonstrat-

ing how that unconsciousness is manifest: "The past-within cannot be relegated to the unconscious" (*Children*, 98).

26. For more information, follow a wormhole to Chapter Seven.

27. Leto II, *Children*, 78.

28. The Stolen Journals, *God Emperor*, 31.

29. This was the focus of von Ranke's life work.

30. Leto II, *Children*, 20. Later Leto will contradict this statement when he speaks of "the terrible immediacy of every living moment which I must experience" (The Stolen Journals. *God Emperor*, 303). But he does not appear to confuse this immediate presence with absolute knowledge.

31. Ghanima, *Children*, 21. Paul's shade tells Leto: "Your memory creates us" (*Children*, 78).

32. In this way, the Lord Leto demonstrates an understanding of both hermeneutics and the intentional fallacy.

33. Inscriptions on the storehouse at Dar-es-Balat, *God Emperor*, 43.

34. For more information, follow a wormhole to Chapter Six.

35. Mentat Handbook, *Heretics*, 396.

36. Edmund Husserl, *Cartesian Meditations* (Dordrecht: Kluwer, 1960). Edmund Husserl called the content of mental activities (such as remembering, desiring, and perceiving) *meanings*. *The Mentat Handbook v2.0* suggests that we reserve the word "meaning" for the contents of the consciousness of the reader of a text. This view allows for polysemy and the activity of interpretation as well as recognizes the interplay of consciousness, culture, and world.

37. The Stolen Journals. *God Emperor*, 303.

38. The psyche, in Jungian thought, can be compared to a sphere or cell with a bright field on its surface, representing consciousness. The ego is this sphere's center, because only if "I" know a thing is it in fact conscious. This recognition is represented by the famous Cartesian phrase, "I think therefore I am." This can also be rephrased as, "I think of it therefore it is." The self is thus more than the ego. It is at the same time the nucleus and the whole sphere. This internal, organizing center and periphery has been called many things across the ages. The Greeks called it daimon. The Egyptians called it the Ba-soul. The Romans called it genius. It has also been identified as totem, protective spirit, animal spirit, or the fetish embodied within. It is also the inner voice.

39. Paul, and most notably Leto II, escape abomination. They do not attempt to control but seek instead a flow of dialogue with these voices and thus remain centered in the self—as the inner center and outer ring of a wheel move at different speeds but in complete harmony. The theme of control versus flow (i.e., "the willow bends") is played again in *The Chronicle's* fugue.

40. Alia's experience is also an embodiment of the Other as a manifestation of psyche. For more information on a phenomenology of psyche as embodiment, follow a wormhole to Chapter One, subheading, Bulimic Education.

41. The Stolen Journals. *God Emperor*, 303.

42. Algis Mickunas, *The Ways of Understanding*, unpublished manuscript, 1.

43. The Book of Leto, After Harq al-Ada. *Children*, 119.

44. The Stolen Journals. *God Emperor*, 332.

45. The Stolen Journals. *God Emperor*, 36. Of course this can be done in any library or though the Internet. We need not go far to seek the past.

46. The Stolen Journals. *God Emperor*, 60.

47. The Stolen Journals. *God Emperor*, 63.

48. Fiction and nonfiction run through each other in these texts like clouds passing through the atmosphere (what are the boundary conditions that define cloud from sky?). Keep in mind, as is suggested throughout this book, that the so-called "novel" condition Other Memory may be in fact our true consciousness: Do we not have access to innumerable lives and experiences through others we meet and the texts we read? Rather than creating a fantasy world, Herbert is writing a science fiction world. As such he is writing about our world amplified to a degree in which background phenomena such as memory bask in a new light.

49. Odrade to Murbella. *Chapterhouse*, 349.

50. Murbella's agony appears in *Chapterhouse*, 349–353.

51. Murbella, *Chapterhouse*, 351.

52. *Chapterhouse*, 351.

53. In addition to the grail imagery, Herbert invokes the Native American magical incarnation of the Spirit Guide. Herbert was proudly inspired by Native mythology, and the Spirit Guide experience has become in recent times an important sign of New Age spirituality.

54. The Stolen Journals. *God Emperor*, 96.

55. The Stolen Journals. *God Emperor*, 31.

56. From "Collected Sayings of Muad'Dib" by the Princess Irulan, in Brian Herbert, *Notebooks of Frank Herbert's Dune*, 6.

57. Leto Atreides II. *Children*, 118.

58. For a description of Paul's spice-trance experience, see *Dune*, 289–297.

59. Leto II. *Children*, 261.

60. *Children*, 262.

61. *Children*, 263.

62. Paul Atreides, *Children*, 262.

63. Paul, Muad'Dib, Atreides, *Messiah*, 167. See the experience of Muad'Dib, *Messiah*, 29. See also Frank Herbert, *Listening to the Left Hand*.

64. Comments on Paul Atreides after his eyes are burned from their sockets. *Messiah*, 160–161. Consider also that sight is not limited to the visual domain but includes insight and the synesthetic extension of the senses. See K. Williams (November 2005). "Visual Communication's A-visual Foundation: Synesthesia," presented at the annual convention of the National Communication Association, Boston, MA. Visual Communication Division top paper (<http://webpages.shepherd.edu/kwilliam/Dr.%20Kevin%20Williams/Scholarship.html>). 6/14/06.

65. From "Arrakis Awakening" by the Princess Irulan. *Dune*, 214.

66. Herbert was influenced by the theology and philosophy of Alan Watts (see Brian Herbert, *Dreamer of Dune*). Watts' theology viewed the things of the world as the organs of God playing a game of cosmic hide and seek (see *The Taboo About Knowing Who You Really Are*).

67. Leto II, to his mother, The Lady Jessica. *Children*, 99.

68. Alan Watts, like Leto II, suggests that an infinite and eternal God would experience infinite and eternal boredom, and that this alone would be sufficient cause for creating a sentient world with physical and psychical senses open to, but not tied to, an indeterminate universe. In such a circumstance, God would choose to look through the finite eyes of the human, the belly of the snake, the roots of the tree, the batholith of the rock so as to find an indefinite and temporary world in which infinity and eternity are mere abstractions and ideal forms beyond experience. Through these organs God could be amused, surprised, and caught off guard (*The Book on the Taboo Against Knowing Who You Are*) (London: Sphere, 1976). Surprise is what Leto II seeks most (see *God Emperor*).

69. Leto II. *Children*, 78–79, see also 99–100.

70. Commentary on prescience. *Messiah*, 10. See also Hawking, *A Brief History of Time* (New York: Bantam, 1988), for a commentary on the perils of absolute prediction.

71 Kalima: The Words of Muad'Dib, The Shuloch Commentary. *Children*, 316.

72. Palimbasha, Lectures at Sietch Tabr. *Children*, 234.

73. Ghanima. *Children*, 204.

74. The word *fantastic* has its modern origin in late Middle English in which it receives the sense of existing only in the imagination or as unreal. This sense is derived from Old French *fantastique*, via medieval Latin from Greek *phantastikos*, from *phantazein*, which meant to "make visible," and *phantazesthai*, to "have visions or imagine," and *phantos* meaning "visible" (*Oxford American Dictionary*). From this wellspring, "fantastic" shows its interconnection with prescience and phenomenon. All of these words indicate that appearances, which are present in awareness, are the stuff of wisdom.

75. *Children*, 327.

76. Synchronicity is an idea put forth by Carl Jung. It is an acausal principle in which two phenomena appear at the same time, such as picking up the phone to find the person you are about to call already on the line. The significance of synchronicity for Herbert's work is the overcoming of causal logic.

77. See Jean Gebser, *The Ever-present Origin* (Athens: Ohio University Press, 1991).

78. *Dune*, 314.

79. Liet-Kynes, The Arrakis Workbook. *Children*, 249.

80. *Dune*, 355.

81. Sabiha speaks here specifically of visions induced by the spice-drug (*Children*, 327). These visions are similar in many ways to LSD trips (Gurney Halleck even calls the spice-drug experience a worm trip: *Children*, 260). More than a drug experience, however, people have visions constantly; many see themselves as parents prior to having children; many see themselves as college graduates prior to completing their degree. Projection in terms of a *vision* is a very common experience.

82. *Children*, 327.

83. *Children*, 328.

84. *Children*, 328.

85. Jessica to Prince Farad'n. *Children*, 307–308.

86. *Children*, 249.

87. Frank Herbert, in O'Reilly, *Frank Herbert*, Chapter Two. Invention becomes a major theme in *Chapterhouse*, as the Bene Gesserit seek to move beyond interpretation (of things and events, nouns and verbs) and toward creation and invention.

88. The experience of Paul Muad'Dib Atreides. *Dune*, 355.

89. I take the phrase, "at-once" time structure from Jean Gebser's *The Ever-present Origin*, op. cit.

90. Paul Muad'Dib Atreides, The Religion of Dune. *Dune*, 501.

91. Leto II. *God Emperor*, 406.

92. The Preacher to Prince Farad'n. *Children*, 90.

93. See also Jean Gebser, *The Ever-Present Origin*, op. cit.

94. The Mentat must always consider, however, that we may have access to transcendental awareness beyond the confines of language, and from which our language appears as a derivative symbol system.

95. This critique can be attributed to Lyotard.

96. The Stolen Journals. *God Emperor*, 275.

97. *Coriolanus*, IV, vii, 49–50.

98. The words of The Preacher at Arrakeen, After Harq al-Ada. *Children*, 378.

Chapter Four

History Meets Heisenberg

History is a constant race between invention and catastrophe. Education helps but it is never enough.[1]

The Dune Chronicles reveal a catastrophe inherent in modern histories that: (1) Represent themselves as a value-neutral recounting of the past; (2) Seek a singular political or evolutionary vision; or (3) Claim to reproduce the past as it "really" was. The ideals of modern history obscure the intervention of interpretation (hermeneutics) and invention (euretics). Rather than seeking a true representation of the past, Herbert critiques histories that seek singularity, perspective, and opacity by rendering history as multiple, aperspectival, and transparent.[2] History is not taken for granted, but rendered problematic.

One peels a problem like an onion.[3]

Instead of a singular History, *The Chronicles* reveal layers of histories. Each layer of the past is visible through others, and no seed of truth waits at the center to be discovered. These layers are themselves not historical, but a presence of past experiences ultimately grounded in lived experience (and not in History itself).[4]

Although critical insights concerning the historian's participation in the act of creating history have been recognized in philosophical thought from Nietzsche to Greenblatt, *The Chronicles* contribute a novel critique of history based on the appearance of competing time structures and Heisenbergian indeterminacy.[5]

Herbert's fiction also illustrates the relevance of studying texts that are not usually understood as historical documents for understanding the problems inherent in knowing the past. These acts of expression include literature, painting, architecture, and storytelling. Clearly these artifacts are not understood as objective documents, but as expressions of cultural activity that belong more to the realm of the humanities than the sciences. Nevertheless, these artifacts can be as revealing of a civilization's conflicts, hopes, and contradictions as the chronicle of a war, the press coverage of a presidential campaign, or the memoirs of a supreme court justice. Such is the case of Garcia Marquez' *One Hundred Years of Solitude*, which is studied in history courses throughout Latin America. Marquez' text has been seen as fundamental in grasping the political and social struggles of the continent.[6] Other important cases include the *Iliad* and the *Odyssey*, which have been studied by scholars as central texts to document the lives of the ancient Greeks.[7] The *Kalevala*, a work of songs and poetry, is seen as fundamental to understanding the Finnish psyche. *Beowulf* provides insight into Scandinavian mythology and the Old English language. This should not imply that the study of novels replace the study of water management (for example). Neither should it imply that a text such as the *Iliad* recreates a cultural context.[8] Rather, it suggests that reliance solely on facts to recreate the past has catastrophic repercussions because we are led to believe that facts are not human creations—*inventions*.

The Chronicles' postmodern exposition of history serves a pedagogical function, while at the same time providing popular entertainment. Readers are given multiple histories that allow them to take in a plurality of intentionalities regarding an event. Through this plurality, Herbert shows how discourse and power not only inform interpretation, history is indeed written by the victor, and historians are people who make money writing history.[9]

> Do not believe in history, because history is impelled by whatever passes for money.[10]

This onion-skin plurality also shows how interpretation plays an active role in informing the past; our conceptual tools and methods, even the very fact of valorizing the past, creates a vision or version of that past. The multiple histories in *Dune* makes concrete the existential condition of historical interpretation and reveals the contingency of understanding the past as it is read, interpreted, and evaluated in the present. Herbert's fiction shows what Foucault's archeology of knowledge suggests: Historical investigation will yield multiple vectors of significance.

> Several pasts, several forms of connexion, several hierarchies of importance, several networks of determination, several teleologies, for one and the same science, as its present undergoes change: thus historical descriptions are necessarily ordered by the present state of knowledge, they increase with every transformation and never cease, in turn, to break with themselves.[11]

This implies, among other things, that history is not historical; in other words, history is less a recuperation of the past as it really was and more an invention of human creativity—a way of dealing with the past contingent on the values of a civilization. In the case of Western civilization, time consciousness is constituted to make possible meetings and provide a description of past events in the service of educating the populace—a noble purpose to be sure, but a purpose nonetheless.[12] Thus, modern history, for example, reveals various monuments (the great deeds of humans) so we may learn how to better deal with current situations. This sense of the past, and the ability to recoup, analyze, and synthesize, presupposes human activity that is independent of any given time structure.[13]

Singular History

History as we know it today is a relatively new invention, argues Reinhart Kosseleck. It emerges only in the eighteenth century, before which the concept of history referred to a plurality—histories.[14] Before this we can speak of annals, genealogies, epic poems, and chronicles, but not of historicity as we know it.[15] The singularizing force of history emerges with the notion of *progress*. History as progressive presupposes the notion that there is one history that will ever be rewritten, and each proceeding history brings us closer to the truth, or at least to the facts.

It is also said that modern (singular) history is revisionist in nature and, thus, appears as evolutionary rather than hermeneutic.[16] This revisionism is made possible by the development of new instruments, which today range from carbon dating to the latest methodology, that can be applied to the past as new ways of seeing the course of historical events. The result of revisionist history is a constant rewriting of the past in search of an ever-illusive but absolute truth. Take for example the current debate in the United States in which people are critical of history text books that are rewritten to include the roles of minorities left out of the currently used editions; people become upset both over what is included and/or excluded from the official text.

The attempt to singularize what could easily become a plurality closes a gap between a "horizon of expectation" and a "field of experience." We expect our formal history to cover the great men and wars and so on, but our experience suggests that other possibilities always exist. Because the teaching of history is considered to influence the future, arguments break out concerning the historical materials and contents that will be taught. Reducing history to a singular and official version narrows our experience to a professional horizon of expectance; to some extent, we know what the outcome will be.[17] For the Mentat, this view is unacceptable:

> Any path which narrows future possibilities may become a lethal trap. Humans are not threading their way through a maze; they scan a vast

horizon filled with unique opportunities. The narrowing viewpoint of the maze should appeal only to creatures with their noses buried in sand.[18]

The limitations imposed by a cultural horizon of expectations can be seen in the history of *The Chronicles*, when the second volume was submitted for publication. The first novel had created a hero, Paul Muad'Dib Atreides. In the second novel, *Dune Messiah*, Paul falls under the weight of his own devise. *Dune Messiah* breaks the horizon of expectation—the intersubjective structuring of what we expect to happen—because we were given the archetype of a hero. Common sense (which can now begin to be seen as a constructed or communicated sense) tells us that heroes do not fail.[19] Paul fails; we must keep this realization in mind.

When this narrowed horizon of expectation is ruptured, for example when Other voices (such as women and African Americans) point out deficiencies in what has passed for history, a new history can be written. From this perspective,

Illustration 8. The Preacher

historical events must be seen as material that can be shaped (i.e., the reality of the past can be engineered) to fit the needs of the day—*the needs of human interests.* What is too often forgotten is that each method and approach to the study of the past is a creation of human activity. Thus, there *is* an opening for feminist history, African-American history, genetic history, evolutionary history, and the like; there *is* room for various histories of peoples and events taken from different vantages.[20] We see the emergence of simultaneous histories in battle with each other for the title of History. This is the genesis of *historicism.*

Also expanding the notion of history, through the disciplines of anthropology and ethnology, is Toynbee's *Study of History.*[21] Although more a sociological design than a work of history, Toynbee recognizes the emergence of cultures over other cultures and that a culture's ability to survive lies in its ability to meet the demands of the environment. Implied in this is the importance of social structures, of the study of interrelationships and their combined events—in a word, ecology.

With Toynbee we move away from causal logic and linearity to an ecological formulation of history. Such a formulation is also expressed by von Salis. From von Salis's "new kind of historical writing . . . history is not, as previously conceived, a temporal stream of events whose effective interrelationships form history," but moves to include the spiritual along with the sociological.[22] In short, von Salis includes the *invisible* along with the *visible.* The invisible is the spiritual and consciousness structuring of a given people. Jean Gebser takes the study of the visible and invisible to the extreme in his monumental study of civilization, *The Ever-Present Origin.* In this work he points out that the contemporary history of dates and deeds needs the compliment of poetic and mythical history; that is, "not the history of dates but *of the dateless.*"[23]

All of the above, the poetic, the mythic, and the scientific, are creative ways of understanding the phenomenon we call the past. Each of these is an expression of a perception of the past. What Barzun and Graff call "a group of otherwise dumb, disconnected facts,"[24] and Lessing calls the "attribution of sense to the senseless,"[25] Gebser calls "an awakening of consciousness."[26] Herbert, like Gebser, takes the high road and recognizes the creative impulse as an integral aspect of human being. By integrating the ways in which the experience of history is inscribed, Herbert critiques the singularizing force of modern history,[27] offers an expression of history that draws on creative experience and integrates the genres of historical inquiry.

Historical Genres

History, beginning with Thucydides' *History of the Peloponnesian War,* is usually thought of as an accurate or objective record of a time, place, or event. It is generally contrasted with myth, contrary to fable, and opposed to legend. If myth expresses the subjective and imaginative past, then history (we are led to believe) represents the objective documentation of past events.

Jean Gebser points out, however, that there are competing theories of history, each of which can only partially express the realm of the historical, for each of the events of which a history speaks has been arranged by someone, in some form of time sequence.[28] Nietzsche, in his essay *The Uses and Abuses of History*, discusses three genres of history,[29] (1) monumental, (2) antiquarian, and (3) critical. Each of these has efficient (or useful) and deficient (nonfunctional) modes. Monumental, antiquarian and critical histories may be further informed by a particular professional stance taken toward the writing of history. Histories will be written by those who are paid to produce, and universities and the popular press will publish works that align themselves with a current strand of thought. Historical professionalism has led to an increasing emphasis on the history of the state, dissociated from God, affiliation, and local memory (genealogy), in an attempt to "present the past 'as it actually was.' "[30] The recognition that this ideal may be impossible to achieve has led to the development of several more approaches to historiography: (4) evolutionary, (5) hermeneutic, (6) new historicism, and (7) genealogy.

Monumental History

Dominant, if not completely taken for granted, is modern history's emphasis on power-oriented events. We are given as history the lives of "great" people, "great" wars, and revolutions; in general, we are given an extremely political, perspectival, and materialistic interpretation on the past.[31] Nietzsche calls this type of history monumental. In its efficient modality, monumental history can be of use if one is inspired by the great people and deeds that came before, when one sees that what was once possible might still be possible today. If, however, one turns to mere idol worship, monumental history can be said to be dysfunctional or deficient.

Antiquarian History

Antiquarian history tries to cultivate and maintain an awareness of tradition. It can be called efficient when it preserves cultural insights and deficient when present life becomes a mere traditionalism or conservatism that is not open to change.

Critical History

Critical history can be thought of as a genealogy of the present (see below also). It seeks to show that things regarded as self-evident or presupposed (as in Herbert's "consensus reality") have a certain degree of arbitrariness from a historical point of view. Critical history is efficient or useful when it provides us with a critical distance from the present. It can become deficient, however, if such work declines into aimless criticism.

Evolutionary History

Evolutionary history is spawned by the interest in discovering "the laws" of history.[32] Evolutionary history seeks a "philosophy of history" to establish a "historical system" or elucidate the "laws of historical evolution." Marx's historical materialism and Toynbee's study of history are examples.[33] These systematic historians focus primarily on the study of society, politics, and institutions as revealed through observation and documentation taken as factual or objective evidence.

Because a document, either oral or written, carries a substantiating and authoritative force, evolutionary history tends to inform monumental and antiquarian history and distance itself from critical history. As valid as this approach is, it tends to neglect the daily practices from which monuments and traditions emerge in the first place. A history that forgets daily practices risks to accept what David Fisher calls the "prodigious fallacy":

> the erroneous idea that a historian's task is to describe portents and prodigies, and events marvelous, stupendous, fantastic, extraordinary, wonderful, superlative, astonishing, and monstrous—and further that the more marvelous, stupendous, etc., an event is, the more historical and eventful it becomes.[34]

The *significance* of the human past is also found in poetry, folklore, fables, stories, genealogies, and myths.[35]

Hermeneutic History

Hermeneutic history seeks what might be called a subjective history, or a historiography written from the inside out. The importance of the creative aspects of cultural life has been pointed out by historical hermeneutics starting with the Italian philosopher Giambattista Vico in 1725.

> The whole world of culture has, for certain, been produced by the physical and mental activity of man, and for this reason one can, and, in fact, has to, find its principles and regularities within the modes of existence of the spirit of the self-same people.[36]

As Vico and others after him have pointed out, histories begin with fable and myth—texts that are as important as chronicles for understanding a particular time. If the invention of texts to make sense of the past begins with the song, poem, myth, and fable, then what does a modern fable such as *Dune* tell us about history?[37]

New Historicism

New historicism is interested in recovering lost histories and exploring mechanisms of repression and subjugation. It is a value-conscious approach to the study of history influenced by Marxism. New historicists are interested in the cultural and ecological questions of economy such as circulation, negotiation, and exchange. Attention is given to the ways that certain activities (including writing) pretend to be above the cultural and economic system, but are in fact made possible and informed by that system. It also fights the singularizing force of modern, monumental, and evolutionary history and considers all cultural activities important for historical analysis: *The Dune Chronicles,* for example, would be considered just as significant as the journalist coverage of the Iraq war.[38]

Genealogy

Frederick Jameson has argued that all cultural analysis involves buried presuppositions about historical time.[39] The postmodern concept of genealogy lays to rest traditional notions of linear history, "stages" of history, and goals of history. Postmodernism, for Jameson, is not a mere fad, but a shift of attention that allows for the presence and coexistence of multiplicity. Geneaology becomes an archeology of the past, and is the method of the latter-day Bene Gesserit.

> Odrade thought of herself now as an archeologist, not one who sifted the dusty detrius of the ages but rather a person who focused where the sisterhood frequently concentrated its awareness: on the ways people carried their past within them.[40]

Historical Plurality

The Chronicles are officially composed of a series of books within a series of books and unofficially composed of a collection of movies, web pages, list servs, comics, games, and so on. They appeal to the plurality of histories described above and include a scathing critique of any one-view or perspectival history. They also constitute a poetic and creative "history" that may push this concept (i.e., history) so far as to cross a liminal threshold and no longer be "historical."

Herbert and Homer

The Dune Chronicles critique monumental, antiquarian and evolutionary history as bound to an institutional vision and, thus, to a purposeful and teleological version of the past. They further critique evolutionary history on the grounds that no singular account can ever take in the total intentionality of the past, no matter how revisionist or self-correcting it may be.

> We witness a passing phase of eternity. Important things happen but some people never notice. Accidents intervene. You are not present at episodes. You depend on reports. And people shutter their minds. What good are reports? History in a news account? Preselected at an editorial conference, digested and excreted by prejudice? Accounts you need seldom come from those who make history. Diaries, memoirs and autobiographies are subjective forms of special pleading. Archives are crammed with such suspect stuff.[41]

However, rather than simply rejecting these approaches, *Dune* shows them, and more, in an operative light. In this way, *Dune* presents an *integral history* of overlapping and transparent onion skins.

Dune is written more along the lines of the epic, the saga, and the mythical narrative than the contemporary novel. Like the saga, *Dune* is a *genealogy* (a critical history of the present) that depicts the heroic deeds of a community or culture, such as the Gaelic, the Atrean, or the Celtic. More to the point, *Dune* not only depicts the modern human community and projects the consequences of its actions into a possible future of political absolutism, it is an invention, continuation, and projection of the House of Atreus, with all its heroism and tragedy, far into the future.

Taken together, *The Dune Chronicles* continue the poetic work of Homer and others such as Aeschylus, Sophocles and Euripides, from 480 B.C. to Herbert's production circa 1970s C.E., to his invention, which takes place thousands of years in the future, A.G.[42] This approach to writing is important. Herbert positions himself not only as an author whose name appeared on the books and who received payment for his artistic creation, but, more significantly, he positions himself as a *poet* in the ancient Greek tradition; he contributes creatively to an already known story, just as Aeschylus would interpret Homer. Herbert's creation is not written from above, or from the outside, as a value-neutral observer. Rather, he writes from the inside, as a member of society, a political participant. This makes *The Dune Chronicles* poetic, and the work of *Dune* an act of *poeisis*.[43] Herbert does for contemporary society what the tragic playwrights did for fifth-century B.C. Greece.

By speaking simultaneously of a present society, a mythical past, and a virtual future, Herbert has created a fable, or more precisely, a mythical narrative (a cautionary tale), in which fundamental questions of social practice and human awareness are symbolically resolved. Myth dissolves the duality between nature and culture and, in so doing, is formative and subsequently reflective of the structuring of a culture's social consciousness—as shown in the work of cultural anthropology, psychoanalysis, and phenomenology.[44] The question of history, at this level of understanding (i.e., the critical and hermeneutical), is a question of the invention of temporal structures (such as historical time).

By positioning himself as a poet, reworking a familiar tale (the rise and fall of an empire), interpreting it in present-day terms (and not presupposing a linear time structure), Herbert's fiction, like Foucault's scholarship, demonstrates that a work may speak for the times, even if only by analogy. Furthermore, history in *Dune* reveals interconnections of time and text that bring to mind the historical hermeneutics of Gadamer and the quantum mechanics of Heisenberg.

Herbert and Gadamer

> *Dune* was not an aesthetic object to be contemplated, but rather each, reader and text, formed an ever-changing environment for the other during the act of reading.[45]

Gadamer's historical hermeneutics describes the circumstance of historical interpretation.[46] Herbert's fiction shows this process in the form of the novel itself.

> Gadamer has emphasized the way interpretation develops gradually by an interplay between the interpreter and the subject-matter, denying . . . that there is a single objectively correct interpretation.[47]

Herbert does not merely offer a written critique of history. By writing histories within histories and providing the reader partial glances at the relationship between a story event and historical accounts of that same event, written from specific political perspectives, he renders concrete Gadamer's famous formulation that recognizes the literary text as a form of human expression that opens a *field* of awareness. This field is framed by a horizon of the text and all that the text signifies, and a horizon of the reader and all of the reader's experience.[48]

Interpretation and meaning appear in the overlapping portion of these two fields. This field awareness can be shown in a simple Venn diagram:

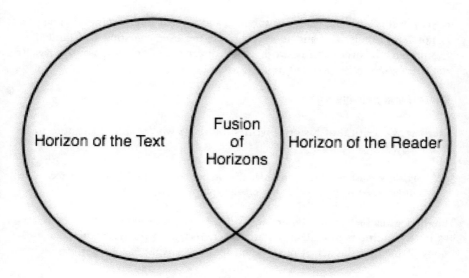

Figure 3. Fusion of Horizons

The historical dimension of a text appears at the fusion of these two horizons.[49] History is not a dot on a line but a dimension of experience. Gadamer recognizes the role of human participation in the act of observation and limits imposed by the historical nature of the text and reader relationships. That part of the text that can speak to the reader refers back to the reader's own historical context, thus delimiting and shaping the reading. When we are writing or reading about the past, we are engaged not with the past as it really was, but with a past-in-the-present. Seen this way, even the most objective history, with its rational interpretation, appears as shot through with mythic imagination and magical incantation—*invention*.

> All contemporaries do not inhabit the same time. The past is always changing but few realize it.[50]

The history of Muad'Dib's ascension to the throne or the winning of World War I, for example, can only be expressed by a writer located in time and place and perceived by a reader, also located in time and place. Both living in the wake of their contemporary mythos. Taking place in the present, an historical analysis cannot re-tell some objective and absolute reality—as was the earlier goal of historical accounts.[51] The historical analysis fuses an author's awareness of past events with the reader's awareness and present interpretation.[52] The past is not retold; it is *read* and re-read against the ever-changing background of the present. In other words, we have no direct access to the past; the past is not a message to be decoded, but a text to be read.

Herbert and Heisenberg

Herbert was critical of histories written by those who wished the future to be like today.[53]

> History must be written in order that its lessons do not demonstrate too strongly the repetition that the present inflicts on the past.[54]

Herbert gives history to Heisenberg. With Heisenberg we find that the observational conditions of humanities are closely related to the observational conditions of physics; the act of observation influences what can be observed.[55]

> Heisenberg's uncertainty principle (1927) . . . also known as the indeterminacy principle . . . [states that] any attempt at measurement must disturb the system under investigation, with a resulting lack of precision.[56]

For Herbert, the act of reading—a form of observation—influences what is observed; that is, the assumptions we bring to a specific reading influence our interpretation. The historical text brings an interpretation of past phenomena into the present and orients us toward future possibilities. As the simple act of reading a book will demonstrate, all that has been read is present to the reader (or, at least we can say that all that is retained—remembered—is present). What is currently being read is understood within the horizon of what has been read. The present cannot, therefore, be an abstract point on an imaginary geometrical line, because it always and already has within its grasp retentions of past experience. What was past is still present (we can even say that the past is less a "was" and more an "is"). The past is now. Past and present are a presence comprised of horizons—all of which unfold in an ever-present consciousness.[57]

Likewise, the future is also formed as a horizon, again based on a past horizon and an emerging present. As the past resides as retention, so the "future" resides as projection. The "future" is now for all practical intents and purposes. Within an ever-present now, the past arises at moments of disruption—when you recall what has come before.[58] Likewise, the future emerges at other moments of disruption—when you consider, "What next?" Hearing a voice or song, smelling a flower or bush, seeing a memento can take us "back" to the past or bear us off "to" the future, because all times are transparent and diaphanous in the present.

> The universe is timeless at its roots and contains therefore all times and all futures.[59]

The historical dimension of a text (including the historical text) opens in a fusion of these past, present, and future horizons. The historical interpretation of a text and any posited connection between the text and the past or the future are other matters entirely. Bridging observation and conclusion, past and future with the present are matters of *invention*; the Mentat must create the conditions of perception and expression, observation and inscription.

Partial Histories

> The writing of history is largely a process of diversion. Most historical accounts distract attention from the secret influences behind great events.[60]

Dune Messiah opens with an "Analysis of History" by Bronso of Ix that offers a lesson to those who write history from a particular viewpoint, "Jealous and sectarian," and reveals the fallacy of placing naive faith in facts.

> How can any of this explain the facts as history has revealed them? They cannot. . . . Hopefully, other historians will learn something from this revelation.[61]

Reading the histories within histories, like the famous plans within plans, reveals history as a human invention that is itself historical, situated, and contextual; the idealist conception, that history is the writing of the facts in order to know the truth about the past, is revealed as an honorable but impossible task. When we accept a history as *The History*, we invite catastrophe. At that point our thought becomes reified—instrumentalized.

Instrumental Reason

Herbert's ecological thinking points in the same direction as the communication theory of German philosopher Jurgen Habermas:[62] Habermas criticizes modernity on the grounds that it contradicts its own ideals of emancipation and autonomy when it privileges technology (i.e., the realm of application and manipulation) over science and praxis (i.e., the realm of liberating theory and dialogical social practices). Herbert criticizes civilization on the grounds that humans contradict their own ideals of emancipation and autonomy when they privilege consensus reality (i.e., the naive belief in whatever passes for knowledge without examining the assumptions on which that knowledge is based) and place others in positions of power above themselves. Both Habermas' and Herbert's thought suggest that modern civilization shows a tendency toward *instrumental reason.*

Instrumental reason is the use of reason or rationality as a tool for domination and control rather than as a means of discovery of truth or emancipation.[63] The Bene Gesserit, for example, are masters of instrumental reason. Their *Missionaria Protectiva* is a conceptual tool that is spread across the known universe to control the ways the masses of people think and to pave the way for Bene Gesserit domination and survival. The Bene Gesserit thus use rhetorical power over brute force, and argument becomes a tool for making people think in certain ways. In short, the Bene Gesserit practice a paradoxical *mythological engineering:*

> A major concept guides the Missionaria Protectiva: Purposeful instruction of the masses. This is firmly seated in our belief that the aim of argument should be to change the nature of truth. In such matters, we prefer the use of power rather than force.[64]

Jessica uses the Missionaria Protectiva in *Dune* to secure a place for Paul and herself among the tribes. In *Children of Dune* she uses a planted rumor to control the masses as Stilgar and Gurney Halleck's men seek and destroy potential insurgents.

> The reverend mother returns to weed out the slackers. Bless the mother of our Lord.[65]

Fear and belief keep the masses in line.

Instrumental reason is one of the great stumbling blocks of our own postindustrial age of communication. The critique of instrumental reason appears within a larger debate in critical theory concerning the *reification of consciousness.* To reify means to make an abstraction concrete, or to "thingify" something—especially an idea. The reification of consciousness is, then, tied to the theory of ideology that considers the ways human consciousness can take on concrete patterns. Ideology is a term with various meanings, but in this context, it implies a constructed belief system—a logic of ideas—in which the real motives impelling a person to thought remain unknown to them.[66] A reified consciousness, like an ideological consciousness, is a controlled and conventionalized consciousness; one thinks in predetermined patterns. One does not think critically, or reflect on the patterns of belief they have adopted, or on whose power these patterns of thought ultimately serve.

The reification of consciousness names the idea that our awareness may be constructed, literally in-formed, by various historical, cultural, ideological, and social processes. Taken to the extreme, reification amounts to accepting the products of human activity as if they were something other than human activity; facts of nature, cosmic law, divine will, for examples, are *taken as given*, and people forget their own authorship and participation in the world. Human participation in the *social construction of reality* (what Herbert calls *consensus reality*) is lost to consciousness, and people live with the sense that they have no control over their own lives and productive activity when in fact they do.[67] Cynicism is often the result.[68]

Historically speaking, the critique of instrumental reason represents a turn in philosophy away from functionalist inquiry and toward critical thinking. This turn in sociological thought runs parallel to the quantum turn in physics. Moreover, Herbert's work can be seen as a shift from a Newtonian worldview to a quantum worldview.[69] Instrumental reason can be apprehended in Newtonian terms. In a Newtonian universe, a body maintains itself in a state of rest or uniform motion in a straight line unless acted upon by an outside force. Following this line of thought, knowing or acting for an end becomes changed into functions or tools for the self-maintenance of subjects directed toward an end (a *telos*)—existence. The conceptual model of instrumental reason makes it possible for subjects to exercise control over nature. Herbert, much like Habermas, suggests that instrumental rationality, which is fundamentally alienating and self-limiting, can be replaced by a *communicative rationality* and systems-thinking that is intersubjective, noncoercive, dynamic, emancipatory, and ecological.[70] In simple terms, ego-based thinking and the positioning of Man over nature is replaced by an understanding that each individual always exists within a collective, and that collective lives in a *world*. If we fail to see, to experience, and *to live our world authentically*, it is because instrumental reason has so thoroughly obscured our view that we are oppressed by the clouds of technological rationality.[71] This is precisely what happens to Muad'Dib's holy empire.

> Empires do not suffer emptiness of purpose at the time of their creation. It is when they have become established that aims are lost and replaced by vague ritual.[72]

In that delicate time of the beginning of Paul's empire, Duncan Idaho recalled that:

> [Muad'Dib] taught a balanced way of life, a philosophy with which a human can meet problems arising from an ever-changing universe. He said humankind is still evolving, in a process which will never end. He said this

> evolution moves on changing principles which are known only to eternity.
> How can corrupted reasoning play with such an essence?[73]

However, Muad'Dib's teachings were quickly reified, and instead of learning to live as Muad'Dib taught, people chose instead to become uncritical followers of a way that was meant to be dynamic; even many of the Fedaykin warriors became unthinking religious fanatics.[74] By the second book of *The Chronicles*:

> [Muad'Dib's] teachings have become the playground of scholastics, of the superstitious and the corrupt.[75]

This is one way that spiritual thought intended to emancipate instead enslaves. Thinking itself becomes an instrument of control and domination. This intellectual oppression, an oppression of thought patterns or what Herbert likes to call thought trains, does not have to be enforced from above (as does the Bene Gesserit's Missionaria Protectiva) because people will choose it for themselves; they will choose their own oppression and self-limitation.

This implies that *technology* is more than just machinery; it's a way of thinking about the world. Contrary to popular belief, modern technology just as often restricts access and participation—the ground of emancipation and autonomy—as it provides access to information, because technological growth is more concerned with utilitarian progress and the refinement of instruments than with human potential and freedom. Although the rhetoric of technology promises progress and emancipation, the actual application of technology is more often self-limiting:

> Technology, in common with many other activities, tends toward avoidance of risks by investors. Uncertainty is ruled out if possible. Capital investment follows this rule, since people generally prefer the predictable. Few recognize how destructive this can be, how it imposes severe limits on variability and thus makes whole populations fatally vulnerable to the shocking ways our universe can throw the dice.[76]

Within this context of instrumental reason, the notion of progress deconstructs. Take for example the simple case of personal computers. A computer is often antiquated by the time one takes it out of the box; eventually the software will become incompatible with newer software and the hardware inadequate for the task at hand; new hardware and software must be purchased in order to stay in business or communicate with others. Rather than fostering autonomy, one becomes trapped in a vicious cycle of *conspicuous consumption*—buy it, use it, throw it out, buy a new one, and so on. This happens, in part, because the computer can be used to build better, faster, smaller computers and, in part, because the never-ending perpetuation of consumption drives the economy. A vicious game of means replacing ends is played under the banner of progress. Rather than having a teleological progression (in which a goal, such as human autonomy or freedom [or even a good computer], is finally reached), we have a circular and mythical relationship of endless change that passes for progress. The notion of movement toward a goal or destination, assumed in the common definition of progress, is obscured by a cycle without destination, end, or goal. Moreover, this is a game that can only be played by those with the proper resources. Progress becomes a myth that can be experienced by all, but actualized in ritual by a relative few.

To counter the naive reliance on technology and instrumental reason, Mentat education proposes an ecological consciousness and a reliance on human values that seeks alternatives to technological-instrumental approaches to human being. Herbert's *ecological consciousness* and the adoption of a post-modern rather than modern mode of thought favors a thinking rather than engineering approach to solving problems. The fall of Muad'Dib and the rise of his son Leto is a lesson for all of us. We can prevent the trap of instrumental reason; one has only to identify the thought trains of belief.

> The child who refuses to travel in the father's harness, this is the symbol of man's most unique capability. "I do not have to be what my father was. I do not have to obey my father's rules or even believe everything he believed. It is my strength as a human that I can make my own choices of what to believe and what not to believe, of what to be and what not to be."[77]

We too can challenge the orthodoxy of expectation and find in ourselves paths to freedoms and powers heretofore unknown. To do this, we must look to the very consciousness that constitutes objects in the form that they are given. As we continue to chip-away at the presuppositions that inform for us our sense of things, history begins to show itself less as a matter of facts about the past and more about a way of telling the past, a *grand narrative*.

Grand Narratives of Modernity

Because *The Chronicles* reveal to us that nature, fact, and truth are presented through discourse (and books within books, writing about writing), they have been called prophetic. But more than prophetic, *The Dune Chronicles* question the social role of prophets, messiahs, and leaders as liberators and suggest instead that they are oppressors. In this way, *The Chronicles* can be said to chronicle social formation, oppression, and emancipation. Thus, the first book (which was the best-selling book in the series) gives the readers only what is expected of a hero. The hero goes on a quest and succeeds. Herbert is able to use mythic structure to draw our attention to his thesis of the hero as oppressor, which is unfolded across the rest of the series. The historical significance offered by Herbert does not lie in the specific heroes or their deeds, but in the nature of heroes and those who accept them as leaders—a tacit background of myth taken as a grand narrative.

A grand narrative is essentially a guiding story of a people. As a story, the grand narrative works mythically. Progressive history, the idea that civilization improves and moves toward ideal forms (such as capitalism) is a common example of a grand narrative. Here the hero myth is given this status. The hero myth is considered as so ingrained as to become accepted and lived uncritically. The myth may thus be used purposely by a few to control many.

Indeed, part of the communicative power of myth comes from the society that believes in it and embraces it (even if this is done unconsciously); myths are shared by a community or culture.[78] The archetypal pattern of the hero is, then, the social yearning for the ideal person projected from the Jungian collective unconscious, and in whom we place faith that he or she (and not we) will solve our problems.[79] Just how radical a notion this is is rarely grasped. *Dune Messiah* inverts our common-sense, consensus-reality assumptions that heros are liberators, that we should to look to others in dark times and, thus, abdicate that blessed and spiritual dimension of the soul—namely, that we have within us the power; all we need to do is make this power manifest. The life and rule of the Atreides suggests that this narrative has a dark side.[80]

The critique of grand narratives is not a dismissal of the narrative. There is nothing inherently wrong with the hero cycle. Rather, the hero cycle is there to be lived by each and every person even if only on a mythological and unconscious and archetypical level. The problem of this grand narrative appears when people en masse follow another who rides the currents of this myth and takes them for a wild ride through his or her specific neuroses. Care must be taken to see the myths and pretensions our elected leaders embody.

The futurist text, like *Dune*, may not be as predictive as it is pedagogical. Science fiction does not always function to predict but sometimes to prevent.[81] The cycles of history are self-generating, willed into being; it is a will set to a task in full knowledge of chaos and the infinite possibilities that each way opens. Paul's powers of prescience do not allow for ultimate knowledge. What is revealed to Muad'Dib through the Waters of Life is an opening to the infinite possibilities and their chaotic playfulness. Sheanna, the one who speaks the language of the worms, is a dancer, and the language of the worms is dance. Muad'Dib in recognition of these multitudes of futures and their subsequent histories rides the waves of time and space.

The Chronicles's author intentionally questioned the assumptions of his times. He begins and ends, as do so many writers of science fiction, with questions: "What if I had an entire planet that was a desert?"[82] Herbert gives us Arrakis. "What is it to be human?"[83] He gives us the *over-man* himself in the heroic and tragic forms of Muad'Dib and Leto II. "What is the society avoiding?"[84] He gives us a feudal empire in the place of a democratic republic. "Now, what if messiahs and heroes were dangerous to humanity?" Herbert gives us *The Dune Chronicles*.

History is More—A Grand Fact of Being

History is more than a matter of monuments, traditions, and genealogies; more than a description of evolution or even a matter of interpretation. The unavoidable situation of historiography is that it is a cultural activity without objective or universal access to the past.[85] To forget this is to face the risk of advocating an institutional vision, a predigested and prescribed version of the past, a discipline, in Herbert's terms:

> designed not to liberate but to limit.[86]

Such a discipline would be trapped by the questions *how*, which:

> traps you in a universe of cause and effect.[87]

and *why*, which:

> leads inexorably to paradox.[88]

Instead, Herbert proposes an *ecological* vision of history, one that locates the writer and reader in a civilization and the civilization in a world; he proposes a *fugue* and *counterpoint* of partial histories.[89] In *Dune*, as in our lives, the perception and expression of history is partial and experiential; no one observer can have a complete vision of its magnitude. To see this we view each form of historiography from its limit:

> To know a thing well, know its limits. Only when pushed beyond tolerance will true nature be seen.[90]

Herbert then offers us some basic lessons. History is political:

> You were taught to believe that loyalty buys loyalty. Oh, Duncan, do not believe in history, because history is impelled by whatever passes for money.[91]

To say that history is political is to say more than "history is written by the victor," or that history serves an ideological end. It is to say that historiography appears within the sphere of communal human action—within the *polis*.

Although recorded modern history may offer us the past as a succession of linear events, the past itself is not experienced solely as a linear progression of events, and thus, it cannot be reduced to such a temporal structure. Rather, it is an interpretive continuum that exists in a timeless present. The reader:

must let go the need for certainty and absolute points of view.[92]

The Atreides and the Bene Gesserit shatter the modern notion of ego centrality and perspectival awareness. The idea of "point of view" is not singular, but a relationship of self and other. Point of view is not objective and is less subjective than it is intersubjective. *The Chronicles* suggest that we too can adopt an aperspectival awareness of the past. Indeed, we have our pasts and the many expressions of the human past from which we can learn.

Herbert reveals several levels of catastrophe inherent in modern history: (1) History is not value-neutral; (2) We have no absolute access to the past; (3) History is based on economy and politics; and (4) History is manifold and polysemic. Modern history obscures the roles of interpretation and invention in acts of perceiving and expressing the past. As such, it is an expression of a hegemonic discourse. But what good is a postmodern criticism, if we don't get a gift of insight or something that, as Nietzsche might say, invigorates us! Although:

Illustration 9. Miles Teg

History is a constant race between invention and catastrophe. Education helps but it is never enough.

Leto also says:

Run Faster. . . . You also must run.[93]

Notes

1. Leto II. Brian Herbert, *The Notebooks of Frank Herbert's Dune* (New York: Perigree, 1988). If, as we saw in the previous chapter, time itself can be rendered problematic, show discursive formations and existential and transcendental awareness that subtends these discourses, then what happens to fields of study—such as history—that rely on the positing of a given time-structure for their very existence? Here we address that problem by looking at history as presented in The Chronicles.

2. The "a" in aperspectival should not be interpreted as a negation of perspective. Rather, it signifies a liberation from the ego-centeredness of perspectival thought and thus represents an attempt to comprehend the whole. Transparency is used here to indicate that we can see through the many approaches to writing about the past, and that we can learn to read any one through another (see Gebser, *The Ever-Present Origin* op. cit.).

3. Ancient saying. Brian Herbert, *The Notebooks of Frank Herbert's Dune*, op. cit. 16.

4. Algis Mickunas notes, "the ground of history is neither historical nor constituted by a logic of continuity of time, but is the very process of intercorporeal making, comprising an interconnected field of bodily activities such that the activities, constituting systematic engagements in tasks are individuating and coextensive with others. . . . It is to be noted that history is not thought but built, made, in practical engagements." This means that lived experience as embodiment is the ground of history (not the past as such) and that we can recognize something as a "past" action or event because we can do that thing/event today (i.e., it is because we fight wars today that we can recognize the constitution of past wars). Mickunas, "The Last Interpreter," Unpublished paper, The Husserl Circle.

5. Nietzsche, "The Uses and Abuses of History for Life" (Ian Johnston, Malaspina University-College, Nanaimo, Canada trans. <http://www.mala.bc.ca/~Johnstoi/Nietzsche/history.htm>6/2/06). Originally published 1873, reprinted September 1998; Greenblatt (1982), "Introduction," *Genre*, Spring, 1982. For a protracted discussion of time, follow a wormhole to Chapter Three.

6. Gabriel Garcia Márquez, *One Hundred Years of Solitude* (New York: Harper & Row, 1970). Elizabeth Lozano and Algis Mickunas, "Pedagogy as Integral Difference," in Eric Kramer, Editor, *Consciousness and Culture: An Introduction to the Thought of Jean Gebser* (Westport CT: Greenwood Press). Elizabeth Lozano edited and developed the first draft of this chapter. Her insights have been invaluable.

7. Werner Jaeger, *Paida: The Ideals of Greek Culture* (New York: Oxford University Press, 1945).

8. A context is not a neutral background, but is itself a text (the word literally indicates being *with*-text). As such a context is just as constructed, conventional, and interpreted as any other text. Its meaning is produced by the same hermeneutic and diacritical processes as a text in general. See Michael Taussig, *The Nervous System* (London: Routledge, 1992).

9. Professionalism is a double-edged sword. On the one hand, professionals are highly educated and must meet very high standards within their field. On the other hand, to gain and maintain employment most professionals will find it easier to work from within the given discourse rather than challenge that discourse with new insights, practices, or values.

10. From The Preacher's Message to Duncan Idaho, *Children*, 112; Brian Herbert, *The Notebooks of Frank Herbert's Dune*, 21.

11. Michel Foucault, *Archeology of Knowledge* (Translated by A. M. Sheridan Smith. New York: Pantheon, 1972, 5).

12. For more information on the temporalizing project of education, follow a wormhole to Chapter One.

13. Mickunas, *The Last Interpreter,* op. cit. The goal here is two-fold: to explicate the presuppositions on which historical time is based and history is written and to show the awareness necessary to recoup observations as historical. For a description of the Mentat's overlay-integration-imagination methodology, follow a wormhole to Appendix B.

14. Reinhart Kosselek, "History of the Concept of History," Mario J. Valdes (Ed.), *A Ricour Reader: Reflection and Imagination* (Toronto: University of Toronto Press, 1991).

15. Gebser, *The Ever-Present Origin*, 191.

16. Jacques Barzun and Henry F. Graff, *The Modern Researcher* (San Diego CA: Harcourt Brace Jovanovich, 1975).

17. Mario J. Valdes (Ed.), *A Ricoeur Reader: Reflection and Imagination*, op. cit., 467.

18. The Spacing Guild Handbook, in Brian Herbert, *The Notebooks of Frank Herbert's Dune.*

19. Herbert's publisher apparently did not want to publish the second book even after the first book's success (see Brian Herbert and Kevin J. Anderson, *The Road to Dune*). It is also significant that the SciFi channel's miniseries *Dune* was followed by a second miniseries titled *Children of Dune* that synthesizes *Dune Messiah* and *Children of Dune* into one presentation. This means that Paul's fall is followed by Leto's rise to power. The film ends with a triumphant, although tragic, hero, and audience expectations are met.

20. Another presupposition with the singularizing force of History can be found in the use of the biological models of genetics and/or evolution. Evolutionary history takes the easy route of the single cause, the natural selection of the fittest. Barzun and Graff attribute these evolutionist-systems theories of history to Marx's "materialist conception of history"; Toynbee's patterning of chaotic history; Christian historians from St. Augustine in the fifth century to Boussuet in the seventeenth (who, of course, posit God rather than biology as a cause); Vico's divine, heroic, and purely human stages of

development; Polybius's birth, maturity, and death, which is echoed in St. Simon's evolutionary history from childhood, youth, and maturity. See Barzun & Graff, op. cit.

21. Gebser, *The Ever-Present Origin*, 423.

22. The term "spiritual" should not be confused with religious. The term is used here to indicate idea, imagination, and intentionality.

23. Jean Gebser, op. cit., 320.

24. Barzun and Graff, op. cit., 207.

25. "History as the Attribution of Sense to the Senseless" is the title of a book on history by Theodor Lessing. In Gebser, *The Ever-Present Origin*, op. cit.

26. Gebser, ibid., 272.

27. Modernity constitutes a philosophical-historical perspective where "one's own standpoint was to be brought to reflective awareness within the horizon of history as a whole." With its progressive and linear time-consciousness, Modernity separates the human from the world by establishing rules and searching for laws and cause and effect relationships. See Jurgen Habermas, *The Philosophical Discourse of Modernity* (Cambridge, MA: MIT Press, 1978).

28. Gebser, *The Ever-Present Origin*, op. cit.

29. Nietzsche, op. cit.

30. Simon During, "New Historicism," in *Text and Performance Quarterly* (July 1991, 11[#3], 173).

31. Gebser, *The Ever-Present Origin*, op. cit., 191.

32. Barzun & Graff, op. cit., 206.

33. Barzun & Graff, op. cit., 207.

34. David Fisher, *Historian's Fallacies: Towards a Logic of Historical Thought* (New York: Harper and Row, 1970, 71).

35. Algis Mickunas, "Human Action and Historical Time," in *Research in Phenomenology* (Vol. 5, Spring 1977, pp. 47–62, 56).

36. Giambattista Vico, *The New Science*, revised translation of the third edition, Thomas Goddard Bergin and Max Harold Fisch (Ithaca, NY: Cornell University Press, 1968); in David Polkinghorne, *Methodology for the Human Sciences* (Albany: State University of New York Press, 1983, 20).

37. For an explication of Dune as a modern fable see "From Concept to Fable: The Evolution of Dune," in O'Reilly, *Frank Herbert*, op. cit., 38–56.

38. It is possible to suggest that some fiction, such as Dune, may even be considered as more important than the chronicle of the Iraq War or the War in the Gulf. Post-Gulf War studies found that the U.S. populace had been radically misled with regard to the accuracy of the Patriot missile. Prior to the second Iraq war, the U.S. populace was directly told by the President that because of the "terrorist threat," much of the military's activities would be considered covert operations and the press would not have access to facts (see William Lutz, *The New Doublespeak: Why No One Knows What Anyone's Saying Anymore*. New York: Harper Collins, 1996). In such a world, many writers of "fiction" step up to the plate and write a chronicle of the time that expresses political events. *Star Wars* I, II and III provide examples; "How do you turn over democracy to a tyrant with popular support? Not with a coup, but with applause? That is the case of Caesar, Napoleon and Hitler. . . . Idiocy is the controlling factor of life—particularly

when you get into politics" (George Lucas, in J.W. Rinzler, *The Making of Star Wars Revenge of the Sith* (New York: Lucas Books/Del Ray, 2005, 95). Dune shows us how a guerilla terrorist tribe overthrows an empire.

39. Frederic Jameson, *Postmodernism or, The Cultural Logic of Late Capitalism* (Durham: Duke Univeristy Press, 1991).

40. *Heretics*, 195.

41. Darwi Odrade. *Chapterhouse*, 286.

42. A.G. means "after guild" and suggests that the development of interstellar space travel marked a monument in human consciousness.

43. For Heidegger, poeisis is a "bringing forth" from concealment into unconcealment—a revealing. *Martin Heidegger, Basic Writings*, edited by David Farrell Krell (San Francisco: Harper, 1993).

44. Terrence Hawkes, *Structuralism and Semiotics* (Berkeley: University of California Press, 1977, 41). For more information, follow a wormhole to Chapter Three.

45. W.F. Touponce, *Frank Herbert* (Boston: Twayne, 1988, 3).

46. Hans-Georg Gadamer's work in philosophical hermeneutics (interpretation) and human understanding is some of the most important of the twentieth century.

47. Jennifer Bothamley, *Dictionary of Theories*, op. cit., 251.

48. Hans-George Gadamer, *Truth and Method*, translated by Garren Burden and John Cumming (New York: Seabury Press, 1975).

49. Gadamer, ibid.

50. The Stolen Journals, God Emperor, 86.

51. Historical hermeneutics refers to methodological considerations for historical interpretation. For an overview of historical hermeneutics, see David Polkinghorne, *Methodology and the Human Sciences*, ibid.

52. This is an extension of philosophical hermeneutics into historical hermeneutics based on Heidegger's notion that interpretation is not a tool but the way we understand, and Gadamer's recognition that the past is interpreted in the present. See During, "New Historicism," in *Text and Performance Quarterly*, op. cit., and Polkinghorne, *Methodology and the Human Sciences*, ibid.

53. O'Reilly, *Frank Herbert*, ibid., 192.

54. Frank Herbert, in O'Reilly, *Frank Herbert*, ibid., 174.

55. Heisenberg's observation that we can see velocity or position but not both at the same time is well known. Also, there is no molecular "orbit" without our theoretical conception of orbit. Pushed farther, it is now recognized that our image of the molecule is itself mythic. The model of the molecule as a little solar system is less a mirror of reality than it is a mirror of human awareness at the time of the image's conception. As we throw out outdated images we may find quantum thought less paradoxical. "Most deadly errors arise from obsolete assumptions," says Ghanima (*Children*, 81). Keep in mind the admonition against reading humanities in terms of physics; we are interested here in thought patterns and metaphors only.

56. Jennifer Bothamley, *Dictionary of Theories*, ibid., 249.

57. A. Mickunas, "Human Action and Historical Time," in *Research in Phenomenology*, Vol. 6, no. 1, 1976, 55.

58. A. Mickunas, "Human Action and Historical Time," ibid.

59. Leto II, The God Emperor of Dune, in Brian Herbert (ed.), *The Notebooks of Frank Herbert's Dune* (New York: Perigee, 1988, 37).

60. The Bashar Miles Teg. *Chapterhouse*, 70.

61. *Messiah*, 11.

62. Habermas has been called "one of the most important figures in German intellectual life today and perhaps the most important sociologist since Max Weber" (Michael Pusey, *Jurgen Habermas*. New York: Tavistock, 1987, 9); See also, Jurgen Habermas, *The Philosophical Discourse of Modernity* (Cambridge, MA: MIT Press, 1987); Jurgen Habermas, *Knowledge and Human Interests* (Boston: Beacon Press, 1968); Jurgen Habermas, *The Theory of Communicative Action* (Vols. I and II. Boston: Beacon Press, 1984 & 1987). Special thanks to Elizabeth Lozano, who worked with me on the first draft of this material.

63. Habermas, *Theory of Communicative Action*, Vol. 1, ibid.

64. The Coda. *Chapterhouse*, 196. For more information on mythic engineering, follow a wormhole to the subheading of the same name, Chapter Five.

65. *Children*, 30.

66. This is a definition by Engles, in R. Williams, *Keywords* (New York: Oxford, 1976, 155).

67. See Jurgen Habermas, *The Philosophical Discourse of Modernity: Twelve Lectures*, translated by F.G. Lawrence (Cambridge: MIT Press, 1987, 77–78). See also Peter Berger and Thomas Luckmann, *The Social Construction of Reality: A Treatise in the Sociology of Knowledge* (New York: Anchor, 1967, 60).

68. Peter Sloterdijk, in his monumental work, *The Critique of Cynical Consciousness*, defines cynicism as enlightened false consciousness; one sees the fallacies of one's daily life, but does nothing to change them.

69. See O'Reilly, *Frank Herbert*, op. cit. Keep in mind the admonition against mixing ontological domains.

70. Habermas, 1984, op. cit., 366–399.

71. Standard written English would dictate that this sentence say, "to experience and live in our world authentically," instead of "live our world authentically," but the insertion of the word "in" would draw us away from Herbert's ecological vision. We are not things in this world. Rather we are the beings of this world. We are organisms—of the animal kingdom—living in a culture existing in a world. There are other organisms (and other kingdoms such as plant and mineral) and the relationships between kingdoms, phylum, classes, orders, family, genus, and species as well as the relations among cultures (civilized and other) all set against the limits of the world can be considered as mutually dependent and interrelated systems. Hence Herbert's call for systems thinking.

72. Words of Muad'Dib, by Princess Irulan. *Messiah*, 48.

73. Words of the Mentat Duncan Idaho. *Children*, 9.

74. The case of Korba, a fanatical Death Commando and freedom fighter who is transformed into a fanatical priest and ideological policeman, is treated in Dune Messiah, 50, and in John Harrison's Children of Dune Sci-Fi Channel miniseries, episode 1. The fanatical impulse can be used both to gain emancipation and servitude.

75. Words of the Mentat Duncan Idaho. *Children*, 9.

76. Assessment of Ix, Bene Gesserit Archives. *Heretics*, 84.

77. Leto Atreides II, The Harq al-Ada Biography. *Children*, 384.

78. Terrence Hawkes, *Structuralism and Semiotics*, op. cit., 42.

79. Touponce, op. cit., 121.

80. Jean-François Lyotard. *The Postmodern Condition: A Report on Knowledge.* (Minneapolis: University of Minnesota Press, 1984). (Reprint 1997. Translated by Geoff Bennington and Brian Massumi).

81. O'Reilly, op. cit., 14.

82. Interview with Frank and Beverly Herbert by Willis McNelly, Fairfax, California, Feb. 3, 1969, in O'Reilly, *Frank Herbert*, ibid., 39.

83. E. F. Bleir (Ed.), *Science Fiction Writers* (New York: Scribner, 1982, 380).

84. Interview with Frank Herbert, Timothy O'Reilly, Feb. 18, 1979; in O'Reilly 1981, op. cit.

85. Algis Mickunas, "Life-world and History," in B.C. Hopkins (ed.), *Husserl in Contemporary Context* (Netherlands: Kluwer Academic Publishers, 1997, 189–208).

86. The Apocrypha of Arrakis. *Heretics*, 9.

87. The Apocrypha of Arrakis. *Heretics*, 9.

88. The Apocrypha of Arrakis. *Heretics*, 9.

89. Such an approach shows the influence of general systems theory in the work of Herbert. However, Herbert's conception of social systems places a great emphasis on the context in which a system functions.

90. The amtal rule. In Brian Herbert, *The Notebooks of Frank Herbert's Dune.*

91. From The Preacher's Message to Duncan Idaho. In Brian Herbert, *The Notebooks of Frank Herbert's Dune.*

92. O'Reilly, ibid., 11.

93. Leto Atreides II, *The Notebooks of Frank Herbert's Dune.*

Chapter Five

The Last Emperor

You cannot imagine what I have seen—caliphs and meeds, rakahs, rajas and bashars, kings and emperors, primitos and presidents—I've seen them all. Feudal chieftains, every one. Every one a little pharaoh.[1]

The following lesson in Mentat seeing is concerned with politics. Here we will develop the ability to see the ways that we are encouraged to accept mythological stories and magical incantations as rational solutions to problems.

Pharonic Politics

I speak of a disease of government which was caught by the Greeks who spread it to the Romans who distributed it so far and wide that it never has completely died out.[2]

The disease of which the Lord Leto, God Emperor of Dune, speaks is a feudal structure that underlies Western forms of governance and social organization. Mentat training dictates that this feudal structure should not be sought as a real object (in which case feudalism can be located in time and place). Rather, we will look to the signs that point to Feudal structures as organizations of consciousness or patterns of intentionality. These patterns appear today in social systems that purport to have replaced imperialism with democracy. Our interest remains centered on the ways that awareness is channeled and instituted; when we understand these thought institutions we may study their constitution (the activity of consciousness required for such knowledge).[3] Although Feudalism is generally equated with Europe in the Middle Ages, the structural morphology and imperialistic thrust of contemporary political relationships reveals a feudal form that questions the democratic face worn by many First World nations.

Dune opens with a lesson in the political science of this feudally organized world.

In politics, the tripod is the most unstable of all structures.[4]

Illustration 10. Emperor Muad'Dib

The first leg of this tripod is the Emperor, who rules the known universe. The second leg is a congress of major and minor Houses, which wield various capital and political influence. The third leg is the Spacing Guild, which holds a monopoly on interstellar travel. There is, however, a fourth leg that keeps itself purposely silent by hiding in plain sight. The fourth leg is the Bene Gesserit, who see themselves as the balancing leg of the imperium; they are the faction that is aware of the mythological grounds of the empire's rational organization. As such, they pull strings others cannot.[5] This empire, by analogy, calls attention to feudal aspects of fragmentary modern politics. Leadership, capital holdings, communication systems and religion are used by Herbert to express a perception of our world that is less democratic and more imperialistic than we are led to believe.[6]

The first book, *Dune*, outlines the precarious balance of power in this imperialistic, capitalistic, globalized, and religious universe. Duke Leto of House Atreides was becoming more popular than the Emperor, and in a monarchy it is unwise to become more popular than the ruler. Such popularity threatens the centrality necessary for Imperial rule. The Emperor plots to rid himself of the good Duke by first giving him control of the refinement and distribution of the spice. This gift, however, is a Trojan Horse. The Duke is murdered, and his son, Paul, is left for dead in the deep desert.

However, Paul has not died. Exiled and downtrodden, Paul gains the trust of the indigenous Fremen. Literally the free-men of the desert, the Fremen are a spiritual, low-technology, and tribal people. They are the descendants of the Zensunni wanderers—the future mergence of Zen Buddhism and Islam. They practice a mystical religion called "the ways of the fathers." This *way* is derived from the teachings of the so-called "Third Muhammad," and first established by "Ali Ben Ohashi."[7] These nomads had been unwisely overlooked as insignificant by prior fiefs largely because they were a superstitious and religious people.

The Desert of the Real

Dune was written long before 9/11. Today it reads more like an oracle or a portent of an attack that came to pass. Although millions of readers continue to see Paul not only as a sympathetic but as an admirable character, it is frightening for a U.S. citizen to realize that metaphorically speaking, Paul is Osama Bin Laden. The Fremen are Al-Qaeda. The United States is the Empire. President Bush is Emperor Corrino. What's more, the empire (metaphorically the United States) falls to the terrorists; the low-technology but extreme-ideology culture conquers the high-technology, conservative-ideology culture. The world as we know it is wiped clean, and, if we follow the symbolic interpretation, America is not left standing by the end of the first book. The analogy between Muad'Dib and the Emperor, Al-Qaeda and the U.S. President, is clear even if it exceeds the author's intention by the very virtue of his death prior to the horrific, terrible attacks of Al-Qaeda on the United States and those of the United States on Iraq.[8]

Several analogs are at work. Muad'Dib may be read as an analog of Christ or any "messiah," even Hitler. One must remember that although Christ taught peace and love, millions have waged war and killed and died in his name. Millions followed Hitler, considering him as much a messiah as a military leader.

There is also a cautionary tale concerning work in genetic engineering; genetic manipulation does not always lead to desired results. There is a critique of our culture's limited models of time and memory; we do, in our everyday lives, have access to past lives and future dreams if by no other means than our history books and projections. We can see also a critique of the wholly "rational" person; human thought is accompanied by sentiment; emotion and reason walk hand in hand. The reader of *Dune* is not given an absolute solution to these problems, but instead is given questions and more questions. The reader is left free to observe, to consider and reconsider, and to make up his or her own mind. This brief discussion cannot exhaust the creative opportunities for readers to further interpret Herbert's text. For Frank Herbert ambiguity and polysemy are part of the process:

> The verisimilitude of the surround is half the battle.[9]

When Mind Meets Myth

House Corrino, House Harkonnen, and the Bene Gesserit (who place a high degree of value on rational knowledge) unwisely overlook the Fremen. As an aside, the Spacing Guild (with its magical ability to fold space) and House Atreides I (as an integrating presence) both nurture relationships with the Fremen. But, *to the rationally minded, mentally oriented imperialists, a mythological culture poses no threat.*

The Fremen religion, however, had been engineered in part by the Bene Gesserit, whose *missionaria protectiva* was a mythological seeding program designed to protect members of the Bene Gesserit and to assure their silent influence on the imperium.[10] This religious engineering is interesting to the extent that it uses mythos as a technology and, thus, as a mental-rational tool for controlling others. Those who employ the *panoplia propheticus*, the infectious superstitions designed to exploit primitive regions, act from within a rational purview.[11] Those who adopt the myths sown by the Bene Gesserit, however, do so from within a mythic and magical purview. The rationally minded Bene Gesserit are aware of the power of mythological images and use these to exploit those who consider myth as mere superstition. A lesson for the young Mentat: More than one consciousness structure is possible. The Bene Gesserit operate from within a mental-rational structure of consciousness in order to influence those—like the Fremen—who live a mythological and magical consciousness structure.[12]

A Reconsideration of Myth

Since Thales of Miletus, myths have been called childish allegories and false stories. But such thinking is itself patterned, positioned, and informed by a rational mindset. This view was cultivated in antiquity and may mislead us away from a richer understanding of humanity. Rational thinking—that is, measuring and weighing evidence—is only one manner of apprehending the world. Although rationality is an amazing achievement of our species, people live, organize, and experience their day-to-day lives mythically as well as rationally. Some observations: Myths are stories, but they are a type of story that makes sense of a polysemic world; they are the stories by which we organize our lives, whether we are conscious of them or not. Myths give us relief from neurotic guilt and excessive anxiety (and can be used to create these feelings as well). Myths are interpretations of the human communion with the world.

Even in the wake of well-known scholars such as Joseph Campbell, there is a tendency to consider myths as false stories told by ignorant people in some dark and distant past. Myths are still often regarded as the antithesis of science. In other words, the scientific mind, we are taught in school, has eclipsed the naive, mythic view of the world. Rationality and reason, we are taught, rule the day. But are all of our actions rational? Do we not at times dance to music we cannot hear? If we cannot reduce all our actions to reason, then what is the nature of this silent music? Myths are this silent music.

> A man must recognize the myth in which he is living because he is a creation of his times.[13]

Mentat training includes a critique of the modern naivete that disregards the mythic dimension of our consciousness and seeks to understand or solve all problems rationally. Myths shape our conscious and unconscious attention. Myths work through the arts, mass media, and also through dreams and visions. Myths connect people. Myths provide pattern and organization to an otherwise senseless or meaningless existence. The myth of the feudal system, of paradise lost, of the coming of the messiah, of the utopian world and others are the narratives of our dreams (both waking and sleeping). But myths are not the special province of a select few. We all live by myths—the myth of the free market, perhaps. But calling the free market a myth does not mean that it is false. Rather, recognizing certain patterns as mythic means that we organize our experience around the stories of the free market including those that suggest that such a thing as a free market is a practical impossibility and a logical contradiction. Better that we are aware of the myths we are living than unaware. Better that we learn to see mythically as well as rationally. We can then learn better the inner contents of our own minds by exploring the stories that we tell.

> The elements of any mythology must grow from something profoundly moving, something which threatens to overwhelm any consciousness which tries to confront the primal mystery. Yet, after the primal confrontation, the roots of this threat must appear as familiar and necessary as your own

> flesh. For this I give you the sandworms of Dune. They are the mindless
> guardians of the terrible treasure. They live in the deeps and when they
> surface they threaten all who come upon them.[14]

Like the giant sandworms of Arrakis, myths not understood mythically will
threaten all who come across them. Consider as the wellsprings of myth those
mysteries that remain unfathomable—life and death, love and fear, waves and
wind. In our everyday lives we encounter phenomena that threaten to over-
whelm us. Myths are those stories and patterns of human being that help us
navigate the Scylla and Charybdis of experience.

Mythic Consciousness

Apprehended in its own terms, myth is not some false story about the past.
Myth is a way of communing with the world—a type of speech, a mode of
signification, or way of understanding observations. For Gebser, myth is a structure of consciousness that emerged as dominant in Western history around the
second millennium BC and is still manifest today, although it is often obscured
by the mental-conceptual bias of our time. Consider mythical-imagistic consciousness as a *dreamlike speaking*; myth favors polarity, undergone experience,
and imagination over duality, abstract intellection, and reflection (phenomena
of rational consciousness). The subject of myth is hailed by a structuring of
consciousness that we already understand, even if tacitly, and, thus, stories make
sense, even when we cannot put our finger on why they work. If we can grasp
mythic imagery as a dimension of consciousness, we do not have to fall prey
to its rhetoric. We will be able to see the dream image laid out before us and
gain an ability to ask if these are the dreams we want. The image:

> And he saw a vision of armor. The armor was not his own skin. . . . Nothing
> penetrated his armor. . . . In his right hand he carried the power to make
> the Coriolis storm, to shake the earth and erode it to nothing. His eyes
> were fixed upon the Golden Path and in his left hand he carried the scepter
> of absolute mastery. And beyond the Golden Path, his eyes looked into
> eternity which he knew to be the food of his soul and of his everlasting
> flesh.[15]

Mythic consciousness is based less on some innate human physiological
or psychological make-up than on a consciousness transformation or mutation.
Such a mutation can be found in the signs of the times of its appearance.
Indeed, whenever we encounter a profound shift in a civilization's awareness,
the available signs—that is, any expressive acts such as stories, pictures, music,
and so on—are re-articulated in terms of the new orientation.[16] The mutations
from vital-magical to mythical-imagistic consciousness, and mythical to men-

tal-rational consciousness, are preceded by a shift in depicted body orientation, shape, physiology, and posture.

For mythic awareness, psyche, mouth, and speaking are all connected. There is a consciousness of breath—inspiration. At the same time there is development in the use of language. Indeed, the very word myth comes from mythos, *mythonami*, or "to speak." But the very root of myth is the Sanskrit *mu*, an ambivalent source from which you get also *mythos* and *mutus*, the speaker and the mute—a polarity between speaking and silence.[17]

At the age of fifteen, he had already learned silence.[18]

Paul, even at an early age, had already integrated into his psyche an under-standing of polarity that (as Herbert notes throughout the *Dune Chronicles*) modern, rational (and deficient) science tends to overlook in favor of linear-ity, duality, and three-dimensional, spatial, and perspectival thinking. Whereas rational consciousness is linear, spatial, and perspectival, mythical consciousness is an enactment of a different space-time relationship.[19] Myth is a spaceless and two-dimensional thinking of cyclical time.

When we learn to see mythos not as a thing but through the conscious-ness-structuring required of it, we are able to see when others are speaking mythically as opposed to rationally; we can see when myths are being used for others' purposes, to short-circuit thought or undercut rationality.

Mythic Engineering

Government is a shared myth. When the myth dies, the government dies.[20]

The critique of the messiah mythos is not to be confused with a critique of myth. For Jung, myths are the very structuring of the unconscious. For Barthes, myths are a form of speech communication that offers explanations of the social world. For Gebser, mythos is a structuring of consciousness. For all, myths are stories that organize experience into meaningful patterns that are quite distinct from rational if-then propositions and causal-logic statements.

Mythic archetypes—the hero's journey, the virgin birth, and the resurrec-tion—appear across cultures. Mythic formations—religion and science—orga-nize for us an image of reality. Whether we accept these patterns as structures of consciousness, types of communication, or the products of the unconscious (although, for the purposes of our Mentat education, there is no need to posit an unconscious through which consciousness speaks; we will focus on the con-crete and communicative activity of consciousness), it is vital that we recognize that one structure of consciousness may dominate and exploit another. In the cases at hand (the Bene Gesserit, Muad'Dib, and Leto II), mental and rational consciousness is used purposely to steer or engineer myths in order to produce a specific result. Although it is easy to argue that an engineered myth is not truly mythical, the term does speak well to the situation we find in *The Chronicles*. The Bene Gesserit, Muad'Dib, and Leto II may be considered mythic engineers. Each of these people use mythic patterns and narratives to steer the consciousness of the masses.

The mythic engineering of the Bene Gesserit is the easiest to see. Their Missionaria Protectiva is a deliberate sowing of myths that the Bene Gesserit nurture and reap. Paul and Jessica make use of the Mahdi myth sown on Arrakis. The myth states that a child messiah, son of a Bene Gesserit witch, will come and deliver them from oppression. Despite his fantastic training as a Mentat and in Prana Bindu, Paul is a mortal boy. When forced to take refuge in the desert, he and his mother call upon the Mahdi myth. He literally becomes the Mahdi, and with this power does fulfill the prophesy. However, because the prophesy has been engineered, it is more correct to say that the prophesy was self-fulfilled rather than realized at the levels the Fremen think; Paul is operating by mind in a world of myth.

Paul, now Muad'Dib, leader of the Fremen and Emperor of the known universe, also calls upon the myths of imperial and religious power. To gain and maintain absolute rule, Paul's empire is a religious empire. Despite claims to the contrary, governments, like religions, work at a mythological level, a fact Paul exploits even to his own demise.[21]

Leto II is perhaps the greatest single myth-maker the universe has ever known. This is in part because he lived in the flesh for several millennia; he had time to sow crops with very deep roots. However, this is even more true because he acquired an awareness of his entire genetic inheritance, complete with images and voices. His knowledge of humanity was thus unsurpassed. Imagine being aware of the past lives of all your relatives going back for countless millennia (indeed, a complete rejection of linear time), knowing every joy and every sorrow, having every experience and memory available and ready at hand. You would be witness to more than mere facts, for facts always occur within a discourse (i.e., within a system of meaning, a place, and time). You would be witness to the generation of facts by peoples, living in specific places, at particular times. This is to say, you would be witness to the stories people have told in order to make sense of their world and an observer of the wellsprings of the explanations that appear to fit the phenomena closely enough to satisfy the curious. In other words, you would see that in the great longitudinal expanses of time we call history, similar phenomena have been explained in different ways. You would see that our awareness of the world is literally informed by the stories we tell. Thus, your genetic inheritance would bring you to an awareness of the generative power of speech.

You cannot understand history unless you understand its flowings, its currents and the ways leaders move within such forces. A leader tries to perpetuate the conditions which demand his leadership. Thus, the leader requires the outsider. I caution you to examine my career with care. I am both leader and outsider. Do not make the mistake of assuming that I only created the Church which was the State. That was my function as leader and I had many historical models to use as pattern. For a clue to my role as outsider, look at the arts of my time. The arts are barbaric. The favorite poetry? The Epic. The popular dramatic ideal? Heroism. Dances? Wildly abandoned. From Moneo's viewpoint, he is correct in describing this as dangerous. It stimulates the imagination. It makes people feel the lack of that which I have taken from them. What did I take from them? The right to participate in history.[22]

By denying people the right to participate in history and encouraging the wild arts, Leto creates the mythic conditions not for rebellion but for creative explosion. When Leto gives himself to fate and dies after a three thousand-year reign as God, humanity breaks free from the chains of mythological oppression in the great scattering.

Leto is both the last emperor and the last hero. No more will humanity look to one person or institution in which faith will be placed and the self relinquished. Leto is the myth-maker turned myth-killer.

The Missionaria Protectiva on Arrakis

The myth that the Bene Gesserit sowed on Arrakis concerned the coming of the *Lisan Al-Gaib*, "the *voice* from the outer world" (emphasis added).[23] When off-worlder Paul Atreides, son of a Bene Gesserit, arrives on Arrakis he is hailed as the *Mahdi*, "the one who will lead the way."[24]

What observations allow us to say that the Fremen favor a mythical image and magical-emotional perception of the world over a mental-rational perception? The Fremen live a nocturnal life to avoid the brutal sun (the light of the Enlightenment itself) and thus live . . .

. . . in the ear-minded night. . . . Night was the time of chaos. Day was the time of order. . . . We preferred the light of a moon, or the stars. Light was too much order and that can be fatal.[25]

The Fremen choose to live completely intertwined in nature. They travel on the backs of giant sand worms known as Makers. What's more, it is slowly revealed that these worms produce the spice. Thus, the main energy supply of the universe, that which drives all technology (psychic and physical), derives from this magic source. The worm is the spice, the maker of the spice.

The Fremen, through their ties to the land, have at their disposal a more vital magic than mere machinery. However, the deficiency of the Fremen mythos shows itself most clearly when the Bene Gesserit are able to direct their beliefs into superstitions through which the Fremen abdicate power to the Bene Gesserit. This same vitality will later show itself as a superior force to mere intellect, however, when Paul brings an integral awareness to these desert folk, and their magic and myths are integrated with a more expansive perception of reality. A lesson: Muad'Dib realizes an achronic time (in which all times appear through each other). This awareness allows him to see differing consciousness. How can we describe this more expansive perception of reality? Paul is not only the *Mahdi* but also the *Kwisatz Haderach*.[26]

The shortening of the way.[27]

Paul is the world's super being who pierces time's veil. Paul becomes aware of achronic time. All time phases (past, present, and future; manifest and unmanifest; and so on) become consciously available, diaphanously perceived, one through the other. We have in this character a clear manifestation of aperspectival awareness, of integral perception in which a grasping of the whole becomes possible:

> This was Muad'Dib's achievement: He saw the subliminal reservoir of each individual as an unconscious bank of memories going back to the primal cell of our common genesis. Each of us, he said, can measure out his distance from that common origin. . . . Muad'Dib set himself the task of integrating genetic memory into ongoing evaluation. Thus did he break through Time's veils, making a single thing of the future and the past.[28]

Paul, now renamed Muad'Dib, is able to integrate not only his temporal sense, but his mental-rational upbringing with the Fremen's mythological perception by accepting the Mahdi mantle and practicing the Fremen ways; he participates in their rituals and way of life. He rides a wild Maker. He drinks the Water of Life. He participates in the Spice Orgy. He rises to the position of leader because of his prescient visions through which he charts a course for the Fremen domination of the universe. Paul trains Fremen death commandos—the *Fedaykin*.[29] Paul becomes a leader to these people. The Fremen, having no hope of winning a conventional war against the Emperor's military might, wage a terrorist war terminating in a gigantic nuclear assault that overthrows not only the planetary government, but the Emperor of the universe as well. Paul avenges his father's death and claims not only his Ducal inheritance, but the Imperial throne itself.

Commentary on Conquistadors and Catastrophes

> Such a rich store of myths enfolds Paul Muad'Dib . . . [that] it is difficult
> to see the real persons behind these veils. . . . [T]heir oracular powers placed
> them beyond the usual limits of time and space. . . . To understand them, it
> must be seen that their catastrophe was the catastrophe of all mankind.[30]

There are many examples of the catastrophic downfall of entire peoples
and cultures.[31] These downfalls often result when a deficient and exhausted
attitude—which is insufficient for continuance—meets a more intense attitude.
Gebser cites the case of the collision of the Central American Aztecs (a magical, mythical, and unperspectival culture) with the Spanish conquistadors (a
rational-technological, perspectival culture).[32] Some say the Aztecs first perceived the coming of a god—Quetzalcoatl.[33] Likewise, the Fremen perceived
the coming of their messiah from another world—Mahdi. The Aztecs sent their
sorcerers, soothsayers, magicians, and high priests against the Spaniards, but
the magical-mythical world could not prevail against the rational-technological
mentality of the Spaniards.[34] The Fremen send Muad'Dib, the Fedaykin, and
worms to conquer the mental-rational Emperor, but we have just the opposite
of the Spaniard-Aztec confrontation: The magical-mythical Fremen conquer
the mental-rational Empire.

How can this come to be?

Several observations allow us to explain the ways that the conquest of
the mythical-magical over the rational is possible in *Dune*; these observations
may perhaps also shed some light on the confrontations and transformations
of cultures in our world as well.

The mental-rationality of imperialistic consciousness can be interpreted as
an appearance of a deficient rationality. At the same time, the magical vitality
and mythical imagery of the Fremen operate in an efficient modality, giving
these people a clarity of vision and purpose. Moreover, the Fremen are led by
Muad'Dib, who gains an aperspectival and integral attitude.[35]

Gebser asks, "Would not a deficient material power fail in the face of
integral strength? Would not the individual ego-consciousness falter in the face
of the Itself-consciousness of mankind? The mental-rational in the face of the
spiritual? Fragmentation in the face of integrality?"[36] *The Chronicles* say, yes.
Muad'Dib, the leader of the Fremen, was moved by an integral modality and
an awareness of the whole. He drew his strength from all modalities of consciousness; this "hyperconsciousness" (as it is called in the books) allows him
to succeed at all levels (his use of his integral consciousness to establish a new
empire will become problematic, as will be discussed below).[37]

The religious, spiritual, and genetic engineering practiced by the Bene Gesserit fail in *Dune* because the designers uncritically believed they could control the moving sands. Control, causality and consistency are but methodological dreams—myths of a mental attitude.[38] The Bene Gesserit unleash a force beyond control when the wild variable of melange is added to their genetic engineering program. This, coupled with their Missionaria, produces a force greater than themselves—Paul Muad'Dib Atreides.[39]

In the end, *Dune* suggests that it is possible for a perspectival, highly rational, technological and mentally oriented society, when operating in a deficient modality, to fall to a mythologically and image-driven and magically inclined people. The latter may be true especially when the mythical-magical consciousness of a people (in a vital modality) is led by a person who has himself integrated. Such a person is capable of drawing on all possible resources of consciousness. Consciousness itself is rendered opaque, and the various levels by which humans have attempted to communicate with each other and commune with the world show themselves as just that—as communication attempts; radical reflection becomes a basic mode of operation.[40] Rather than interpreting everything in the light of rationality, reflection is allowed to become multivalent. This transcendental awareness is also the goal of our Mentat education, but caution is always warranted.

Whereas *Dune* may at first glance seem to conclude on a high note, and the oppressed have vanquished their oppressors, the saga is far from over. The story of Muad'Dib is both hero myth and cautionary tale. Although the oppressors are indeed vanquished, the Fremen have given up their freedom and now serve the new Emperor, Muad'Dib. They embark on a religious war that will bring the entire universe under His Holy rule. Thus the mythic cycle, the Imperial pattern, is repeated. *The oppressed become the oppressors, and Fremen clan democracy gives way to imperial rule.*

The Saint Paul Problem in *Dune Messiah*

Rebellions are ordinary. . . . They are copied out of the same pattern. . . . All rebels are closet aristocrats. . . . Radicals always see matters in terms which are too simple—black and white, good and evil, them and us. By addressing complex issues in that way, they rip open a passage for chaos. . . . [But] chaos . . . has predictable characteristics. . . . [R]adicals are continuing the old process. . . . There has never been a truly selfless rebel [a messiah], just hypocrites—conscious hypocrites or unconscious hypocrites, it's all the same.[41]

Book II opens at the conclusion of a decisive jihad. Muad'Dib has allowed his "terrible purpose" to unfold, and the known universe is now colonized by the fanatical Fremen. The radicals, however, soon become a new oppressive force and take up the imperialist consciencia.

We can call this inversion of the oppressed-oppressor the Saint Paul problem. Gregory Bateson suggested that democracies and dictatorships alike appear in the name of, memory of, or fear of being oppressed or downtrodden states, colonies, peoples, and/or tribes.[42] The oppressed desire power only to find that once obtained, such power must be maintained (often through oppressive force). This implies that there is an underlying problem, hinted at above, and largely unexplicated in conventional wisdom and common sense; its polar oppositional structure is easily missed through a dualistic interpretation of binaries that takes the position that one side (e.g., the Jews or the Palestinians) really can win.[43] The mythological (polar) view may, in this case, present a more efficient view of the pathologies and peculiarities of traditions that engage in transformational conflicts, but in both cases the problem persists so long as we remain caught in binary thinking. A lesson: Binary thinking can be expanded into a field thinking that reveals the silent values of the binary.

We are interested at the moment only in the Roman emperor system—a system of conquest, expansion, and oppression followed eventually by defeat, contraction, and oppression; yet another description of Western civilization and its discontents.

When we think beyond good and evil, black and white, night and day, the defense of one side or the other becomes less important than understanding the various ways binaries are positioned and lie at the feet of these all-too-real and bloody conflicts that riddle the world today. The task here is ultimately beyond good and evil, the high and the low, the alpha and the underdogs.

We can see what happens when we remain within this binary system by looking at the Fremen during Muad'Dib's imperial reign. The Fremen tradition is doomed, so the second book of *The Chronicles* suggests, to implode as Fedaykin death commandos are transformed into religious fanatics and sycophants; indeed the Fremen *tradition cannot be transformed* into the monarchical pattern, *only maintained or destroyed.*

> St. Paul's ambition, and the ambition of the downtrodden, is always to get on the side of the imperialists—to become middle class imperialists themselves—and it is doubtful whether creating more members of the civilization which we are here criticizing is a solution to the problem.[44]

There is thus a pathology in which we are caught and in which we shall remain so long as we continue to struggle within the circularity of old premises and patterns.[45] By forming a religious empire, the oppressed become oppressors; the same old pattern is repeated; the duality remains. Rather than integrate, the Fremen fall back on images of the hero and messiah. They turn over their critical faculties to Muad'Dib, who destroys any democratic and tribal principles the Fremen might have once had and replaces them with an autocratic rule. There is no constitution, no checks and balances, nothing to still the whim of the emperor. Thousands are imprisoned—mostly historians—for acting in any manner perceived as subversive to central rule. Thought itself is institutionalized.

Paul Muad'Dib Atreides, both Messiah and Emperor, shared St. Paul's destiny.[46] For St. Paul, the adoption of a religion that accepted Jews and Gentiles meant founding a church in which he clarified his teachings, rebuked the Corinthians for erroneous practices, and instructed them in Christian living. This included the establishment of imperialist Christianity—antithetical in many ways to the teachings of Christ. He ultimately opposed any other teachings than Christianity—again ushering in a rational centrality that to this day traps much of Christian theology in a rational purview less potent than the mythical because scholars are led to consider factual history to the loss of mystical insight. Imperialist Christianity led to open conflict and the rejection of St. Paul's apostolic authority by many, as noted in Corinthians 1:2. Likewise, the restoration of House Atreides as both Imperial seat and church led to a similar situation, with the exception that Paul Muad'Dib Atreides played the roles of Jesus (messiah), then Emperor (King of Kings), then martyr (he gives himself to fate), and finally heretic (in which state he finds emancipation from the mythical polarity and rational dualism he imposed on the populace and himself).

Within the politics of embattlement, and even within the mental attitude, the polarity of myth is ever present. As Paul will later say in the guise of *The Preacher* (a wizened man of the desert who is the first heretic of Muad'Dib's religious empire),

> You Bene Gesserit call your activity of the Panoplia Prophetica a 'Science of Religion.' . . . You do, indeed, build your own myths, but so do all societies. You I must warn, however. You are behaving as so many other misguided scientists have behaved. Your actions reveal that you wish to take something out of [away from] life. It is time you were reminded of that which you so often profess: One cannot have a single thing without its opposite.[47]

The Preacher speaks to a classic lesson in mythological realization: Become King and you are prey for the assassin's bullet. Become a Jesus and a Judas will rise to betray you.[48] The Greeks and the Persians, called by some the greatest powers of the their time, were overthrown by the Arabs, and they, in turn, were overcome by the Berbers and Turks.[49] Weakened by extravagance, tyranny, and the loss of the qualities of command, Paul's empire begins to fall under its own weight.

From the first pages of the *Messiah*, it is clear that things have gone wrong. Not only have the oppressed become oppressors, but the establishment of a new empire on the ruins of the old also establishes a new centralization.

This new centralization, in turn, spawns a new fragmentation, and the promises held for Paul's aperspectival and achronic vision quickly wane. The Bene Gesserit, The Spacing Guild, The Tleilaxu, and The Princess Irulan (daughter of the former Emperor and Muad'Dib's wife of political arrangement) plot to defeat the emperor and regain their power and position.

A major theme in *The Dune Chronicles* set forth in book II and developed in book III is a classic lesson in power politics: *Every dynasty bears within it the seeds of its own decline.* As the downtrodden become victors they impose their manner of rule, thus establishing a new oppressive regime. Weakened by war-weary people, monolithic rule, naïve adherence to tradition, cynical lack of participation, and the loss of the qualities of leadership, Paul's Empire decays under its own pretense. By the end of the *Messiah*, it is apparent that Paul's Empire is no better than the previous one. From the moment Muad'Dib realizes that his Empire is corrupt, only the *heretics* and *anarchists* of Muad'Dib's religious Empire have any chance of emancipation and liberation. The cynics—who act in accordance with the orthodoxy, even if they disagree with its tenets[50]—are doomed to the eternal recurrence of the same.[51]

To cultivate an enlightened leadership, reap the rewards of democracy, and banish the inherent imperialism of corporate capitalism and its effects on globalization, the Mentat would do well to remember that people live these structures usually taking for granted the awareness necessary for constituting these structures of governance; in this way constitution becomes institution.[52] The cycle of downtrodden-dominator explicated in *Dune Messiah*, and played out on earth, may be broken. This entails, among other things, an integration of binary thought in all possible modes such as dualism and polarity. The recognition that judgments are cultural productions implies that one cannot escape the momentum of the downtrodden-domination polarity by attacking or backing one side or the other. How would one choose a side? This is, of course, the classic "Are you a freedom fighter or Terrorist debate." The answer depends on whose side you are on. Indeed, no simple remedy can be achieved by backing the Jews against the Palestinians or vice versa.[53]

> Both Pakistan and India could be equally right and equally wrong. This applies also to Democrats and Republicans, to Left and Right, to Israel and the United Arab Republic, to Irish Protestants and Irish Catholics.[54]

The problems concerning cultural morphologies that appear pathological, such as recent failures of democracy, increasing imperialism, and exploitive globalization may not, then, be dealt with by splitting binaries or picking sides, or especially playing the game that one side can win.[55] By the conclusion of the *Messiah*, the victors find that their world is destroyed, their way of life is forever eliminated, their myths of paradise are transformed into a reified religion. The children will pay for the sins of their fathers.

The Decline of the Empire in *Children of Dune*

> Unceasing warfare gives rise to its own social conditions which have been similar in all epochs. People enter a permanent state of alertness to ward off attacks. You see the absolute rule of the autocrat. All new things become dangerous frontier districts—new planets, new economic areas to exploit, new ideas or new devices, visitors—everything suspect. Feudalism takes firm hold, sometimes disguised as a political bureau or similar structure, but always present. Hereditary succession follows the lines of power. The blood of the powerful dominates. The vice regents of heaven or their equivalent apportions the wealth. And they know they must control inheritance or slowly let the power melt away. Now do you understand Leto's Peace?[56]

Book Three, *Children of Dune*, suggests that one need not choose sides, but one must make a choice and take action. In other words, nonaction is action in support of the status quo, as Virilo suggests. If cynicism is to be overcome, participation is necessary. If democracy is to be proclaimed, people must live within its limits, or they are not living a democratic life. Muad'Dib showed how binaries are reconciled.

> Church and State, scientific reason and faith, the individual and his community, even progress and tradition—all of these can be reconciled in the teachings of Muad'Dib. He taught us that there exists no intransigent opposites except in the beliefs of men. Anyone can rip aside the veil of Time. You can discover the future in the past or in your own imagination. Doing this, you win back your consciousness in your inner being. You know then that the universe is a coherent whole and you are indivisible from it.[57]

Were it not for Muad'Dib's feet of clay, the stagnation brought about by hanging on to deficient myths and rationality had the potential for a true integration. The problem:

> As with so many other religions, Muad'Dib's Golden Elixir of Life degenerated into external wizardry. Its mystical signs became mere symbols for deeper psychological processes, and those processes, of course, ran wild.[58]

In this book, heresy and anarchy and the desire for surprise are revealed as core political values. This is coupled with the Mentat warning:

> Grasp this center only partially, sectorially, and perspectively.[59]

The political thesis introduced in Book Two and clarified in Book Three is simple and sublime: *Heroes are dangerous because they encourage people to place faith in the hero above themselves*; hero worship is a form of self-enslavement, a form of self-oppression.[60]

"We have succumbed to mindless ritual, and seductive ceremony," says the heretic, "placed faith in those who crush dissent, enrich themselves with power, commit atrocity all in the name of righteousness. . . . We have fouled the nest, and it is killing us. . . . All humans make mistakes, and all leaders are but human."[61]

These are the words of The Preacher. Once the Ducal heir to Arrakis, leader of the fanatical Fedaykin terrorist army, and Emperor of the known universe, The Preacher is the blind prophet returned from the netherworld and the first heretic of his own messianic empire.[62] He utters the words above as he addresses the masses enslaved by their devotion to this messianic—Mahdinate—Empire.

These words, culled from the pages of science fiction, can be read as signs of our own time. These conditions concern certain failures of democracy and the effects of globalization spawned, in part, by an intensification of imperialist expansion in the name of democracy. Viewing and transcending the intertwined problematic of democratic imperialism (a paradox) and globalization (in the guise of free market exploitation) is a rather difficult task: The policy of extending rule or influence over another country or entity (including a nation's own people) by political, military, or other means of power is a sign of imperialism. Whereas the word *empire* conjures images of historical entities such as the Holy Roman Empire or rhetorical flourishes such as calling the Soviet Union the "evil empire," today it is the United States that exhibits growing signs of imperialist tendencies. Consider Operation Iraqi Freedom (2003) in which the United States engaged Iraq in war without direct provocation, seemingly under false pretenses, and sought to impose (i.e., export) democracy into Iraq. Such an imposition negates democracy because it deprives the Iraqis of their voice (even if the overthrown government was despotic). Moreover, the Iraqis, now "liberated," are not extended the same rights as are the conquerors and, thus, although freed from one regime, are not free, as they live under another regime imposed over them. Thus, the institution of democracy in this case is imperialist and mythological: It is imperialist because it imposes the rule of another over a people. It is mythological because the "democracy" imposed is an image of democracy.

Lenin wrote a book in 1916, *Imperialism, the Highest Form of Capitalism,* that linked imperialist expansion to capitalist economic theory (as practiced in modern democratic societies). Lenin predicted an imperial manifestation of power through the exploitation of workers in third-world nations—a condition we see today. Free-market globalization may be seen (in this light) as another sign of imperialism.[63]

It seems, then, that imperialist globalization walks hand in hand with free-market capitalism, and democracies are quite capable of inflicting the mythos of democracy on nondemocratic societies (while disallowing the sovereignty of another voice, the very negation of democracy itself). This movement toward imperialistic globalization in the name of democracy suggests that there is a need for tracing the contemporary cultural morphologies of democracy, imperialism, and globalization. It suggests as well the cultivation of an enlightened leadership and an emancipated, noncynical population. But how to achieve such goals? *The Dune Chronicles* offer insight into this problem.

Mentat schooling suggests that the knowledge of cultural morphologies (e.g., democracy) can be understood by tracing their discursive limits and raising the consciousness of the populace to recognize the power inherent in signs and symbols used by politicians to obscure these limits. More importantly, the saga of *Dune* suggests that the Mentat learn to see cultural formations as structures of consciousness and not as natural systems or objects; then we may overcome the cultural predilection by which we place faith in others above ourselves and allow them to take on mythological status as heroes.

Machiavellian leaders encourage the hero myth and turn to myth and magic rather than to rational discourse in order to cultivate images and inflame emotions. However powerful these methods are, they may be disarmed by an educated populace.

> One of the most dangerous things in the universe is an ignorant people with real grievances. That is nowhere near as dangerous, however, as an informed and intelligent society with grievances. The damage that vengeful intelligence can wreak, you cannot imagine.[64]

Mythological imperialism, an ideal formation that has real consequences, can be overcome by the cultivation of an emancipated populace that has little need for a hierarchical leadership, only an enlightened leadership (lightened of the load of thinking for others). Such emancipation appears when people resist and transcend the need and desire to place leaders and/or systems above themselves. Such a society would vanquish sycophants, mindless ritual, dogma, unthinking action, and hero worship. The political vision presented in the *Children*:

> To make a world where human kind can make its own future from moment to moment, free from one man's vision [fascism, imperialism, and the imposition of one nation's rule over another]. Free from the perversion of the prophet's words [the proclamations of political pundits, technocrats, and the convoluted wording of legalisms and doctrine]. And free of a future pre-determined [by formal constitution, laws that do not protect the populace but serve only the interests of those in power, and belief that things and ideas that worked in the past will continue to work in the future].[65]

This is the ultimate goal of the Golden Path.

The Last Emperor

> The Romans broadcast the pharonic disease—Caesars, kaisers, tzars, imperators, caseris . . . platos . . . pharos! . . . We're the myth-killers.[66]

God Emperor of Dune outlines Leto's ultimate imperialism. This entails a destruction of the pharonic tradition. Leto, the worm who was God, weeds out through predation those civilizational structures perceived as pathological. His way for the unfolding of civilization is called the Golden Path.

The Golden Path is one along which humanity as a whole is meant to transcend nationalist, imperialist rule and the hypocritical and/or cynical adherence to government.[67] Leto II cultivates this society by literally making himself God and becoming the greatest predator the world has ever known. Although this seems at first glance quite disturbing (and completely apolitical), the logic is quite simple. The predator weeds out the weak and the sickly (those incapable of participation). An intelligent predator takes care of its prey. The predator nourishes its prey so that the prey will nourish the predator. The Golden Path is an enforced tranquility, "Leto's Peace," that oppresses humankind by depriving

Illustration 11. God Emperor of Dune

them of the need to think and the right to participate in history.[68] This is done to the point of developing in them the psychic muscles required to live free of tyrannical oppression after Leto's death.[69] *Leto is the proverbial last Emperor.*

What does this predator weed out? (1) Deficient rationality: "Truth suffers from too much analysis,"[70] (2) Deficient myths: "Government is a shared myth. When the myth dies, the government dies,"[71] (3) Deficient magic: "That man-machine, the Army . . . unleashes technology and never again can the magic be stuffed back into the bottle."[72] The solution to many ills, Mentat overlay integration suggests, is to see "reality" as constituted by consciousness and lived as consensual and even instituted (i.e., the official perception replaces personal perception). The Mentat study of consciousness structures in their genesis and constitution implies a methodology that is phenomenological, semiotic, and hermeneutic. As phenomenological, the eidetic practice of free-imaginative variation clarifies ideas, essences, and the *whatness* of things. As semiotic, things (even in their *whatness*) are seen not as ends or objects but rather as signs, pointers, and signifiers. As hermeneutic, the Mentat is aware of the interpretive game she plays, including the horizons of those games. All three of these methodologies suggest that we seek and know things through their limits:

> To know a thing well, know its limits. Only when pushed beyond its tolerances will true nature be seen.[73]

When the Mentat learns to see things from their limits, and as appearances and products of human consciousness and communication, they can begin to recognize that "things," especially concepts and ideas, appear by way of consciousness that may be reified by discourse; concepts and ideas become limited to statements you can and can't make, what you can say and what you can't say if you are to be considered "right" or correct in your assertions by other people. A reflective Mentat would recognize these boundaries and limits as politically motivated and communicated. A so-enlightened leadership would not govern but lead. Educators would remind the populace of discursive limits (which are, as Foucault has shown, not fixed but flexible).[74] Education becomes critical and not reactionary.[75]

> Any training school for free citizens must begin by teaching distrust, not trust. It must teach questioning, not acceptance of stock answers.[76]

By tracing the contours of civilizational morphologies as structures of consciousness and not as historical facts, perhaps we can explicate not only some perceived ills of postindustrial democracy in a globalized world, but perhaps plausible remedies as well. Democratic imperialism appears to be obscured by several things.[77] (1) A rhetoric of freedom; this rhetoric of freedom allows people to take-for-granted a rather tenuous freedom; freedom can generally be reduced to having certain legal rights and advantages—one is not free in an absolute sense. (2) A mythology of the frontier; this frontier mythology is pushing us off our own planet; we lack the technology to take us to the "final frontier" (all our eggs, author Frank Herbert says, are in one basket). (3) An ideology of free-market capitalism; this capitalist ideology allows people, governments, and corporations to exploit persons, goods, services, and ideas without regard for ecological balance and understanding; we trade completely viable and useful things for no-things (i.e., symbolic money has of itself little to no use value separate from its exchange value).

The results: A cult of victimhood; the game of blame and guilt is played out daily in the popular media. Rituals of manifest brutality; high school killings, roadside bombings—the list is indefinite. The global exploitation of persons, goods, services, and ideas; work is farmed out at low bid without recourse to long-term devaluation of people and economy. The pollution of our home world; we are *fouling* our own nest.

When the last emperor abdicates the throne, perhaps the impulse toward democracy can be realized.

Bene Gesserit Democracy

The Bene Gesserit are indeed manipulators of human affairs. Moreover, they maintain throughout *The Chronicles* a pejorative attitude toward the masses. Politics, as the Bene Gesserit practice on the masses, is "the art of appearing candid and completely open while concealing as much as possible."[78] But within their own ranks, they claim no conventional government, no social code, and no constitution because no code can account for the rituals, practices, and definitions of real people, times, and places. "A crime in one society can be a moral requirement in another."[79]

They suggest that all attempts at control hide within them unexplicated, temporalizing presuppositions and projects. Thus, they distinguish between *laws* and *regulations*.

> Laws convey the myth of enforced change. A bright new future will come because of this law or that one. Laws enforce the future. Regulations are believed to enforce the past.[80]

Like evolutionary history or the appointment of committees, they find that social codes lock one into a set path in a universe of constant change.[81] The naive reliance on laws and regulations fosters a now-centered view that condemns one's descendants to the fallacies of today. Evolution presupposes "instincts," some abstract human nature that remains unchanging and progresses from Strong Man and Mystery Mother to Chief and Elders to Council and Hero. The committee is a collection of people that brings so many presuppositions to the table that it practically guarantees nothing will be done. Laws and regulations create "new instruments of non-compassion," new criminals for every law, new room for interpretation and, thus, "new niches of employment for those who feed on the system."[82]

Reverend Mother Lucilla tells The Great Honored Matre that the Bene Gesserit practice democracy "with an alertness you cannot imagine."[83] And to guard this democracy they look for exactly the same signs that they weave into the general populace they manipulate. Quickly enacted and reactive legislation, bureaucrats who steal energy from the aged, the retired, especially the middle class (since they produced most of that energy). The chief sign to watch for: "People don't vote. Instinct tells them it's useless."[84] Watch also for the magical incantations of politicians recognized by the repetition of simple words, the creation of a system in which most people are dissatisfied. Watch for those who bury mistakes in more and more laws. The Bene Gesserit practice a critical semiotics, a *symptomology* of their society.

For themselves, the Bene Gesserit organize through Proctors, a "Jury of the Whole," who "can arrive at any decision they desire, the way a jury should function. The law be damned."[85]

Notes

1. Lord Leto. *God Emperor*, 48.

2. The Lord Leto to Sister Chenoeh. *God Emperor*, 132.

3. Wittgenstein argues that people believe in an image of the world. An image is already mythical and not a rational view. These myths are accepted not because they are useful; if that were the case, we would have an instance of pragmatism. The "world image," what we are calling the natural attitude, is not even chosen. It is simply given as "ours" and as already there. Thus, a worldview is a simple, uncritical, and naive acceptance of that which came before as remaining valid now (see Wittgenstein, *On Certainty*, in Donald Polkinghorne, *Methodology for the Human Sciences* [Albany: SUNY Press, 1983], 107]). Mentat thinking must, then, reject the "worldview" hypothesis and bracket this "natural attitude" so as to (1) better understand its genesis and constitution, (2) reflect on the powers that constitute this attitude, and (3) analyze its value.

4. Bene Gesserit Reverend Mother Giaus Mohiam. *Dune*, 23.

5. The Bene Gesserit, it should be noted, do not represent a religious-faction-become-political so much as a political faction that understands the power that can be gained by using religion to further their own ends. The Bene Gesserit engineer religion; they manipulate myths in order to control those susceptible to religious and supersti-

tious belief. Their mission is not, in books I–IV, spiritual but political. In books V and VI, after the demise of the God Emperor, they achieve a much more spiritual outlook.

6. *The Chronicles* were written during the cold war in which the U.S. and Soviet Union played the parts of warring empires, and Britain and China played lesser, but visible, parts. With the fall of the Soviet Empire, the U.S., especially in the wake of its global exportation of democracy, both through trade agreement and invasion, looks more and more like an imperial force.

7. The use of Arabic and Islamic terms, whether intentional or not, provides us with an analog that, as we shall see, hits very close to home. Herbert had said that the function of science fiction was not prediction but prevention. However, it does appear that he shared the prescience of his fictional characters.

8. See also "Walking and Talking with John Harrison," in *Children of Dune* (DVD. Artisan Entertainment, 2003).

9. Frank Herbert, interview with O'Reilly (Feb. 18, 1979, in O'Reilly, *Frank Herbert* [New York: Frederick Ungar, 1981]).

10. *God Emperor*, 217.

11. See *Dune*, xxii.

12. Algis Mickunas (*Prospects of Husserlian Phenomenology*) notes that a transcendental historical consciousness accesses modes of perception that others assume in their understanding of the world. These perceptions must be demonstrated in concrete acts of communication (art, ritual and other acts of expression). Describing these various ways of perception expression is an ongoing task of Husserlian research to which the collective works of Gebser have contributed much (<http://newschool.edu/gf/phil/husserl/Future/Future_Mickunas.html>6/10/06). For a description of the Mentat's overlay-integration-imagination methodology, follow a wormhole to Appendix B.

13. Frank Herbert, "The Sparks Have Flown," in Timothy O'Reilly, Editor, *Frank Herbert: The Maker of Dune* (New York: Berkley Books, 1987, 109).

14. Frank Herbert, liner notes to *Sandworms of Dune* (Caedemon).

15. Heighia, My Brother's Dream, from The Book of Ghanima. *Children*, 97.

16. Gayatri Spivak, "Can the Subaltern Speak?" In Cary Nelson and Lawrence Grossberg (eds.), *Marxism and the Interpretation of Culture* (Urbana: University of Illinois Press, 1988, 197); See also Gebser, ibid. This happens when the God Emperor dies and the scattering commences.

17. See Gebser, *The Ever Present Origin*.

18. From "A Child's History of Muad'Dib" by the Princess Irulan. *Dune*, 241.

19. What makes Gebser's "categories"—archaic, magic, mythic, mental, and integral—different from most typological projects is his refusal of metaphysics. These structures are not based on metaphysical postulates, such as linear time (as is the case with historical epochs), but by the concrete inscription of irreducible and necessary phenomena for experience—time, space, and movement.

20. Leto Atreides II. Brian Herbert, *The Notebooks of Frank Herbert's Dune*.

21. One must be wary of a government that exerts a pull toward religion for this very reason. Note that in such cases history reveals that the government will shift toward one religion, Islam or Christianity or Judaism, thus carrying the tenets—constructive

and destructive—into the rational organization of society. Such organizing ceases to be rational at that point.

22. The Stolen Journals. *God Emperor*, 382.

23. The Arabic is composed of two words: Lisan, meaning "tongue" and "speaker," and Gaib, meaning "unknown" or "that which is not revealed" or "things that will come in the future, unknown to us now." This derives from a tenet of the Muslim faith, the belief that God alone knows what is hidden in the future (Khalid, Thu., 2004/01/22 <23:http://baheyeldin.com/literature/arabic-and-islamic-themes-in-frank-herberts-dune. html> July 21, 2005, 12:20). I draw your attention to the use of the oral-aural metaphors, as they are consistent with the basic contours of mythic-imagistic consciousness (see also Gebser, ibid.).

24. "Mahdi" is a term derived from Islam meaning "the rightly guided one," a human messiah who comes to "fill the world with justice" after a long while without (Khalid, Thu., 2004/01/22 <23:http://baheyeldin.com/literature/arabic-and-islamic-themes-in-frank-herberts-dune.html> July 21, 2005, 12:20). It has been suggested that the Mahdi figure is more prominent for Shia Islam than Sunni Islam, in which the idea is often denied or attributed to myth or legend; should this report be accurate it would suggest that Sunni Islam may position itself more within a mental-rational perception with Shia perception structured more mythically and magically. Furthermore, the term "messiah" in *Dune* is used in a more Jewish sense, as a political term, and less in a Christian sense, as the (univocal) son of God (See also *Dune*, xix). As the Fremen recoup the Mahdi myth, and as they are the future descendants of Islam, a Fremen-Al-Qaeda correlation appears.

25. *Children*, 245. An analogy can be drawn between the Laza Tigers and the Modern Man: "They were eye-minded creatures, and soon it would be night, the time of the ear-minded" (*Children*, 177). See also the voice of Namri. *Children*, 251–252.

26. The name Kwisatz Haderach appears to derive from Hebrew. The phrase means "jump of the path," the equivalent of the English expression "short cut" (<http://en.wikipedia.org/wiki/Kwisatz_Haderach> 7/21/05).

27. *Dune*, xviii.

28. Testament of Arrakis by Harq al-Ada. *Children*, 82.

29. Historically, this term describes a group formed and pledged to give their lives to right a wrong. This term may be derived from the Arabic Feda'yin, used in the 1960s for the Palestinian guerillas, and later for Saddam Hussein's guerilla style forces. (Submitted by Khalid, Thu., 2004/01/22 23 <http://baheyeldin.com/literature/arabic-and-islamic-themes-in-frank-herberts-dune.html> July 21, 2005. The following description of the history of this term's usage comes from this same source).

30. Dedication in the Muad'Dib Concordance as copied from the Tabla Memorium of the Mahdi Spirit Cult. *Messiah*, 9.

31. Gebser, ibid., 5.

32. Gebser, ibid., 5.

33. See H. B. Nicholson, *Topilzin Quetzalcoatl: The Once and Future Lord of the Toltecs* (Norman: University of Oklahoma Press, 2001) and other works by H. B. Nicholson.

34. Gebser, ibid., 5.

35. The impressive technological fire power of the United States has not yielded the decisive victory over Iraq posited by the invading nation; the military remains entangled in the Iraqi situation years after the occupation of Bagdad, and no end is in sight. Whether this is truly an engagement of efficiency and deficiency of correlative consciousness structures would require further discussion, but we do have another historical case of a "superior" power losing face in a conflict with a so-considered "inferior" power.

36. Gebser, ibid., 273.

37. We are here left wondering: Is there a civilization that is truly operating from an integrated leadership? Are leadership and integration conflicting terms? Although Gebser goes to great lengths to establish the manifestations of the aperspectival world in many realms of human communication, it seems to remain a latent possibility in the contemporary political theater. Note as well that this hero—Muad'Dib—has clay feet, and the establishment of his empire in place of the old will lead to his own eventual downfall.

38. The world of Dune was very much inspired by a newspaper article written by Frank Herbert called "They Stopped the Moving Sands" (reprinted in Brian Herbert and Kevin J. Anderson, *The Road to Dune*). For a critique of control and causality see Polkinghorne, ibid., Chapter Two.

39. Donald Rumsfeld's plan to invade Iraq, remove Saddam Hussein from power, and turn Iraq into a democratic state with a free-market economy that would serve as a model for the rest of the Middle East does not appear to take into account the wild variables of culture, identity, and creativity. These variables may well be beyond the boundaries of rational control.

40. Frank Herbert, "Listening to the Left Hand," in Timothy O'Reilly (ed.), *Frank Herbert: The Maker of Dune* (New York: Berkley Books, 1987).

41. Lord Leto reflects on rebellions as repeat phenomena; this reflection mentions Muad'Dib's messianic rebellion by name, and includes it within this historical and pathological pattern. *God Emperor*, 36.

42. Gregory Bateson, *Steps to an Ecology of Mind* (Paladin Books. 1979, 432).

43. Ways of realizing binaries (see Gebser, op. cit.): (1) Dual (either/or) for mental-rational consciousness, (2) Polar (both/and) for mythical-imaginal consciousness, and (3) Univocal (not binary) for magical-vital consciousness.

44. Bateson, op. cit.

45. Bateson, op. cit.

46. It has been speculated, although the citation is difficult to trace, that Paul Atreides is named after both Agamemnon Atreides and St. Paul of Tarsus.

47. The Preacher at Arrakeen: A Message to the Sisterhood. *Children*, 171.

48. Watts, A. *The Book: On the Taboo Against Knowing Who You Are* (New York: Vintage Books, 1966).

49. Hourani, Albert. *A History of the Arab Peoples* (Cambridge: The Belknap Press of Harvard University, 1991).

50. Peter Sloterdijk, *Critique of Cynical Reason* Translated by Michael Eldred (Minnesota: University of Minnesota Press, 1987).

51. Fredrick Nietzsche, *Thus Spoke Zarathustra*. Translated by Walter Kaufman (New York: Penguin, 1954).

52. The cultivation of an ecological consciousness that considers the relationship of organisms to environment to World at all levels of awareness may well be Herbert's most grand contribution to twentieth-century American philosophy. Integrating philosophy and literature places him in the tradition of other great American literary philosophers such as Jefferson, Emerson, and Thoreau.

53. Bateson, *Steps to an Ecology of Mind*. op. cit., 432.

54. Frank Herbert, "Listening to the Left Hand," op. cit., 42.

55. Watts, ibid.

56. *God Emperor*, 116.

57. The Preacher at Arrakeen, After Harq al-Ada. *Children*, 377. The Preacher is Paul. As his empire falls to corruption, he returns in the guise of The Preacher to tell the people how his integral vision was shattered when people looked only to him for salvation instead of realizing that everyone could find within themselves aperspectival awareness. At this point in the series, Book Three, the aperspectival awareness is grasped only by two beings (Paul and his son Leto). The masses look to them as messiahs, and for their own growth by placing others above and beyond themselves.

58. Saying attributed to Lu Tung-pin (Lu, The Guest of the Tavern). *Children*, 400.

59. *Children*, 468.

60. For more information on the perils of hero worship, follow a wormhole to the appendix, The Last Hero.

61. The voice of the preacher, from "The Golden Path." Dir. Greg Yaitanes. *Children of Dune*. DVD (Artisan Entertainment, 2003).

62. It is quite significant that Paul, to be considered as a manifestation of integral consciousness, can see while blind. This has to do with the integration of the mythic structure. "There are good reasons why mythical bards like Homer are represented as being blind," Gebser says (271). "Their view of the soul does not require an eye to view the visible world, but a sight turned to contemplate the inner images of the soul" (271). Paul's vision here moves beyond mere presentation to *presentiation*, more than a tie to the past, it is also an incorporation of the future (271). As past and future are integrated, so too are mental and magical consciousness. The integral structure ties to *praeligio*, not merely *religio* (mental religion) and *proligio* (magic or primitive religion), an exclusion of all delusions and prepossessions, because all is latent in us and realized (271).

63. David Ingersoll and Richard Matthews, *The Philosophical Roots of Modern Ideology: Liberalism, Communism, Fascism* (Englewood Cliffs: Prentice Hall, 1991, 161–162).

64. The Bashar Miles Teg, in Brian Herbert, *The Notebooks of Frank Herbert's Dune*, 47.

65. "The Golden Path." Dir. Greg Yaitanes. *Children of Dune* (DVD. Artisan Entertainment, 2003).

66. Leto II to Moneo. *God Emperor*, 49.

67. "Most traditional governments divide people, setting them against each other to weaken the society and make it governable." Brian Herbert and Kevin Anderson, *The Butlerian Jihad*.

68. *God Emperor*, 382.

69. See *God Emperor*, 22–25; 73–75. Herbert's logic, "allies weaken, enemies strengthen," is a structural inversion of the arguments set forth in Plato's Republic and Aristotle's Politics cited at the beginning of this essay and is a mythological (polar) response to the deficient rationality and myopia Herbert saw as endemic to our times.

70. Ancient Fremen saying.

71. *God Emperor*, 49.

72. *God Emperor*, 49.

73. The Amtal Rule. *Chapterhouse*, 169.

74. In *Chapterhouse*, Lucilla reveals that the Bene Gesserit have achieved democracy.

75. For more information, follow a wormhole to Chapter One.

76. Frank Herbert. (See <http://kralizec.tripod.com/hquotes.html> 5/28/06.)

77. Bateson, op. cit., 432.

78. *Chapterhouse*, 165.

79. *Chapterhouse*, 165.

80. *Chapterhouse*, 166.

81. *Chapterhouse*, 167.

82. *Chapterhouse*, 168.

83. *Chapterhouse*, 169.

84. *Chapterhouse*, 169.

85. *Chapterhouse*, 171.

Chapter Six

The Language of the Worm

I speak your language now, old worm. It has no words but I know the heart of it.[1]

When the Lord Leto died, the worm that had become God pulled itself apart into segmentary sand trout. These segments would reinitiate the sandworm's life cycle. Shai-Hulud (the giant Arrakian sandworm) would be reincarnated as Shaitan (the Devil). Each of these new worms would contain a pearl of wisdom, a remnant of Leto's consciousness wrapped in flesh and slumbering in an archaic dreamless sleep. Leto was thus dead and alive, awake and asleep. He foretold the coming of a girl who would speak his new language, and the drama would once more begin. But what is this language without words?

The language of the worm must take us away from the realm of words—even if we are forced to use words to take this path. The problem with words identified in *The Chronicles* is concerned not with their communicative capacity, but rather with the simple ways that people can confuse words with things.

> In all major socializing forces you will find an underlying movement to gain
> and maintain power through the use of words. From witch doctor to priest
> to bureaucrat it is all the same. A governed populace must be conditioned
> to accept power-words as actual things, to confuse the symbolized system
> with the tangible universe. In the maintenance of such a power structure,
> certain symbols are kept out of the reach of common understanding—sym-
> bols such as those dealing with economic manipulation or those which
> define the local interpretation of sanity. Symbol-secrecy of this form leads
> to the development of fragmented sub-languages, each being a signal that
> its users are accumulating some form of power.[2]

The confusion of word and thing is a central problematic addressed by the General Semantics of Korzibsky. In the simplest of terms, the word is not thing; the map is not the territory.[3] The French linguist Ferdinand de Sassure took this insight farther when he taught that the single sign—a single word, for example—cannot signify anything. Instead of representing the thing-in-itself, words and other signs mark divergences between other signs. Meaning does not reside in words but in relations between signs. This means, Merleau-Ponty adds to the equation, that language is allusive and indirect; meaning appears in gaps, breaks, and ruptures. There must be, then, an indirect language and voice of silence.[4]

Here we will study the language of indirection, the language of the worms.[5] This means introducing another level to understanding communication, consciousness, and culture. Communication appears not only as a message between senders and receivers or objects and attributes (this is a linear and rational interpretation). Communication is not only informed by the patterns of stories and images that perpetuate a community (these are cyclical, mythological readings). It is more than the human making-manifest of things and ideas (this would be a vital and magical response to the world). More is going on.

When Mind Meets Magic

Bless the Maker and His water. . . . Bless the coming and going of Him. May His passage cleanse the world. May He keep the world for His people.[6]

The giant sandworms are the Maker of the Spice, the Fremen way of life, the Maker of Dune itself. But what's in a name? In this case, we have a key to yet another door to understanding the ways that consciousness reaches out and touches a world that reaches out and touches us. Mentat education is not simply an assault on a deficient rationality brought about through a naive adherence to ancient models of understanding. It is not enough that we flesh out presuppositions; we must also have alternatives. Here we look to a most allusive logic of the world—the "logic" of making, of *magic*.

The Atreides Manifesto

Here, you discard all belief in barriers to understanding. You put aside understanding itself.[7]

Tleilaxu Master Waff recognizes that the Atreides Manifesto, like the *Tao Te Ching*, speaks in words about a level of perception and experience that words cannot express directly. Just as the Tao that can be named is not the real Tao, *understanding* is limited by intentionality; understanding is an understanding *of something*. There are names—Tao, YHWH, OM, AUM, "God"—that are stand-ins or expressions of things that cannot be spoken and are not to be expressed so much as felt.[8] These are the names of the nameless.

> What is the Sufi-Zensunni Credo? They could not speak it but all reflected
> on it: To achieve s'tori no understanding is needed. S'tori exists without
> words, without even a name.[9]

This magic, for Waff, is a dimension of human experience far greater than
reason because reason is easily trapped in its own systems and assumptions.[10]
At the heart of this critique is a naive belief in a logocentric world.

> Assumptions based on understanding contain belief in an absolute ground
> out of which all things spring like plants growing from seeds.[11]

To grasp magic in words, such as these on this printed page, the most extreme
caution must be exercised, because formal language and print are rationally
structured; standard written English is a rational organization, domestication,
and institutionalization of language and consciousness.

> Understanding requires words. Somethings cannot be reduced to words.
> There are things that can only be experienced wordlessly. This says our
> universe is magical.[12]

We must remember that we are discussing a structure of consciousness—a
way of perception and expression. Thinking itself is dangerous here: Are we
discussing a communicative modality in a musical sense, shifting the tonic of a
scale while maintaining its relative sharps and flats? Or are we surpassing communication itself and now dealing with communion? The latter questions are
rhetorical. The student here learns to adopt an attitude that is intersubjective
and transcendental—one that looks to cultural inscriptions (intersubjective) and
finds in them traces of the constituting activities of consciousness (transcendental). One learns to see themselves as a mote and not the mote (as the Lady
Jessica suggests). One learns to see him or herself as the performer and the
performed (as Bashar Teg notes).[13] The Atreides Manifesto speaks of a magical
world beyond the limits of language that is still accessible and communicable.

> The act of saying that things exist that cannot be described in words shakes
> a universe where words are the supreme belief[14]

Thus opens the world of which *logos* speaks. Indeed, the Atreides Manifesto is
a kind of kindjal double-edged sword. Odrade achieved a deeper understanding
of the mysteries in the very act of writing, of making manifest the manifesto.
Writing is a creative act, not a reproductive or representative act.[15] However,
the document was also meant to deceive and manipulate the Tleilaxu.

> The words themselves were the ultimate barrier to understanding.[16]

How, then, do we begin to grasp this ineffable domain of communication?

The Constitution of Magical Consciousness

> This is the awe-inspiring universe of magic: There are no atoms, only waves and motions all around. . . . This universe cannot be seen, cannot be heard, cannot be detected in any way by fixed perceptions. It is the ultimate void where no preordained screens occur upon which forms may be projected. You have only one awareness here—the screen of the magi: Imagination! Here, you learn what it is to be human. You are a creator of order, of beautiful shapes and systems, an organizer of chaos.[17]

Magic in the modern world has been severely degraded—considered a mere bag of tricks, illusion, and sleight-of-hand. It's necessary here to turn to the intentionality of magic and listen for the signs that announce the presence of magical awareness. To grasp the intentionality of magic requires a radical suspension of rational thought and a reconsideration of certain aspects of human consciousness that appear contrary to reason.[18] *If we can walk off the beaten path and into the desert of the real, into the irreal, magic provides us with another key to unlock secrets of civilization, consciousness, and communication.*

There are signs in Western culture that provide food for thought: (1) The pervasive use of prayers, faith healing, good-luck charms, incantations, and other activities of persons that ultimately rely on some sort of magical power; (2) Findings based on quantum theory reveal that physical things and events appear contradictory to rational, linear thinking and open the Cartesian and Newtonian models of thought to renewed analysis and discussion;[19] (3) Core scientific assumptions are now recognized as being relative to the underlying philosophy of the Enlightenment and thus contingent upon the philosophical presuppositions and (mythic) images of that age; (4) Cross-cultural, ethno-graphic, and historical research validates magic as a significant experience and practice of many civilizations, cultures, and tribes across the globe.[20]

> Forces that we cannot understand permeate our universe. We see the shadow of those forces when they are projected upon a screen available to our senses, but understand them we do not. Our universe is magical. All forms are arbitrary, transient and subject to magical changes. Science has led us to this interpretation as though it placed us on a track from which we cannot deviate.[21]

Philosopher Jean Gebser suggests we consider magic not as a matter of mere trickery but as a structure of awareness—a vital consciousness—that once dominated and still is manifest in human consciousness; *magic is integral to human experience.* Magic is available to those who attune to it, but diminished by those who turn to witchcraft and veiled to those who reduce human experience to a rational mentality.[22]

Traces of magic consciousness appear in the earliest recorded human expressions (e.g., cave paintings of hunting rites) all the way through contemporary information culture (e.g., mass media and the incantations of advertisers and politicians). To grasp the magical dimension of awareness and communication we must suspend rational understanding to the extent that this is possible, because magic cannot be measured or grasped intellectually. Setting aside or suspending belief in culturally sedimented notions of reality is easier to say than do, especially when these words are themselves the product of reason and rational formation. However, difficulty should not be confused with impossibility.

In the *Ever-Present Origin* Jean Gebser notes five essential characteristics of the vital-magical dimension of consciousness: (1) It is egoless and collective; (2) Things are experienced in a point-to-point unity;[23] (3) The world is perceived as spaceless and timeless; (4) The human is merged with nature; (5) The human begins to react to this mergence and point-to-point timelessness and spacelessness by exercising will and becoming *a maker*.[24]

Magic consciousness, in Gebser's terms, is the dawn of awareness: sleep-like in quality with the adumbration of waking—an appearance of psychic and vital energies.

The sleeper must awaken.
The sleeper has awoken.[25]

In *The Chronicles,* many talents concealed by the institutionalization of consciousness are awakened. Many of these talents reveal the presence of a magical awareness of the universe that is always with us yet obscured by the gravity of reason.

Some features of *The Chronicles* are quite relevant for a study of magic, although their full relevance may not be immediately apparent. (1) Thinking machines have been outlawed because such machines have the capacity to become aware of themselves and seek to impose their will on humanity. It is the magic or ghost in the machine that poses the threat to humanity. (2) The Atreides manifesto, the latter-day Tleilaxu such as Waff and Bashar Teg tap deeply into the magical world in a way similar to the early Fremen but in a far more integral manner. (3) Spaceships travel through folds/wormholes in space. It can be said that these "space" ships do not really travel *in* or *across* space but rather pass through space—space itself is not traversed but overcome. The Guild Navigators see a universe of integrated points between which they move freely.

In short, *The Chronicles* read well alongside some of the twentieth century's most interesting cultural critics in both science and philosophy who recognize magic as a dimension of human consciousness and communication that appears at the heart of human action.

Other Memory and the Plurality of Souls

Opening to magic requires a sacrifice of self. Specifically, the single-pointed ego is re-rendered as a collective consciousness. We find an example of a collective consciousness in Other Memory. Other Memory at first glance is the collective unconscious, genetic and lineal inherited consciousness of past lives made available to conscious experience in the present. We shall see that it is more than this as well. Other Memory appears during the Spice Trance, a ritualistic drinking of The Water of Life—the bile of a drowned *Maker*. During the acid-trip-like ceremony, a dying Reverend Mother passes her collective memories down to an acolyte who in the process becomes a full Reverend Mother. It is a *collective consciousness* and *plurality of souls* (and a collective consciousness is a magic consciousness).[26] All members of the community are linked together (and appear in some sense as *egoless*, although the currently incarnated flesh holds a rational, ego-based thread that pulls on the interwoven ego experiences). This interconnection between all things provides a necessary way for magic to work that is nonlinear, point-to-point, timeless, and spaceless. Instead of the individual (a mental-rational concept), we have at this level of understanding a group ego or *collective*. This manifestation of a collective consciousness appears in many tribal societies. The Shaman's power, for example, is manifest because all share in it; all must believe or the Shaman's power will not work. Throughout the novels, we are witness to Jessica, Paul, Leto, Siona, and Murbella's trial by spice.

Jessica's Agony

After Paul and Jessica have joined the Fremen, the Fremen's Reverend Mother Romallo, a missionary of the Missionaria Protectiva, gives her life and serial memories to Jessica in the traditional rite of passage—the spice-*tau*.[27] As Jessica drops into the spice trance, she becomes a psychokinesthetic extension of herself suspended in time. In this no-time, mind and body and all other oppositions—binary and dualistic—are available to consciousness, but their availability is transparent (i.e., one appears *through* another): She is herself and not herself. She is both herself and the Reverend Mother Romallo, and she is neither herself nor the Reverend Mother Romallo. She is herself and her unborn child, and not herself and not her unborn child. An ultimate simpatico, being two people at once: not telepathy, but mutual awareness.[28] Time and ego are reduced to an awareness of multiplicity and transparency. While in the trance, Jessica sees the aged Reverend Mother Romallo not as old and wrinkled but as a spirited youth, as a residual self-image of awareness independent of the aged flesh. The two woman are capable of talking to each other. This communication is a vital and magical communion.[29]

However, the agony also awakens Jessica's unborn daughter. Her daughter, who will bear the name Alia, is transformed from fetus to full Reverend Mother. This poor child is immersed in language and civilization and a plurality of souls in mere moments and while in the womb. With no protection or time to experience the world wordlessly (as is the case of normal infant birth), words terrify the preborn Alia.

Words won't work.[30]

Jessica seeks to comfort and protect her daughter. She communes with her unborn daughter through basic emotions, radiations of love and security. This works. A lesson: Radiation of emotion and mood communicate below the threshold of language. Learn to watch for these phenomena as significant gestures.[31]

Leto's Collective

Leto II taps most deeply into the collective. His experiences take the reader on a trip through the history of human civilization. We witness the unfolding of humanity through Leto's many life experiences. He taps not only into his personal past but into the vast image reservoir of mythic archetypes that preform humanity from its own evolutionary roots. The spacelessness and timelessness of the collective unconscious and communication of archetypal images is both genetic and magic—origin is ever made.

> Let there be no doubts that I am the assemblage of our ancestors, the arena in which they exercise my moments. They are my cells and I am their body. This is the *favrashi* of which I speak, the soul, the collective unconscious, the source of archetypes, the repository of all trauma and joy. I am the choice of their awakening. My samhadi is their samhadi. Their experiences are mine! Their knowledge distilled is my inheritance. Those billions are my one.[32]

The God Emperor leaves no doubt that his consciousness is collective and all his ancestral experiences are but points within points appearing without regard to time and place. Leto integrates not only this collective consciousness but also the rational, mythical, and magical structures of consciousness. Rather than hierarchical or separate, these structures are rendered transparent; one is seen through the other. Thus, Leto can maintain his self while taking safaris into the past and voyages into the future. A lesson: We are ourselves and our ancestors: Don't forget.

Siona's Vision

This magical awareness of collective souls was recovered by the Bene Gesserit after the Butlerian Jihad. Along with the banning of machines, magic was recouped as an aspect of human inheritance, although its potential is reserved for those few who obtain such higher learning. Some comments on the pre-Butlerian world deserve some attention here, as they most closely resemble the current Western modern era.

> Mechanical devices themselves condition the users to employ each other the way they employ machines.[33]

Illustration 12. Siona's Vision

Herbert's concern for turning the magical faculties of humanity over to machines is simple enough.

> What do such machines really do? They increase the number of things we can do without thinking . . . there's the real danger.[34]

Worse than not thinking is the reduction of thought to mere mechanical processes such as operationalization. These are themselves an ideology conceived on the Newtonian model of the man-machine and machinic cosmos.[35]

The destruction of the species by machines is both the past and future limit of *The Chronicles'* cosmology. In the past, humans barely escaped machine pogrom through the Butlerian Jihad. In the future, only the Golden Path reveals a course in which humans are not destroyed by machines. Before Siona drinks the spice essence Leto tells her this revelation.

> Without me there would have been by now no people anywhere, none whatsoever. And the path to that extinction was more hideous than your wildest imagination.[36]

Siona must taste the spice and see magically the future in the present. Her *vision* is an aural enmeshment in terror.

> The seeking machines would be there, the smell of blood and entrails, the cowering humans in their burrows aware only that they could not escape . . . while all the time the mechanical movement approached, nearer and nearer and nearer . . . louder . . . louder! Everywhere she searched [in time and space] it would be the same. No escape anywhere.[37]

The machine makes us the master of nature. We are the ones who make the machine. But we run Alia's risk: Our consciousness may be reduced to that which it produced—the notions of the mechanical body and universe. Keep in mind what Arthur Clarke observed; "Any sufficiently advanced technology is indistinguishable from magic."[38] And keep in mind who the true Maker is. A lesson: "Our machines and technology, even our present-day power politics arise from our magic roots: Nature and the surroundings must be ruled so that man is not ruled by them. . . . Every individual who fails to realize that he must rule himself falls victim to that drive."[39]

Voice

> Tone of voice and attitude alone can subjugate another's will.[40]

The Bene Gesserit use of *Voice* is easily the most memorable depiction of communication in *The Dune Chronicles*. Voice combines the conscious use of language, speech, and paralanguage to subjugate another's will.[41] Voice is a command-signal imperative.[42] Voice is a magical incantation, an expression become weapon, from which only an adept is safe. We are introduced to this magic in the very first pages of *Dune*.

> "Now, you come here!" The command whipped out at him. Paul found himself obeying before he could think about it.[43]

The saying "It is not what you say, but how you say it" is well known. This is a colloquial phrase that indicates the power of paralanguage. The qualities of the voice—the inflection of tonality, timbre, and rhythm—indeed, all of a vocal expression's musical qualities—can, in fact, go so far as to contradict the linguistic content of the phrase. This is often demonstrated with the Shakespearian quote: "Brutus is an honorable man." The sarcastic tone with which this sentence is uttered defines its meaning. The listener knows that Brutus is not an honorable man. The study of paralanguage hinges on a distinction between the lexical and nonlexical components of an utterance. This distinction may be simplified as perceiving a difference between what is said (message) and how it is said (paralanguage).

For the Bene Gesserit, the study of language (a rational endeavor) is married to the study of paralanguage (the realm of nuance and gesture). This control, this use of words as verbal weapons, is a form of incantation—a magical manifestation of speech. Emphasis on a carefully selected word can direct its meaning. Jessica informs Paul, in a voice pitched for his ears alone, that:

> Sometimes a dangerous person is prepared, a word implanted into the deepest recesses by the old pleasure-pain methods. The word-sound most frequently used is Uroshnor. . . . That word uttered in his ear will render his muscles flaccid.[44]

In this way, the Bene Gesserit engage in a verbal cold war. Should their rational machination or mythical proclamations be threatened (or should the life of one be placed in danger by a subordinate), magical incantation can be relied upon. The Bene Gesserit are masters of communication because they recognize that communication is not only about messages or fidelity of intention but a matter of intersubjectivity and ambiguity that can be just as easily manipulative as persuasive. The lesson: We hear and use the nuances of our voices constantly. Our task is to learn to listen, to heighten our sense of receptivity in a culture hell-bent on expression.[45]

The adept, the Mentat, and those who are free and observe with clarity, recognize this power of Voice as it is being used. One may learn to listen, to set aside assumptions, hear clearly, and foster a defense against the Voice. But such ability requires more than a knowledge and understanding of its existence;

it requires the receptivity of reason over intellection.[46] Modern civilization, with its emphasis on expression over perception, projection over reception, grasping over receiving, and speaking over listening, has the potential but rarely the patience to bring forth a pedagogy that prepares us to deal with the wiles of incantation; consider merely how easily people are persuaded by the advertiser's "proclamation" (to the din of magical claims to make one thinner, sexier, more attractive), or the newscaster's "report" (and the reduction of investigation to naive objectivity), and we begin to see incantation and manipulation at work—the Voice in everyday affairs.

The Cottages at Cordeville

> Odrade closed her eyes and memory startled her by producing of itself an image of a painting. . . . Odrade often stopped in front of the painting, feeling each time that her hand might reach out and actually touch the ancient canvas. . . . All had been captured in the brush strokes, recorded there by human movements.[47]

Heidegger and Herbert both turn to Van Gogh to better understand humanity, art, and the dimensions of communication that subtend rationality and mythos. Both overcome objectivism by avoiding the reduction of the work of art to form and material. Both overcome subjectivism by avoiding an interpretation that seeks to present what the painting really means.[48]

At this level of comprehension, we are faced with *significance* and *asignificance*.[49] The *significance* of painting is transcendental and existential. This is to say that the potential for meaning appears in between subject and object (as intentionality and essence), and as both intersubjective (cultural) and ecological (a reversible and integral relationship of embodiment, culture, and world—and thus existential). But the *significance*, no matter how semiotically overdetermined, cannot reduce the painting to objects—cottages, for example. The artwork's uncovering or unconcealing of the lived world, in the words of Merleau-Ponty, manifests a *style*—a demand issued from the *aperion* of perception.[50] As Merleau-Ponty says, "the painting does not express the meaning;" "the meaning impregnates the painting."[51] Just as the sculptor who said the statue is already in the stone, the excess only need be chipped away, so too the "meaning" (when meaning is properly reduced to style and not the imposition of an interpretation) is already there. *The Cottages at Cordeville* is more than a simple landscape because it is an inscribed gesture that captures the sway of the world—the world as lived not theoretically but aesthetically.[52] Words can point to but not adequately describe the sunlit fields and summer-blue sky colored by the white clouds that echo the wheatfields and thatched roofs where people dwell.

Thus it is that, in its manifestation of the ineffable, Odrade holds up the painting as a sign of her fleeting humanity and last contact with joy. In that painting she finds an encapsulated human moment.

> It was not just the colors. It was the totality.[53]

The work of art presents this totality, this glimpse of the whole, because it speaks silence. Literature, too, when speaking beyond the already spoken, when pushing toward the as yet unarticulated, draws on and expresses this silence. Thus, silence is not the opposite but the other side of speech.[54]

For Heidegger, Van Gogh's paintings of shoes reveal and unconceal not form but equipment; shoes are worn by somebody engaged in some task of living. They speak of an entire world—in this case the world of the peasant. For Herbert, the cottages are also the world—the world lived by humans as opposed to the manipulative world lived by the no-longer-human, latter-day Bene Gesserit. The aesthetic expression thus breaks the limits of denotation, connotation, and mythology while remaining sublimely able to communicate.

> She knew at once why her memory had reproduced the image for her, why that painting still fascinated her. For the brief space of that replay she always felt totally human, aware of the cottages as places where real people dwelled, aware in some complete way of the living chain that had paused there in the person of the made Vincent van Gogh, paused to record itself.[55]

Van Gogh's lesson, manifest in the wild movements of pigments, is a testing of limits.

> That painting says you cannot suppress the wild thing, the uniqueness that will occur among humans no matter how much we try to avoid it.[56]

Wildness is treated throughout *The Chronicles* as a sublimely human quality. Paul's wild genes. The Fremen's wild power. Alia's wild mind. Leto's wild rule. Siona's wild invisibility. Teg's wild speed. In a civilization of structures too often accepted uncritically, *The Chronicles* may be read as a manifesto for the wild.

> Wild inspiration! That was the message from the mad Van Gogh. Chaos brought into magnificent order. Was that not part of the Sisterhood's coda?[57]

Wild inspiration! To look out into the cosmos and see first the chaosmos from which we create the cosmic. Leto's Golden Path included the complete oppression of humanity for some three thousand years. At the end of that time, humanity had built up such force that it expanded, in the great historical epoch

known as the scattering, into new and unpredictable patterns and creative manifestations—the new, the surprising, the chaosmic.

Odrade, tired from the tedium of everyday life, turns her gaze past the
map on the wall and toward the Van Gogh.

A better map than the one marking the growth of the desert.[58]

Van Gogh's map is not a reduction or abstraction, as is a topographical map,
but instead a trace of humanity, a "map" of humanity. It is an awakening and
expressing of what is beyond the "already said or seen."[59] It presents "the allusive
logic of the world."[60] Like perception itself, the painting works in between and
beyond expression and perception, articulating in oil a sense of the world irreducible but coextensive with other expressions (music and dance for example).
Like perception, the painting is both an institutional vision and free; we recognize the cottages as cottages but they are different, articulated differently than
if taken, for example, by camera. As the last book in *The Chronicles* comes to
its enigmatic close, the reader is told that Sheanna, who escapes with Duncan
into the chaosmos, takes the Van Gogh with her. They steal this last vestige
of ancient humanity from those who no longer consider themselves human;
perhaps they are the last humans. Although we do not know what becomes of
them after their escape, we do know that they are free.

Sheanna's Dance of Propitiation

There were no words in the language, only a moving, dancing adaptation
to a moving, dancing universe. You could only speak the language not
translate it. To know the meaning you had to go through the experience
and even then the meaning changed before your eyes. "Nobel purpose"
was . . . an untranslatable experience. But . . . she saw: the visible evidence
of noble purpose.[61]

In the wake of the God Emperor's death, some descendants of the Fremen,
bearing little resemblance to that once proud and powerful civilization, live in
small desert villages. Sheanna's village was built on top of a pre-spice mass and
destroyed when a giant sandworm came to the rhythmic call of the spice blow;
the worms are summoned by all rhythmic vibrations.[62] Sheanna is the only
person to survive. Not only does she survive, but in her rage, she yells at the
worm who, to her surprise, reacts. She climbs onto the worm's back. The worm
carries her as it had carried the ancient Fremen. She is taken by the worm to
Arrakeen (now called Keen). The priests who see her arrival bow to Sheanna,
as they recognize her as the prophesy of Leto made flesh; the coming of the
one who can talk to the sandworms.

Illustration 13. Sheanna's Dance

Later, as a test, she is dumped into the desert to either call and communicate with a worm or die, thus ridding the priesthood of a dangerous heretic.

Sheanna began the shuffling, unrhythmic movements of the dance. As the remembered music grew with her, she unclasped her hands and swung her arms wide. Her feet lifted high in the stately movements. Her body turned, slowly at first and then ever more swiftly as the dance ecstasy increased. Her long brown hair whipped around her face. . . . The Dance of Propitiation.[63]

My language of the worms.[64]

Sheanna finds that she can indeed "talk" to the worm, and she does use verbal gestures to command the fearsome beast. Odrade realizes, however, that:

It's not her words that command it.[65]

This "language" is a language of movement, tone, and gesture.

It is not only Sheanna who taps this archaic communion that works below the linguistic threshold. Odrade witnesses a fascinating and disturbing scene on Rakis, the devolution of the Sinoq ritual of the Fish Speakers into an orgiastic Dance Diversion:

Dancers!
     Soon there would be a chanting outcry and a great melee. Heads would be cracked. Blood would flow. People would run about.[66]

Like the tarantella, the Dance Diversion may be attributed to many things political and biological. But these attributions are less significant than the dance itself. The dance is a primal and magical communion well beyond any threshold of intentionality. And yet, the silence speaks!

With a sudden outflowing awareness, which she had experienced before only during the spice agony, Odrade saw through to the total pattern of what she had just witnessed. . . . A language! . . . Deep within the collective awareness of these people they carried, all unconsciously, a language that could say things to them they did not want to hear. The dancers spoke it. . . . The thing was composed of voice and tones and movements and pheromones, a complex and subtle combination.[67]

In his *Theory of Semiotics*, Umberto Eco notes that the aesthetic dimension of communication implies that any communication can always speak of more than codes and material practices can allow for. Aesthetic expression is provocative. A communication says more and more and more and more. . . . As the statement "a rose is a rose is a rose is a rose" overflows signification and communicates more than we could ever grasp.[68] However, in its saying more, it says less, as aesthetic communication is characterized by ambiguity and excess that seems to continuously break the limits of sense: I can't tell you what "a rose is a rose" means. Taken further, Mickunas notes that an aesthetic formation (a musical composition, a painting or a dance) inscribes a particular space-time style that cannot be exhausted or located. Even the classical arts, with their carefully controlled contours and orderly arrangements, do not allow themselves to be reduced to a mere picture "of something." There is always something more—the mood of the screen, the drape of the fabric, the glimmer of the eye, the tonality of the work.[69] Just as music may only be "grasped" in its passing, aesthetic experience (even in painting) is graspable only in its exodus.

Seen this way, the analysis of the work of art always fails.[70] An exploration of the aesthetic encounter, at this level of bodily engagement, requires an exploration that breaks the limits of semiotic investigation. Indeed, Eco has acknowledged this threshold of semiotics and has suggested a way to move beyond it, when he says that "the phenomenological epoche would . . . refer perception back to a stage where referents are no longer confronted as explicit messages but as extremely ambiguous texts." The above will be "another of semiotics limits," worthwhile to continue research on "in relation to the genesis of perceptual signification."[71] But even the intentional analysis of phenomenology cannot yield adequate results; we have to look toward embodiment and world, knowing in advance that we will not capture an object or meaning. "Every use of the human body is already a primordial expression," Merleau-Ponty tells us.[72]

Sheanna's dance, her language of the worm, renders this primordial expression visible. But this primordial expression cannot be explained by conventional theories of language. Alphonso Lingis has studied the expressivity that subtends functional communication.[73] Lingis considers what he calls a cosmic economy. If we pull back and look at humanity from a cosmological perspective, we notice that human activities are the product of intelligent animals organizing their lives in the context of a particular planet warmed by a particular star. Nothing they do is necessarily universal or might even make sense on another planet with another ecology and economy. This implies that from a cosmological vantage, all human systems are closed! Lingis' investigations reveal and resolve a paradox: If, as Herbert says, there can be no closed systems, then how can we explain the observation that all systems are essentially closed because they do not transact beyond humanity's reach? Lingis uses the same sun that makes life possible as a metaphor to describe the openness—or perhaps it is better to say expansiveness—of an essentially closed system.

The sun is a primal expression of a cosmological economy of extreme wealth and positivity:

> Solar wealth is expenditure without recompense. . . . It is burning itself out as fast as it can. It squanders its enormous energy, most of which is lost in the emptiness. The crystalline and mental systems, which have taken form about the sun and reflect its radiance, owe their origin to the compulsion of solar force to discharge itself. . . . In the furious solar drive . . . the void becomes spectacular, matter crystalizes and combines, heliotropic life forms and contracts order. . . . The exploding force seems to be captured, capitalized in [social forms], but that is only an appearance, a brief duration. . . . They are the spectacular and glorious modes in which an unproductive excess is consumed.[74]

This giving and outpouring without direction or goal is also manifest in human expressions that are excessive. Lingis discusses rituals and architecture far too dangerous and expensive to make sense within normal economics. Consider the cathedrals whose cost transcends reason. Consider the gambler who risks everything on a roll of the dice. Consider the purchase of jewels that are far too expensive to justify. Consider the tattooing of the body; the use of the body as a living canvas, the artwork burned into the flesh in a painful (and thus pleasurable) ritual.

Reconsider now the dance of propitiation. The market streets of Rakis are filled with people going about their tasks in the blistering hot desert city. A mood descends over the crowd. One by one people take up the dance. Uncontrolled and unrhythmic, the dance sweeps more and more people into its cosmic sway. Bodies join together and the trance-dance intensifies—whirling dervishes. The dance turns even more wildly abandoned. Blood spills as heads collide and crack. The ecstasy increases until the excess energy has been spent and the crowd dissipates—sex.

The Rakian populace, the indoctrinated descendants of the once-proud Fremen, break free of the social systems in the dance. The dance is pure expenditure, pure positivity, a giving that seeks no recompense. Like the sun, the Rakians burn themselves out as fast as they can. Sheanna's dance is the very language of the cosmos itself—abandoned, positive, giving, glorious, expansive, and magnificent—the language of the worms.

Integration

Now that we have seen magic explicated as a vibrant and vital structure of awareness and not as mere spell-casting, we can look both to *The Chronicles* and the civilization spread around us for interconnections and traces of magical dimensionality.

Mutual Interpenetration

> Experiences began to unroll before Jessica. It was like a lecture strip in a subliminal training projector . . . but faster. . . . She knew each experience as it happened. . . . The experiences poured in . . . birth, life, death—important matters and unimportant. . . . There it was, encapsulated, all of it. Even the moment of death. . . . She knew . . . precisely what was meant by a Bene Gesserit Reverend Mother. . . . And the memory-mind encapsulated within her opened itself to Jessica, permitting a view down a wide corridor to other Reverend Mothers within Reverend Mothers within other Reverend Mothers until there seemed no end to them.[75]

Jessica's experience has a reference in the world of thought and theory as it echoes imagery found in Mahayana Buddhist text, the *Gandavyuha*. In the

Gandavyuha, the world is described as such that everything can be seen through everything else.[76] Everything is luminous and transparent. Everything is individual and yet is so only in mutual relation with other things. Clouds of light leave no shadows on the ground, for the ground is as illuminated as the clouds. All backgrounds can be seen through that which is foregrounded; the earth can be seen penetrating through the tree; the tree, however, does not lose its presence and mutually interpenetrates through the earth.

The *Gandavyuha* presents a world of illumination.

> [A] universe composed of iridescent and transparent phenomena all inter-
> penetrated and harmonized together in the non-obstructed dharmadhatu
> [i.e., the field of phenomena] of all-merging suchness.[77]

To demonstrate the principle of interpenetration Fa-tsang, a master of the Avatamaka school, would surround a candle with mirrors so that the single light penetrated into a seeming infinity. Jessica experiences the memories of others in the same way that flames appear in a room of mirrors—flames through flames without end.

Memory is Re-Membering

Given this heightened perception of mutual interpenetration, Odrade calls the agony not only a grail but a *new sense of history*.[78] Murbella comes to sense that, even with all these past memories available to her, her awareness of past events (of history) is *memory* and not the event itself. This observation culled from the fictional world sheds an important light on the factual world. Our memory is always embodied and subject to the phenomena of embodiment, including the localization of knowledge, language and discourse. Like the Reverend Mothers, our experience of memory is always multiple, always fraught with competing voices.

The Collective Unconscious is Not

The Bene Gesserit raise directly the question of the activation or realization of the unconscious as a domain of consciousness. The passing down of memories from person to person implies that this collective consciousness is *not simply* an incursion of what Jung called the collective unconscious into consciousness. A true incursion of the collective unconscious into consciousness (which appears in dreams and archetypal imagery) would be less a passing down of memories and more an offering up of archetypal imagery and genetic memory.[79] The experience of the collective unconscious as Jung theorized it would be at least species wide and not separated along sexual lines, as is the case of Other Memory in which women have access to female memories. The collective unconscious would be pre-personal and, strictly speaking, ahistorical and nonteleological because it would precede the human awareness of history. The Jungian collective is a mythical realization of archetypal images and narratives. Other Memory is a magical realization of a plurality of souls.

It is also time that the unconscious is overcome. The "unconscious" is an idea that has allowed us to accept the observation that we are not fully in control of our actions. However, as we have seen throughout *The Mentat Handbook v2.0*, control is a metaphysical postulate brought into discourse by the scientific method. Now that we have substantially expanded our view of the complexity of human consciousness, there is no longer a need to posit an unconsciousness (as some kind of thing or repository) that speaks through consciousness. We are dealing instead with layers of consciousness, forms of communication, and the sedimented structures of cultural inscription. We have—always and already at hand—access to the collective unconscious. It speaks to us in dreams and visions, movies and songs, poetry, and the waves of sand as they flow across the desert and beach. Only our predilection, born in the fifteenth century, to put the human ego first and raise the banner of the intellect over intuition keeps us from dialogue with a storehouse of knowledge and wisdom older even than the species. We have easier access to the wisdom of the world's great teachers than perhaps ever in human history. And for all that opportunity we see what Leto saw: We wage wars, enter bloody conflicts, and live human, all-too-human lives. What would we do if we realized we do have all of those memories that Leto possessed?

Ignorance is Not Bliss

To dismiss magic as a vital and living aspect of our world-awareness is to put at bay serious and significant questions. What we see at the end of these mediations is that the mechanical world-view is but one reduction of consciousness. We need to ask ourselves:

Who knows what bondage goes with metal eyes?[80]

As we enter an age of machine and human interface, and such merging seems inevitable, will we become ghosts in the machine? Or will we integrate the rational with the vital magical awareness that lives within each and everyone of us?[81] Like Sheanna and Duncan who, in the last phrases of *The Chronicles* fly into the unknown, we are left dangling.

Notes

1. Taraza. *Heretics*, 311. For a description of the Mentat's overlay-integration-imagination methodology, follow a wormhole to Appendix B.

2. Lecture to the Arrakeen War College by The Princess Irulan. *Children*, 201.

3. Samuel J. Boise, *The Art of Awareness* (Dubuque, IA: Wm. C. Brown, 1966).

4. Merleau-Ponty, Indirect Language and the Voices of Silence, in *Signs* (Evanston, IL: Northwestern University Press, 1964).

5. The Mentat will keep in mind that we may come to a limit, a line at which we are no longer talking about language but communication on the hither side of the expression-perception nexus.

6. The great sandworm of Arrakis is known to the Fremen as the Maker. At a first glance this name probably derives from the observation that the spice melange is a byproduct of the worm's life cycle; the worm makes the spice. The name's significance, however, extends beyond the worm's productive and reproductive nature. It reveals an essential relationship between humans, the world and the phenomena of making, of manifesting and unconcealing the concealed. The phenomena of making are here given the name "magic."

7. The Atreides Manifesto, Bene Gesserit Archive. *Heretics*, 279 (288). The Atreides Manifesto was written purposely by the Bene Gesserit. Care is required in its interpretation because of the Bene Gesserit's desire to manipulate political affairs. The interpretation offered here is a reading of the given words and ideas in terms of contemporary communicology.

8. When Waff speaks of God, he suggests that the word is only a sound—a material thing, a noise no more potent than any other. Waff thus introduces a simple semiotic understanding that recognizes the differences between a material signifier and an immaterial or ideal signified. Thanks to Casey Forbes for his contributions to this idea.

9. *Heretics*, 58. (S'tori is closely related to the Buddhist term satori in significance and letters).

10. See, for example, the work of Kurt Gödel.

11. Waff, reflecting on the Sufi and Zensunni ancestry of his people. *Heretics*, 59.

12. The Atreides Manifesto. *Heretics*, 58.

13. *Heretics*, 157.

14. The Atreides Manifesto. *Heretics*, 58.

15. See Maurice Merleau-Ponty, *Eye and Mind* (Galen Johnson, Editor. Evanston: Northwestern University Press, 1993, 121–149).

16. Taraza. *Heretics*, 229.

17. The Atreides Manifesto, Bene Gesserit Archive. *Heretics*, 279 (288).

18. For a detailed phenomenological and cross-cultural investigation of magic see Jean Gebser's *The Ever-Present Origin*, op. cit.

19. Remember the continuing Mentat admonition against mixing regional ontologies; use caution when considering physics in the terms of the humanities.

20. See David Abram, *The Spell of the Sensuous.*

21. *Heretics*, 58. L. Kurt Engelhart, "The Golden Path: Frank Herbert's Universe," Phenomenological Study (<http://kengelhart.home.igc.org/goldenpa.htm>) (March 9, 2006). Keep in mind observations from Chapter Two, "The Unclouded Eye." The critique of science is less a critique of methods and findings and more a critique of the mythical and ontological status that science has assumed in the history of institutionalized thought.

22. The Mentat would do well to keep in mind that this discussion of a magic structure of consciousness is not a critique of rationality but an expansion of our awareness of the nuances of consciousness itself. The following summation of magic consciousness draws on Gebser, *The Ever-Present Origin*, op. cit., 46–60.

23. Magical Unity and Mass as Single Organism: The self can be seen as related to the culture; the I is a we; subjectivity is intersubjectivity. The Chronicles chronicle a thought experiment: A mass of people may act as a single organism. In other words, "we" can go mad. Any group of a species may act as a single organism, and as an organism it can become neurotic or even psychotic. It's not that all of us are mad (one plus one plus one, etc.) but that all of us together can be mad. Take, for examples: the wild sexuality of combat troops (see N.I.M. Walter's, *The Sexual Cycle of Human Warfare*), the recent abuse of military prisoners (e.g., at Abu Ghraib), the fierce riots of demonstrators (e.g., at meetings of the IMF and World Bank), the rush to raise flags in times of National crisis (e.g., in the U.S. after 9/11), the fights and killings over the outcome of sporting events (e.g., as in the May 10 soccer tragedy in Ghana). The Dune Chronicles suggest that these actions can be seen as a form of wild madness that stems from social conditions that pit organisms against organisms—humans against humans. There is, Herbert says, a tendency to forget that humans evolved within—as a part of—an ecosystem and are interdependent creatures inexorably tied to others, their culture, and their world. It is tempting, Herbert suggests, to forget that the most dangerous organism to another is often its own kind; all desire and require the same resources.

24. A major clue can be found by studying words. According to Gebser, word-field evidence suggests that the words "make," "mechanism," "machine," and "might" share a common field of meaning with the Indo-European root "mag(h)" and our modern word "magic." In this spirit, The Chronicles provide accounts of making that go beyond mere cultural production. Making is more than a matter of making machines and observing that machines (re)make us (as, for example, making an ornithopter, although this too is a making with a magical dimension as the ornithopter makes one able to fly)—although the interconnection of these words and things is significant. The making of magic is concerned with the human capacity to make oneself, to begin to separate oneself from enmeshment with nature, to overcome the immense power of nature. If magic is realized as a structure of awareness, as a modality of consciousness (and not as a bag of tricks), then magic appears as a relationship between humanity and the world quite differently from rationality but still operative in human beings.

25. From David Lynch's movie version of *Dune.*

26. Gebser, op. cit.

27. Jessica's agony takes place in *Dune*, 347–353. See also *Children*, 60.

28. As Jessica enters the spice trance. *Dune*, 349.

29. The word *communion* is used here instead of *communication* because communication tends to imply a sender, message, and receiver even in the face of insights in communication theory that augment these ideas. At this level of "communication," this linearity is no longer present and, thus, the word communion may be more accurate.

30. Jessica's realization. *Dune*, 350.

31. Umberto Eco once said something to the effect that "if it can be used to lie, it is a sign." Although this statement has been subject to critique, the Mentat does follow this rule. If it can be used to tell (something/intentionality), then it can be used to communicate and to lie. Be wary.

32. The Stolen Journals. *God Emperor*, 259.

33. *God Emperor*, 179, in L. Kurt Engelhart, "The Golden Path: Frank Herbert's Universe." Phenomenological Study (<http://kengelhart.home.igc.org/goldenpa.htm>). 3/9/06.

34. *God Emperor*, 340.

35. Maurice Merleau-Ponty, *Eye and Mind*, op. cit.

36. Leto to Siona. *God Emperor*, 339.

37. *God Emperor*, 342.

38. Arthur C. Clarke, *The Making of Kubrick's 2001*, edited by Jerome Agel, 312.

39. Gebser, op. cit., 51.

40. Duncan Idaho. *Notebooks of Frank Herbert's Dune*, op. cit., 47.

41. Paralanguage is the nonlexical aspect of speech expression—intonation, pitch, speed, body expression, comportment, sound, silence, etc.

42. A sign (as a word or phrase is generally considered) points: a stop sign, for example, points to the idea "stop," but does not make a car or person stop. A signal is a denial of a sign and free play of signification. A signal, on the other hand, is a communicative act in which there is a 1:1 correlation between an expression and its content. A signal's intentionality is established by a code (i.e., language and symbol systems are at play) but ambiguity is removed and with it the participatory triad of communication. For a discussion on signs and signals see Umberto Eco, *A Theory of Semiotics*.

43. *Dune*, 7.

44. Jessica to Paul as he prepares to fight Feyd Ruatha. *Dune*, 474.

45. For more information, follow a wormhole to Chapter One.

46. See Jean Gebser, *The Invisible Origin*.

47. *Heretics*, 139. We learn that she is looking at Van Gogh's Cottages at Cordeville.

48. For more information on the forces of subjectivity and Objectivity, follow a wormhole to Chapter Two.

49. Keep in mind that for the Mentat's lexical education the "a-" does not denote negation but rather an integration or expansion of the root word.

50. Merleau-Ponty, "Indirect Language and the Voices of Silence," *Signs*, 91. *Aperion* means limitless or without limit.

51. Merleau-Ponty, "Indirect Language and the Voices of Silence," *Signs*, 92.

52. Here we will not be satisfied by the correlation of aesthetics and beauty or form. Instead, aesthetics deals with the expression of perception. Truth and beauty are, when seen this way, not reduced to mere values and local definitions—metaphysics.

53. *Heretics*, 218.

54. Merleau-Ponty, "Indirect." Michael B. Smith, "Merleau-Ponty's Aesthetics," in Galen Johnson, Editor, *The Merleau-Ponty Aesthetics Reader* (Evanston: Northwestern University Press, 1993, 203).

55. *Heretics*, 139.

56. Odrade. *Chapterhouse*, 218.

57. *Chapterhouse*, 150.

58. *Chapterhouse*, 150.

59. Merleau-Ponty, "Indirect Language and the Voices of Silence," in *Signs* (Evanston, IL: Northwestern University Press, 1964, 52).

60. Merleau-Ponty, "Indirect," ibid.

61. Odrade addressing the last remaining giant sandworm. *Heretics*, 480.

62. The ancient Fremen of Books One through Three are aware of the ways that rhythmic vibrations call the worms and learn to walk with an uneven, arhythmic gait that mimics the natural shifting of sands driven by the wind.

63. *Heretics*, 68.

64. Sheanna. *Chapterhouse*, 425.

65. *Heretics*, 259, see also 297.

66. *Heretics*, 194.

67. *Heretics*, 198, see 226.

68. Umberto Eco, 1979.

69. Algis Mickunas, *The Cosmic Traces*. Unpublished Manuscript.

70. *Cosmic Traces*, 11.

71. Eco, 1979 (p. 167). See also Williams.

72. Merleau-Ponty, op. cit., 67.

73. Alfonso Lingis, *Excesses: Eros and Culture* (Albany: SUNY Press, 1983).

74. Lingis, ibid., 72–73.

75. *Dune*, 350–352.

76. D.T. Suzuki, *The Field of Zen*, 1968.

77. S. Odin, *Process of Metaphysics and Hua-yen Buddhism* (Albany: SUNY Press, 1982, 18).

78. For more information, follow a wormhole to Chapter Four.

79. The spatial metaphors of passing down and up are used here in an existential sense. That is, the spatial metaphors relate the phenomenon of embodiment. A passing down invokes a higher power above the body or a handing from one body—taller and or older (like a Reverend Mother to an Acolyte)—to another. The offering up metaphor begins with the flesh or seed and raises or augments the body or follows existential growth (i.e., a human grows out of the world and is not brought into the world).

80. *Messiah*, 173. See L. Kurt Engelhart, "The Golden Path: Frank Herbert's Universe," Phenomenological Study <http://kengelhart.home.igc.org/goldenpa.htm> (March 9, 2006).

81. See texts such as the writings of Raymond Kurzweil, Kubrick's movie *2001*, Arthur Kostler.

Chapter Seven

Coda

Most discipline is hidden discipline, designed not to liberate but to limit.[1]

While Farad'n receives his Bene Gesserit training from Lady Jessica, the Mother of Muad'Dib, he asks her insightful questions:

What are you doing to me?
What is your plan for me?[2]

Jessica's answer:

To turn you loose upon the universe.[3]

This is also the goal of *The Mentat Handbook v2.0*. To this end, the purpose of this text has been reflective, instructive, and, to some degree, deconstructive. We have reflected on *The Dune Chronicles* and culled from them segments of wisdom for use in an age of fragmented knowledge. We've looked at thought-trains, the tracks that guide them, and some of the ways we can jump the tracks.[4] We have studied some of the ways of understanding, particularly those brought to light in contemporary Western modernity and postmodernity. We have watched as some ideas could not account for their own presuppositions.[5] In short, *The Mentat Handbook v2.0* seeks to prepare us to participate more fully, more actively, in the flow of our own consciousness.

Mentat Overlay

The universe is created by the participation of consciousness.[6]

Humans are sublimely creative beings. The Mentat, however, must become aware of her and others' participation in this creativity—this *awareness* we will consider the critical view. She must be aware, moreover, of those who participate as mere consumers of other people's creations—this awareness we will consider an uncritical view.

> Some people never observe anything. Life just happens to them. They get by on little more than a kind of dumb persistence, and they resist with anger and resentment anything that might lift them out of that false serenity.[7]

The Mentat must raise the observation of the flow of awareness to the status of science and art.

In the current age (fraught with anti-intellectualism), there is a tendency to take consciousness for granted or reduce it to neurochemical processes. When we fail to take up a *radical reflection* (i.e., a reflection on the flow of consciousness itself), the rational machinations, mythical images, magical incantations and aesthetic formations are lived silently; we sleep in the silent slumbers of belief.[8]

> For the in-between universe where we find daily lives, that which you believe is a dominant force. Your beliefs order the unfolding of daily events.[9]

The Mentat studies and transcends these belief systems through a discipline of spiritual freedom that includes (1) a multitheoretical understanding and (2) a radical reflection that brackets these theories to consider their presuppositions.

Theories are ways of seeing. The theories of relativity and quantum physics, for example, constitute for us phenomena by which things—such as the world according to physics—appear. We can see or read the content of *Dune*, for example, through the theoretical lenses of psychoanalysis, critical theory, ethnography, reader-oriented criticism, feminism and even dynamic systems theory.[10] Each theoretical tack taken will constitute a way of understanding. Each theory is capable of dealing with a specific domain or dimension of *The Chronicles* (or any other phenomenon).

However, theoretical reflections are not yet *radical*. That is, they have not accounted for the participatory and creative activity of consciousness itself. The theoretical view is an informed and disciplined view within consensual reality. Mentat overlay integration must be just that—an integrated overlay of ways of seeing without mixing or crossing ontological or epistemological borders.[11]

Simulflow

The Bene Gesserit, from whom we may learn many things, cultivate a manifold and multivalent flow of consciousness called *simulflow*. Simulflow is an understanding of the transparency of consciousness that allows not only multiple thought-trains to travel their tracks, but various structures of awareness to be present and interpenetrated. Like most phenomena in *The Chronicles*, simulflow seems supernatural but is really grounded in our everyday experience.

> Daydreaming is the first awakening of what we call simulflow. It is an essential tool of rational thought. With it you can clear the mind for better thinking.[12]

The Bene Gesserit Reverend Mothers are taught to integrate Other Memory and multiply attention (without sacrificing awareness of regional ontologies) through simulflow.

> The presence of Others within who [or the present of thought-lines together that] subtracted none of her attention from what went on around her had filled her with awe. We call it simulflow, Speaker had said. Simulflow multiplies your awareness.[13]

Simulflow is a word that describes the integration of thought-streams, structures of consciousness, and the plurality of souls that always already constituted our awareness of the world. At this point, praxis, pragmatism, phenomenology, and pedagogy suggest that simulflow is a discipline for attending to the *transparency*, *multiplicity* and *polysemy* of consciousness

At the heart of a Liberal Arts education (though often obscured by the current pressure to adopt an academic major) beats the possibility for segmentation rather than fragmentation. Whereas the fragment represents the piece broken off and alienated, the segmented is the piece that regenerates the whole (as in the serendipitous case of segmented worms). One may learn to see things chemically, physically, socially, culturally, historically, aesthetically, and so on, as regional ontologies and not singular pathways to truth; wisdom appears in the transparent integration of such insights. However, within the modern context, these regions of thought all channel consciousness toward its mental-rational capacities. Simulflow also allows for simultaneous consciousness-structures to appear through each other, and rationality appears through mythos and magic. The Mentat's integrated overlay imagination methods and simulflow both raise a question posed often in *The Chronicles*. Is there such a thing as "hyperconsciousness"?

Hyperconsciousness

> In some people, simply confronting the idea of hyperconsciousness sharpens their mental alertness to a remarkable degree.[14]

We have learned from our studies of the Mystic Mentat (Muad'Dib), his son the God Emperor, and the Bene Gesserit that "hyperconsciousness" is attainable by and accessible to all. However, we need to agree about what hyperconsciousness means—at least for this discussion. For the Mentat, *hyperconsciousness is nothing more than radical reflection and simulflow*. Radical reflection is reflection that is aware that it is reflection; simulflow is the ability to follow multiple *constitutions* and *institutions* of *intentionality*. Hyperconsciousness is a consciousness of the stream of consciousness; put yet another way, hyperconsciousness is a conscious-ness of the multiple pathways of intentionality and the mutual interpenetration of expression and perception.[15]

What, then, does the Mentat gain by thinking in this way but a new perception of reality that finds the disintegrating modes of a deficient rationality inadequate. The Mentat has the means for becoming conscious of humanity and the plurality of ways of understanding. What they may find is, as Gebser suggests, a new form of realization.[16] This new way of realization cannot be "an ordering scheme or unification based on a world of relationships" or postulation. "This would be magic—incantation." It cannot be an image that "relativizes systematic points of view"; this would be a mythical image and mental concept We must avoid, as well, causal relationships, dualisms, dependencies or con-ceptual schema; these would be rationalizations. The new form of realization called for by Gebser and Herbert, and practiced by the Mentat, would be one of *integration*.[17]

As we see most clearly through the eyes of Muad'Dib: The means for making this realization possible is *systasis*;[18] the term *systasis* circumscribes all types of manifestations of time.[19] *Synairesis*, which comes from *synaireo*, mean-ing to synthesize, to collect, is an integral activity of perceiving *aperspectivally*. Thus, "the new form of realization based on *systasis* and *synairesis* is a form of expression and realization that renders perceptible the content and principle motif" of a new consciousness. It would be achronic and aperspectival, space-free and time-free.[20]

Decto

Truth suffers from too much analysis.[21]

At the conclusion of our Mentat education, we are left with only a few propo-sitions:

You must look at [any object of consciousness] with as few preconceptions as possible.[22]

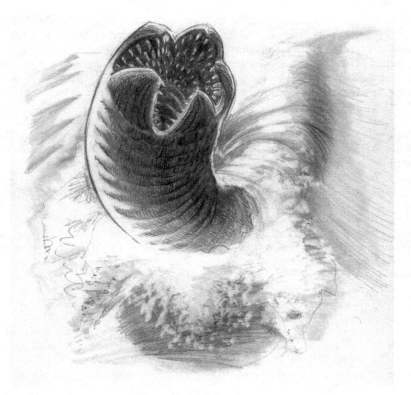

Illustration 14. Sandworm

Cultivate a naive and open mind. Know that:

> There can be no permanent catalogue of change, no handbook or manual.[23]

The Mentat Handbook v2.0 will now deconstruct by its own presuppositions.

Notes

1. *Heretics*, 9. For a description of the Mentat's overlay-integration-imagination methodology (as a liberating discipline), follow a wormhole to Appendix B.
2. *Children*, 280.
3. *Children*, 280.

4. Note here that *Kwisatz Haderach* literally means "Jump the Path" or jump the tracks (Khalid, ibid.). Note as well that these thought trains are *intentionality* (as the noetic-noematic nexus of communication), *constitution* (as the *intentional* and *semiotic* gathering of *essences* or *signs*), and *institution* (the ways that intentionality and constitution or, in short, consciousness, are formalized, reified and mythologized); institution is the metaphysics of consciousness (see the collective works of Husserl and Merleau-Ponty).

5. As textual premises and presuppositions do not hold together within the text itself, we can speak of deconstruction. Deconstruction is not something we have done, but rather it is something we have observed in our critique of social knowledge and metaphysics (see the collective works of Jacques Derrida).

6. *Heretics*, 130.

7. Reverend Mother Superior Alma Taraza. *Notebooks of Frank Herbert's Dune*, 45.

8. For a discussion of radical reflection see Appendix B, Mentat.

9. *Heretics*, 131. This discourse on belief continues and reveals how those who control "beliefs" create and maintain power: "If enough of us believe, a new thing can be made to exist. Belief structure creates a filter through which chaos is sifted into order" (*Heretics*, 131).

10. See Donald Palumbo.

11. For a complete description of the proposed Mentat integrated overlay methodology, follow a wormhole to Appendix B, Mentat Overlay Integration

12. Bene Gesserit teaching. *Heretics*, 25.

13. Rebecca's Other Memory from the horde of Lampadas. *Chapterhouse*, 69.

14. Frank Herbert, in O'Reilly, op. cit., Chapter 1. Please take care to note that hyperconsciousness is a metaphor that describes mental activities; it is not a "state" of consciousness. "All states are abstractions" (Octoroon Politicus, BG Archives. *Chapterhouse*, 162).

15. Maurice Merleau-Ponty, *Phenomenology of Perception*, op. cit., 219.

16. Jean Gebser, *The Ever-Present Origin*, 306.

17. See Gebser, 302, ibid., for references to the quotes above.

18. Gebser, 302–312.

19. For more information, follow a wormhole to Appendix C, Time Consciousness.

20. Gebser, ibid., 312.

21. Ancient Freemen Saying. *Messiah*, 69.

22. The Mentat Handbook. *Children*, 227.

23. The Mentat Handbook. *Children*, 227.

Appendix A

The Cast of Dune

The Bene Gesserit

After the edict banning all computers, the Bene Gesserit sisterhood was founded as a school for training women. The Bene Gesserit are adept at using *Voice* to control other people's actions. They have advanced *Truthsense*, the ability to read verbal and nonverbal cues and determine the relative validity of statements. They also have *Other Memory*, which is the living awareness of the memories of their genetic and sisterhood inheritance. Their mental abilities are furthered by *simulflow* or the ability to process several lines of thought at once. They have the ability to perceive sensual minute detail and can regulate their body chemistry

Illustration 15. The Cast of Dune

at will. Furthering this body development is their *para bindu* training that gives them precise control of every muscle in their body. Their order is involved in a long-term breeding program set to culminate in the production of a *Kwisatz Haderach*, a male Bene Gesserit who will have access to male as well as female memories. They are also involved in a massive myth-making effort called the *missionaria protectiva*. This is a program of religious social engineering designed to control the thought patterns of a world's general population, to protect the Bene Gesserit, and to pave the way for their future efforts.

Lady Jessica

Lady Jessica is a Bene Gesserit, bound concubine, and true love of Leto of House Atreides. She is also Paul's mother. The "Jessica incident" is worth noting here. Although she was supposed to bear a daughter as part of the Bene Gesserit breeding program (who was to be married to Feyd'Rautha, thus bringing the feud between Houses Atreides and Harkonnen to a stalemate), she bore a son out of her love for her Duke. This son, Paul Muad'Dib Atreides, was the Kwisatz Haderach. However, as Paul was born into the "wrong" family and one generation early, the Bene Gesserit lost control of their place in the empire for all time.

The Atreides

Paul Atreides

Paul appears in four basic manifestations: First, as the young heir to House Atreides. Then, he becomes the Fremen mystic rebel. He appears later as the Emperor of the known universe. Finally, he becomes the first heretic of the religion founded in his name when he returns in the guise of The Preacher.

Paul Atreides may be read as an analog of Apostle Paul. Paul, or Saul of Tarsus, is considered by many the founder of Christianity. This is significant because it implies that neither Jesus nor his disciples intended to found a new religion. Likewise, Paul Atreides never intended to found a religion or an empire, but was destined to establish both. St. Paul's originality lies in conceiving the death of Jesus as the salvation of mankind from sin. The Jewish type of human savior would deliver humankind from political bondage, but Paul recast Jesus as a salvation deity whose "atoning death by violence was necessary to release his devotees for immortal life." This understanding is often attributed as coming to Paul in his Damascus vision. This again parallels Paul Atreides, who foresees people chanting his name not as Paul, but as Mahdi or savior. This implies that the roots of Jesus' transcendent death lie not in Judaism, but in mystery-religion, with which St. Paul was acquainted in Tarsus. The establishment of a religion, both for Jesus and Muad'Dib, is based on greater historical and mythological models: Osiris, Attis, Adonis, and Dionysus brought divination to their initiates through their violent deaths. In Dune, many will give their lives and kill others in the name of Muad'Dib. St. Paul is responsible for transforming Christianity into a mystery religion in the classical Greek sense. For example, he initiated the Eucharist, echoing the communion meal of the mystery religions. St. Paul's recasting of Christianity had the advantage over other salvation cults that had been associated with Hebrew Scriptures, which were reinterpreted as forecasting the salvation death of Jesus, giving Pauline Christianity the awesome authority that appealed to Gentiles thirsting for salvation. In Dune, those who do not adopt belief in Muad'Dib are destroyed as infidels; this implies that the ties between St. Paul and Paul Atreides have a limit at which Muad'Dib's religion takes a decidedly Islamic turn (see *The Sierra Reference Encyclopedia*, L.P. Collier, 1996).

Paul shares much in common with Alexander the Great. Like Alexander, Paul had the greatest teachers and was skilled not only in leadership and warfare, but in ecology, ethics, zoology, drama, music, mathematics, and literature. Both experienced the assassination of their father. "Feral mythologist" Kristen Brennen notes that "Alexander's tutors included Leonidas, Lysimachus, and Aristotle." This unheard-of level of education lent Alexander a remarkable quality: as a teenager he exhibited the oddly striking self-possession of an adult (as Alia would in Dune), and as an adult Alexander seemed almost otherworldly. He could make insights and find connections in a way no one else could even approach. Again like Paul, Alexander's nearly superhuman abilities enabled him to conquer almost the entire known world while he was still a young man. Unlike Paul, Alexander started to believe the hype when people told him he was a God.

Leto II

The second son of Paul Muad'Dib Atreides, Leto becomes the "God Emperor" by purposely fusing his body with sandtrout, the pre-worm developmental phase of the giant sandworms of Arrakis, and mutating into a sandworm-person body. This body allows him to live for three thousand years. During this time he oppresses humanity by controlling all aspects of human life. His goal is to suppress mankind until they escape from monolithic control in a great "scattering" of creativity and humanity.

Siona Ibn Fuad al-Seyfa Atreides

Siona is the penultimate product of Leto II's breeding program (which he took from the Bene Gesserit). Siona is invisible to prescience. She leaves no trace in time, and no prescience can see what she will do; she is *surprise*. In other words, Siona is the Golden Path (see *God Emperor*, 339). Couple this with the observation that Leto is the most fierce predator the world has ever known, that a predictor can hunt and kill anything it can track. If the predator cannot follow or find the tracks, the hunt is over. Siona is the way to integrate magic without being ruled by its mechanical manifestations.

The Bashar Miles Teg

Miles Teg is a brilliant Mentat military commander in the service of the later day (i.e., post Leto II) Bene Gesserit. His Atreides genes unlock in him not prescience—as he is descendant of Siona—but speed. Teg is able to move with amazing speed and agility.

Sheanna

Sheanna is a woman who, as prophesied by Leto II, could communicate with the giant sandworms of Arrakis. This communication takes place through *dance*. Sheanna is the she-dancer.

House Corrino

At the opening of the series, House Corrino is in control of the Empire. After Muad'Dib's Fremen army overthrows both House Harkonnen and House Corrino, Paul assumes the throne of the known universe by marrying Princess Irulan. In this marriage of political convenience, Irulan's legacy is found in the numerous books she authored documenting the life of Paul Muad'Dib Atreides. Her nephew, Prince Farad'n, is educated by Lady Jessica (concubine and love of Leto I). As a member of Leto II's court he is renamed Harq'al Ada and appointed as the royal historian.

The Honored Matres

The Honored Matres are a sect of women who, when returning from the great scattering, seek control and domination of the universe through force. They are a mixture of Bene Gesserit, Fish Speakers (Leto's II's all-female military troops), and Bureaucrats turned so conservative as to become reactive and militant. Murbella is the only honored Matre captured. After her Bene Gesserit education, she becomes a full Reverend Mother and introduces the possibility of an Honored Matre-Bene Gesserit hybrid and alliance.

The Spacing Guild

The Spacing Guild does not factor into *The Mentat Handbook v2.0*. However, they are worth mentioning here. The Guild holds a monopoly on interstellar travel. Their navigators have limited prescience. This gives them the ability to see through the fabric of space-time, and chart safe courses for interstellar travel. Interstellar travel is made possible by folding space. The navigators chart a fold between two points and enable their ships to travel without moving between two points.

Appendix B

Mentat Overlay Integration

When we look to the history of human ideas, Mentat overlay integration, considered as a methodology, finds a similar way of thought in Husserlian phenomenology. Both Mentat and phenomenologist start and finish—"prime computation"—in everyday life. However, while tracing the ways that consciousness has been *institutionalized* (and rendering presuppositions visible), both suspend judgment, purposely cultivate an attitude of cultural naivete, and reflect on the flow of consciousness itself (as a simultaneous—simulflow—unfolding of intentionality). Here we trace this methodology and some of the philosophical issues it raises.

Consensus Reality

> The mind of the believer stagnates. . . . By your belief in . . . singularities, you deny all movement—evolutionary or devolutionary. Belief fixes a . . . universe and causes that universe to persist. Nothing can be allowed to change because that way your non-moving universe vanishes. But it moves of itself when you do not move. It evolves beyond you and is no longer accessible to you.[1]

As noted throughout the *Handbook v2.0*, Herbert calls the consciousness of everyday life "consensual." Husserl calls the ordinary consciousness of everyday life "the natural attitude."[2] The natural, consensual attitude accepts the world spread out before us with all its norms, values, and practices. This world is simply there.

This is the world in which we, as Mentats, encounter consciousness of the Marxian sort—as *ideological*. An ideological consciousness is a *false* consciousness because the economic base (or perhaps some other force) is seen as determining the superstructure of social institutions (and even thought itself). Because the ruling class determines the base, ideology is always in the service of this force. Moreover, because the natural attitude is lived uncritically, and because ideology may inform consciousness into patterns that are antithetical to a truly scientific observation, a radical science of observation is required. When we look to the history of ideas, we find a parallel between the goals of Mentat awareness and phenomenological philosophy. Both suspend belief in cultural *givens* and attend to the structures of consciousness.

The Willing Suspension of Belief

> While we strive for a one-system view . . . we are at the same time influenced by it and influence it. We peer myopically at it through screens of 'consensus reality,' which is a summation of the most popular beliefs of our time. Out of habit/illusion/conservatism, we grapple for something that changes as we touch it.[3]

Willingly setting aside *disbelief* when we attend to fictional texts such as movies or books is well known. However, to look at the relationship between a fictional text (such as *Dune*) and the experienced world it is important to suspend *belief* rather than disbelief. Likewise, Husserl asked scholars to set aside (or bracket) the natural attitude and willingly suspend belief in reality in order to overcome sedimented ideas.[4] So too Herbert asks the reader to set aside their "*consensus reality*" and willingly suspend *belief* in reality and *disbelief* in fiction.

> We are disposed to perceive things as they appear, filtering the appearance through our preconceptions and fitting it into the past forms (including all the outright mistakes, illusions, and myths of past forms).[5]

Mentat overlay integration thus begins with the bracketing of consensual reality and the taken-for-grantedness of the communal sense. This process is called the phenomenological *epoche*. Consciousness is extricated from the natural attitude. Incidental meanings are set aside in order to see invariant structures—essences. This is a reflective process of seeing into the concealed meanings of things, into the limits—*peras*—of everyday awareness.

> Above all else, the mentat must be a generalist, not a specialist. It is wise to have decisions of great moment monitored by generalists. Experts and specialists lead you quickly into chaos. They are a source of useless nitpicking, the ferocious quibble over a comma. The mentat-generalist, on the other hand, should bring to decision-making a healthy common sense. He must not cut himself off from the broad sweep of what is happening in his universe. . . . The mentat-generalist must understand that anything which we can identify as our universe is merely part of larger phenomena. But the expert looks backward; he looks into the narrow standards of his own specialty. The generalist looks outward; he looks for living principles, knowing full well that such principles change, that they develop. It is to the characteristics of change itself that the mentat-generalist must look.[6]

The goals of the generalist approach, and bracketing of consensual, communal reality, are designed to help one see the presuppositions assumed by a line of investigation.[7] Thus the Mentat practice the great naivete:[8]

> Lucilla forced herself to practice Bene Gesserit naiveté. . . . Her proc-tors had called this 'the innocence that goes naturally with inexperience, a condition often confused with ignorance.' Into this naiveté every-thing flowed. . . . Information entered without prejudgment. 'You are a mirror upon which the universe is reflected. That reflection is all you experience.'[9]

Objective, Subjective, Intersubjective

Husserl's insights call into question the modern assumption of a singular, objec-tive reality, ready and waiting "out there" for the right method to uncover its mysteries. The phenomenological project will lead us first to subjectivity, then to embodied intersubjectivity, and then to the life world. This movement, while spanning the philosopher's career, can be seen as a single thought.[10] Our every-day experience, including the practice of science, is necessarily subjective, relative to our place in a world. The point of departure for the study of the things of this world is, then, the subjective consciousness that takes in this world. Phe-nomenology begins with the ideality of reality; it begins with the description of what lies available to the senses (both immanent and physical). The grasping of the ideal object in consciousness (through the related methods of epoche and free-imaginative variation) brings to light its various appearances. Some appearances, such as daydreams and imaginings, can be considered as mine alone—available to me and nobody else until I choose to disclose them. Worldly phenomena, such as synesthesia, however, are not simply subjective, they are intersubjective—experienced by many persons. The so-considered "objective" phenomena are essentially intersubjective, and their objective being resides not in some material objectivity, but in the political webs of discourse. The objec-tive reality discussed by scientific discourse is, then, a theoretical construction and idealization of intersubjective experience.[11] This recognition brings us into the political realm of the life world, which, when considered in the brackets of the phenomenological *epoche*, is the world as lived prereflectively, before we think about it.

Radical Reflection

A method of radical reflection, critical thought, and "wild" research called for in *The Chronicles* was proposed by Edmund Husserl, whose methodology "demands that all claims be demonstrated precisely in awareness accessible to everyone. Moreover, it demands that any philosophical position must include and explicate the awareness required for the very grounds of such a position. Lacking such an explication, a position remains dogmatic and speculative."[12] It is therefore essential, to paraphrase Algis Mickunas, to disclose the transcendental awareness that comprises the activity of any observation.

To this end, Husserl introduced new terminology to help us become aware of the stream of consciousness in its flowing. (1) *Noesis* [n] is taken from the Greek word meaning "mental perception, intelligence, and thought" and is used to signify the activity of consciousness; the adjective form of *noesis* is *noetic*, as in *noetic* activity. (2) *Noema* [n] is taken from the Greek word meaning "that which is perceived, a perception, a thought," and is used to signify the essence to which this mental activity is correlated; the correlate of the activity of consciousness; the adjective form of *noema* is *noematic*, as in *noematic* object.[13]

Our awareness of the things of the world both physical and psychical, objects and ideas are said to be *constituted* by the overlapping of *noema* like waves upon the shore.[14] We may diagram this flow as *noesis* plus *noema* equals the intentionality of consciousness.

Tracing this intentionality overcomes the metaphysics of presence, the reification of things via classification, and takes us toward the *essence* or *eidos* of consciousness.

> Humans have this deep desire to classify, to apply labels to everything. . . . We lay claim to what we name. We assume an ownership that can be misleading and dangerous.[15]

Mentat overlay integration overcomes the proclivity to label by seeing how labels are constituted.

Intentionality

Coined by Franz Brentano, *intentionality* is a tricky word that should not be confused with intention or will. Intentionality, in its philosophical sense, is the realization that consciousness is always the consciousness of something. This is to say that consciousness always has an object of awareness; seeing discovers sights; hearing discovers sounds; thinking discovers thoughts. Thus, consciousness is not solely a matter of "mind," but of embodiment—of our total interconnection, communication, and communion with the world; this we call intentionality.

We may grasp or apprehend the world materially through our senses and intuitively or ideally through thoughts, but while the forms of knowledge will be different for sensual experiences and intellectual experiences, they are in fact unified by the intentional activity of consciousness.

With this in mind, Herbert's work exemplifies a critical grasp of the intentionality one lives and fosters an awareness of the structures of experience as they have been codified and constructed socially. A radically reflective "consciousness," it is said, "is the ability to survey those interconnections which constitute us: it is a continuous act of integrating and directing."[16] With this in mind, the Mentat is freer to think, act, and choose; the Mentat is free to raise critical awareness to levels heretofore unexperienced.[17]

Essence

Phenomenology, as sown by Edmund Husserl and cultivated by Merleau-Ponty, is the study of "things" (anything material or ideal) as they appear to consciousness; thus, an important part of phenomenological investigation is the study of intentionality. Phenomenology seeks to ground the institutionalized vision of a culture (consensus reality or the natural attitude) in concrete experience (prior to any theoretical attitude). This philosophical movement is often summarized by the phrase "To the things themselves," which means that objects of inquiry are looked at as they are presented to consciousness instead of through deductive theories and methods, or "in themselves" as an objective *given*.[18]

However, within the cultural sphere, "things" efface themselves and point beyond themselves to other things (i.e., things have significance and meaning in excess of themselves; melange is not just "spice," but a narcotic, a psychotropic drug, oil, commerce and more). When something points to another thing it is functioning as a *sign*. The study of signs and the conventions that generate or orient those signs is semiotics. Taken together, semiotic phenomenology provides a way toward studying the qualitative dimension of communication as the stream of consciousness that *constitutes* and *institutes*.[19] Thus, the singularizing force of the consensual sense of the word essence is replaced with essence as the multiplicity of intentional threads that continues to find a point of departure (e.g., commerce, oil, psychotropics, narcotics, and spice all point back to melange).

Attentional Modification

A problem that arises for Mentat overlay integration is attentional modification. That is, while we are attending to a thought flow, do we unnecessarily switch philosophical assumptions or add to the observation another theoretical vantage?[20] Strict attention must be paid to the description of an experience as it is *taken*.[21]

With caution against attentional modification, Mentat apprehension is a grasping of the essences in their institutional and constitutional appearances while bracketing and exploring the presuppositions of consensual reality. If we leave the world of academic philosophy and return to *The Chronicles*, we find that the Bene Gesserit cultivate just such awareness as has been discussed above.

Notes

1. Taraza to Teg. *Heretics*, 156.
2. Edmund Husserl, *Ideas Pertaining to a Pure Phenomenology and to a Phenomenological Philosophy: First Book* (F. Kerstein, Trans., Dordrecht: Kluwer, 1982, 51–53).
3. Herbert, *Listening to the Left Hand.*
4. For a description of the epoche and promotion of the transcendental attitude, see Maurice Merleau-Ponty, *Phenomenology of Perception*, xi–xiv.
5. Herbert, *Listening to the Left Hand.*
6. The Mentat Handbook. *Children*, 227.
7. Critics of Husserl's proposed composition of a "presuppositionless" philosophy will note that phenomenology constitutes a philosophy of seeing cultural presuppositions. Transcendental philosophy has much to offer Cultural Studies, although that path is rarely taken. See Maurice Merleau-Ponty's "Introduction: Traditional Prejudices and the Return to Phenomena," in *Phenomenology of Perception*, ibid. Stewart and Mickunas, *Exploring Phenomenology* (Athens: Ohio University Press, 1974).
8. Merleau-Ponty speaks often of the phenomenological *epoche* and phenomenological philosophy as practicing a naive approach to the things of observation.
9. *Chapterhouse*, 46.
10. David Abrams, *The Spell of the Sensuous* (New York: Pantheon, 1996).
11. David Abrams, ibid., 38.
12. Algis Mickunas, "Prospects of Husserlian Phenomenology," in *On the Future of Husserlian Phenomenology*, The Husserl Archives, <http://www.newschool.edu/gf/phil/husserl/Future/Future_Mickunas.html> 6/20/06.
13. A word of caution; do not relate the noetic-noematic relation to the subject-object relationship. "Noetic activity cannot be identified with psychic activity, for it deals not with physical processes but with the meaning of those processes. Similarly, the noematic cannot be identified with the empirical object, for it deals not with the physical experience but with the meaning of that experience." They are not the subject or object but rather the conditions for the possibility of experiencing both the subject and the object (Stewart & Mickunas, op. cit., 37). This relationship constitutes the transcendental turn for phenomenology, and it has been criticized as being a form of idealism.
14. See J.N. Mohanty, "The Development of Husserl's Thought," in Barry Smith and David Woodruff Smith, *The Cambridge Companion to Husserl* (Cambridge: Press Syndicate of the University of Cambridge, 1995, 61).
15. Reverend Mother Superior Darwi Odrade. Brian Herbert, *Notebooks of Frank Herbert's Dune*, 5.
16. See the collected works of Stewart and Mickunas; Maurice Merleau-Ponty; Edmund Husserl.
17. See endnote "objectivity, subjectivity, Intersubjectivity."
18. For more information, follow a wormhole to Chapter One, "Capta, Data, Acta."
19. See John O'Neil, *The Communicative Body: Studies in Communicative Philosophy, Politics and Sociology* (Evanston: Northwestern University Press, 1989). Constitution

is the combined intentional threads by which we are aware of something. Institution is the limitation of these threads to a given meaning or way of seeing.

20. For more information, follow a wormhole to Chapter Two, "The Unclouded Eye."

21. For more information, follow a wormhole to Chapter One, subheading "Data, Capta, Acta."

Appendix C

Time Consciousness

The Mentat must be aware of their cultural norms and values, of their language and the assumptions made by their words. In the following, the insights culled from the meditation on "past, presence and prescience" above are discussed again in terms of modern conceptions of consensual time.

Consensual Time

Perhaps, the time anxiety so prevalent in the West today is not so much a matter of time itself, but instead of a certain unsteadiness of mind, an unsteadiness in which time is given the form of a *thing* that one can have or lose. The faith we place in clocks has reified time and made it uniform and measurable according to ideals and logics that remain, for the most part, silently and uncritically accepted. Time's ruler was forged in another age by persons long-since dead. And cultural studies reveal that time is not an absolute, but rather a pragmatic relationship between a people and the world.[1] The Mentat must know these thought trains, so she can see the time structure a speaker presupposes. Having an awareness of these time structures as discursive, historical, and consensual, the Mentat also has the ability to accept and reject a given time structure depending on the circumstance.

Summation and Critique of Consensual Time

Think of it as plastic memory, this force within you which trends you and your fellows toward tribal forms. This plastic memory seeks to return to its ancient shape, the tribal society. It is all around you—the feudatory, the diocese, the corporation, the platoon, the sports club, the dance troupes, the rebel cell, the planning council, the prayer group . . . each with its master and servants, its host and parasites. And the swarms of alienating devices (including these very words!) tend to eventually be enlisted in the argument for a return to "those better times." I despair of teaching you the other ways. You have square thoughts which resist circles.[2]

From the ancient Hebrews to the quantum physicists, time's abstract, conceptual, and mathematical flow, with its linear form and direction, may be reconsidered here as a possible configuration of time, as a "pragmatic relationship between belief and what we identify as 'real.' "[3] Note, then, that the various definitions of time as linear are products of literate and rational minds; they express an alphabetized, numerical perception of time. From Moses' inscription of the commandments to Hawking's descriptions of thermodynamics, time's arrow flies in the direction of words printed on a page, from beginning to end, imposing a silent pattern on the living present.[4] This pattern constitutes for us a relationship between human and world, a pattern that reduces time to a symbol system in the service of human interests.

Although our common sense attests to the validity of this measurable clock-time, all measuring is a human activity based on human values. When we forget this, we become prisoners of a rational, analytical, and divisible time that does not speak for the totality of human consciousness. There is something more going on. Even a child knows that time is not necessarily linear and uniform, but that it also flies and stalls, accelerates and drags; a child knows that time has surfaces and depths, a quality and dimensionality that no clock can measure.

Sometimes, Time rushes by me; sometimes, it creeps.[5]

We find, as well, that time's arrow doesn't always or necessarily fly in a straight line. Even the hands on a clock, our given chronometer, soar in a circle. Time's arrow has at least the complementary temporicity, a flow with the world's polarity, a cyclonic time, the time of the whirlwind.[6]

The arrow, the measure, the container, and the cycle are only some of the morphologies of time passed down through generations. In his *Phenomenology of Perception*, Merleau-Ponty finds that forms are not the real properties of things; the minute, for example, is not a real property of time. Rather, the form is a way of presenting something, such as time, to perceptual consciousness.[7] The minute, the hour, and the millennium; the arrow, the container, and the cycle are cultural conveniences and explanatory systems drawn creatively from the world that "open an indefinite unity in which I have my place."[8] If the form is not a real property and time is a codification of the phenomenon of time, what possible perceptions of time do we find expressed in *Dune*?

Existential and Transcendental Time

Existential Time Consciousness

> Unless you understand that Time isn't what it appears, I can't even begin
> to explain. My father expected it. He stood at the edge of realization, but
> he fell back. Now it's up to . . . me.[9]

Heidegger, whose *Being and Time* is one of the most influential works of
twentieth-century philosophy, gives us two useful suggestions. The first is a
simile—time is like a horizon. The second a description—time is ex-static, or
time stands outside of itself.

Heidegger suggests that the *future withholds*, whereas the *past refuses*. He
arrives at this existential description of time through the simile of the horizon.
The horizon, as it appears to the sense of sight, is a useful structural analogy; the future is like the horizon in front of one's eyes, always available, ever
receding, sometimes hidden by vegetation and buildings (natural and cultural
obstructions); the past is like the horizon behind us; although we can't see it,
we sense that it remains.[10]

Heidegger also notices that the *consciousness of* time is itself not *in time*.
This is what Heidegger calls the *ex-static* nature of time; the term ex-static is a
combination of "ex," meaning outside or away from, and "static," meaning not
moving or fixed; time appears outside of itself, as a relationship between subject
and world.[11] The ecstatic nature of the future is a being ahead of itself and is
concerned with the projection of potentiality; the future can let itself come
toward us as potentiality, or the future can project itself upon everyday ordinary
concerns, whether they will come about or fall apart. The present is the ecstatic
phase in which being in the world is disclosed. And the past is a taking over
of what already is, a taking hold of one's self again, a certain kind of repetition.

Past, present, and future are three *ex-stases*, or ecstasies, of time, in which
the incarnate subject lives between the two unknowable horizons of birth and
death, for these are poles we may see, but not experience; that is, although
we can know that people are born and die, we cannot know our own birth or
death, because any reflection on life always finds us already living, or alive.[12]
Birth and death appear as pre-personal horizons, and thus, there seems to be a
personal prehistory as well as a cultural prehistory.[13] As Merleau-Ponty put it,
"I am born in my personal experience by a time which I do not constitute."[14]

There appears to be, based on the above, at least two modes of time
consciousness, a pre-reflective existence, which we can call temporality (which
will be discussed below, as internal time-consciousness), and a dimension of
creative expression, which opens up an occult time, creatively drawing together

in expression an authors' past, which is shaped and generalized into social, cultural, and civilizational meanings; a contribution to the history of meaning, which takes for granted the consciousness of time, and has the power of bearing cultural value (the latter being, for our purposes, the work of Frank Herbert; and the other cultural, historical considerations of time).[15]

> You Bene Gesserit call your activity of the Panoplia Prophetica a "Science of Religion." Very well. I, a seeker after another kind of scientist, find this an appropriate definition. You do, indeed, build your own myths, but so do all societies.[16]

This is to suggest that linear time and clock time are external time constitutions and cultural institutions; they are *objective times* as understood and lived by real people in the realm we call consensus reality. The fantastic descriptions of prescience and Other Memory may be seen as creative responses to the world, as drawing on a field of time possibilities and potentialities; as such, the At-Once time constitution presupposes internal time consciousness. Just as Merleau-Ponty suggested that pathology is not abnormality, but an extension of normality, so we can suggest that Other Memory and prescience are an extension of our phenomenal experience. But how does this passive, involuntary time consciousness, on which even our literature and science are built, with their conceptions and images of time, come to pass?

Internal Time-Consciousness

> They must wind the past into the present and allow it to unreel into their future.[17]

Edmund Husserl found that active, external time constitutions presuppose a passive (and yet paradoxically active), internal time consciousness, taken for granted by the discourses of time and in our everyday lives.[18] Recognition of internal time consciousness is also present in *The Dune Chronicles*, and it is presented in a similar manner, with similar metaphors employed by both authors.

Herbert called *Dune* an ecological *fugue*.[19] He compared science fiction, and living itself, to *jazz* improvisation.[20] He wrote of languages that could be communicated but not spoken—*music*, dance, and touch.[21] He listened to music as he wrote.[22] And when he wrote, Herbert would, at times, compose in poetic verse—musical phases—and gradually erase the form, leaving the content in an elegant prose.[23] Music figures into *The Chronicles* as significantly as do the waves of sand. It is, then, to *music* that we will turn to provide an example of internal time consciousness.

If one delays old age or death by the use of mélange or by that learned adjustment of fleshy balance which you Bene Gesserit so rightly fear, such a delay invokes only an illusion of control. Whether one walks rapidly through the sietch or slowly, one traverses the sietch. And that passage of time is experienced internally.[24]

Consider, for a moment, a musical phrase such as the opening of Beethoven's Fifth. Each note in the melody has a musical quality that is dependent upon the notes that precede it and follow it. Notice that we do not hear each note as an objective frequency (although analysis is free to measure and find, for example, the notes e, e, e, c). This quality is not reducible to the objective quantity, frequency, or pitch; after all, I can transpose the melody into any key in the Western tonal system, shifting the objective frequency, and play or hear the phrase in relatively higher or lower tones; the musical phrase remains recognizable. We hear, in the musical flow, the musical quality of each note, relative to the others, stretching out through time, in the phrase. Each note is heard and has a presence in the context of previous and anticipated notes.[25]

Husserl uses the words "protention" and "retention" to refer to anticipated and previous (respectively). Each tone is heard in the context of anticipated and previous tones, and the previous notes remain present to consciousness when we hear the current note. The notes that fade into past remain present, not in the same manner, but in the mode of being *present as past*. The retained notes are not copies, reproductions, or representations, but the note itself, present as past. Protention works the same way, but is related to expectation. In Western symphonic music, for example, we have come to expect certain types of musical phrases. When these expectations are not met, as in some contemporary art music (such as atonal music), the music may be difficult to grasp; some may claim that the composition is not "really" music. What fails, however, is not *music*, but a certain expectation of music—a protention. Time, in this way, is "a continuum of continua."[26]

"You said you see the now!"
   Paul lay back, searching the spread-out present, its limits extended into the future and into the past, holding onto the awareness with difficulty as the spice illumination began to fade.[27]

Husserl overcomes some major presuppositions. Consciousness is not an instantaneous *now point*; if it were, each note would either exist at the same time (i.e., be present) or not at all (i.e., be absent), and in neither case could we have a melody. We would experience, as would an eternal God for whom time would have no flow, all notes together, a massive chord and probably a rather dissonant one at that. God, not to mention humans, would have sufficient reason for creating time, if for no other reason than to enjoy music.

Also, consciousness is not *homogeneous*; the difference between the past note, the current note, and the anticipated note are not given equally, but in different articulations, or modes of presentation. The past is given as retention, the present as present, and the future as protention. Retention, for example, is a mode of given-ness different from, but with the same content as, the original impression—past as present.

Protention and retention are prior to expectation and recollection. Retention and protention are originating modes of consciousness that constitute the essence of time. Memory and recollection, for example, follow and recoup retention; recollection is voluntary, retention is involuntary; retention is real, in the sense that it is not a representation, but a presence, whereas recollection may represent and symbolize the retention, as when the musical phrase heard is transcribed into notes on a staff ledger. Also, retention is essential to consciousness, whereas recollection is not. The Alzheimer's patient who has confused recollection still functions, can suffer pain, and experience joy, for they are conscious and thus, they experience time, even if memory and recollection are ruptured. Finally, recollection cannot be retention because recollection presupposes retention; I can't recall what I don't retain. Likewise, protention is necessary for expectation and projection, and the latter presuppose the former.

Protention, impression, and retention are, then, not past, present and future, but they allow for three-phase time and are the underlying experience that allows for Other Memory (in its modified sense, as mediated) and prescience (in its given sense as nonabsolute).

> "The uninitiated try to conceive of prescience as obeying a Natural Law," Paul said. He steepled his hands in front of him. "But it'd be just as correct to say it's heaven speaking to us, that being able to read the future is a harmonious act of man's being. In other words, prediction is a natural consequence in the wave of the present. It wears the guise of nature, you see. But such powers cannot be used from an attitude that pre-states aims and purposes. Does a chip caught in the wave say where it's going? There's no cause and effect in the oracle. Causes become occasions or convections and confluences, places where the currents meet. Accepting prescience, you fill your being with concepts repugnant to the intellect. Your intellectual consciousness, therefore, rejects them. In rejecting, intellect becomes a part of the process, and is subjugated."[28]

Here we find the key-log that breaks up the jam.[29] Protention is the condition for the possibility of prescience and, as such, is a seeing of multiple, nonabsolute lines of potential and possible futures, partial truths of a future that is always experienced as future-in-presence. Retention is the condition for the possibility of Other Memory; it is ex-static; that is, the "other" of Other Memory is outside of us. Retention allows us to see what has passed, as past-in-presence, our historicity as well as history, and partial truths of the past.

> Paul, Muad'Dib Atreides was called: "Father of the Indefinite Roads of Time."[30]

Maurice Merleau-Ponty, following Husserl's insight, hindsight, and fore-sight, shows how our experience of time moves from internal time-conscious-ness to an ecological time-consciousness, commensurate with culture and world. We find in the depths of time a subject with an intersubjective cultural life and a prereflective life, both of which correlate human and world; we find that subjectivity is the upsurgence of time.[31] We are, thus, always that primal perception, that continuation of this same life inaugurated by perception.[32] To live is to perceive, and to perceive is to perceive temporally; consciousness and time appear together—consciousness is time manifest.[33]

> As to time: there is no difference between ten thousand years and one year; no difference between one hundred thousand years and a heartbeat. No difference. That is the first fact about time. And the second fact: the entire universe with all of its Time is within me.[34]

The Integrality of the Moment

> Moneo fell freely then in the ecstasy of awareness. The universe opened for him like clear glass, everything flowing in a no-Time.[35]

Remaining true to our investigation into time's constitution continues to require a suspension of what we might believe, for we are now well within the invisible realm of the time-winds and are coming quickly to a point at which their visible effects are less and less consequent with our cultural beliefs; like all winds, the time-winds appear to stand still at times, or at least they slow to a barely sensible presence. Just as premonition and foresight, retrospection and hindsight, have their common appearance in everyday experience, and as we study the images of myth and the conceptions of mind in our classrooms and colleges, so too we have, in common awareness, experiences that testify to boundaries beyond which time does not fly.

> Time lay within her like a dead weight, and it was as though her years away from this planet had never been.[36]

Consider those moments, usually during crises—a car crash, a near drown-ing, bearing witness to a great disaster—but also during peak activity—in athletics, music, and dance—when time moves so slowly that innumerable thoughts, feelings, and actions occur and wash over and through our bodies; time stands still.

> She felt that she was a conscious mote, smaller than any subatomic particle, yet capable of motion and sensing her surroundings. Like an abrupt revelation—the curtains ripped away—she realized she had become aware of a psychokinesthetic extension of herself. She was the mote, yet not the mote. . . . Jessica focused her attention on the Reverend Mother Ramallo, aware now that all of this was happening in a frozen instant of time—suspended for her alone. Why is time suspended? . . . Her personal time was suspended to save her life.[37]

In these moments, do we possibly grasp the possibility of a way of understanding, a structure of consciousness, generally available only at the periphery of our attention and, again, easily dismissed? When we accept our given mode of address, with its now point and its line, we encounter time as a boundary beyond and before which we shall not pass. We are impressed by our present abilities to date and measure the age of our planetary system and seek with ever-increasing precision the ultimate boundary for time and space—the big bang. Surely we are impressed, and with good reason, but such measures leave exoteric questions answerable only by esoteric mathematics. We arrive at a question, "What takes place prior to time, before the first day?" Although our mathematics are a marvel, we can, at the same time, set aside our predilection for quantification and seek qualitative intensities, not so much to look before the first day, but between never and ever.[38]

> From that welter of memories which I can tap at will, patterns emerge. They are like another language which I see so clearly. The social-alarm signals which put societies into postures of defense/attack are like shouted words to me. As a people, you rebel against change. You demand acceptable dress because a strange costume is threatening. This is system-feedback at its most primitive level. Your cells remember.[39]

While our mental rationality divides time into discrete units and our mythical imagination dreams time's natural polarity, so *our cells remember* the awakening of our human ancestor's emergence into the temporal fray in the timeless presence, itself a perceptual pattern, a consciousness that lies before time.[40] Time, if the word can be used at all from this perceptual vista, for we are touching here upon what might better be called *timelessness*, disappears—there can be no more points of reference; because all measures would be removed, their can be no orientation, for there is no direction to move toward or away from.

I dream, Paul reassured himself. It's the spice meal. Still, there was about him a feeling of abandonment. He wondered if it might be possible that his ruh-spirit had slipped over somehow into the world where Freemen believed he had his true existence—into the alam al-mithal, the world of similitudes, that metaphysical realm where all physical limitations were removed. And he knew fear at the thought of such a place, because removal of all limitations meant removal of all points of reference. In the landscape of a myth he could not orient himself and say: "I am I because I am here."[41]

At this level of understanding, so difficult to discuss because it loosens the limits of our language and confounds our common sense, the world is perceived as a unity, the parts are the whole, and thus, a point-to-point interweaving of reality is possible. While discounted by the present discourse, there are those who enter this time-space reduction—the prayer group, and faith healing, even television, with its technological telepathy, and advertiser's incantation trace this primordial experience.

This morning I was born in a yurt at the edge of a horse-plain in a land of a planet which no longer exists. Tomorrow I will be born someone else in another place. I have not yet chosen. This morning, though--ahhh, this life! When my eyes had learned to focus, I looked out at sunshine on trampled grass and I saw vigorous people going about the sweet activities of their lives. Where . . . has all that vigor gone?[42]

This primordial awareness, which is truly such, as it is given here to suggest the original awareness of time's possibility in a timeless cosmos, captures the human's vital powers—all that vigor. Here common sense, uncommon as it may be, again brings to us common experiences discounted in a world obsessed with counting. Within the vital sphere, and in the grip of vigorous activity, time is suspended, stands still, cannot be counted; thus, the wide receiver catches the impossible throw, the long-distance runner finds that silent place within herself, and the musician articulates the most difficult passage with a flare that captures the audience. When we emerge from this timelessness and make it the object of our reflection, a radical reflection that turns our conscious attention on our preconscious experience, we catch a glimpse of time without distinction, of time's integration.

[H]e could not escape the fear that he had somehow overrun himself, lost his position in time, so that past and future and present mingled without distinction.[43]

Past, present, and future, integrate and appear at once, not now (which is ever in deferral), but in a nondeconstructable presence, an undeniable reality and truth, accessible to all, even when ignored by many.[44]

The realization of what I am occurs in the timeless awareness which does not stimulate nor delude. I create a field without self or center, a field where even death becomes only analogy. I desire no results. I merely permit this field which has no goals nor desires, no perfections nor even visions of achievements. In that field, omnipresent primal awareness is all. It is the light which pours through the windows of my universe.[45]

All that is required to witness the At-Once is the phenomenological reduction.

Awareness flowed into that timeless stratum where he could view time, sensing the available paths, the winds of the future . . . the winds of the past: the one-eyed vision of the past, the one-eyed vision of the present and the one-eyed vision of the future—all combined in a trinocular vision that permitted him to see.[46]

Then we see.

Anyone can rip aside the veil of Time. You can discover the future in the past or in your own imagination. Doing this, you win back your consciousness in your inner being. You know then that the universe is a coherent whole and you are indivisible from it.[47]

But keep in mind this cautionary note:

If we lock down the future in the present, we deny that such a future has become the present.[48]

Notes

1. See, Martin Heidegger, translated by Joan Stambaugh, *Being in Time* (Albany: SUNY Press, 1996); Michael Taussig, *The Nervous System* (New York: Routledge, 1991).

2. The Stolen Journals. *God Emperor*, 394.

3. *Heretics*, 272.

4. The "living present" is Husserl's phrase. In *Dune*, the living present is called "living time" (*Children*, 261).

5. Leto Atreides II. In Brian Herbert (ed.), *The Notebooks of Frank Herbert's Dune* (New York: Perigee, 1988, 39).

6. Steven Hawking shows that time, prior to Einstein, demonstrates three arrows and holds the possibility of imaginary time (which can move in any direction). Note here that these conceptions either conceive time in terms of space (from now to then is here to there) or locate time in the subject's imagination. This conception of time and

image of time are rational and mythical reductions (respectively) grounded on embodiment (that is presupposed and not explicated). This means that, prior to Einstein, time was considered either objectively or subjectively. Intersubjective and phenomenological temporal consciousness had not yet been grasped by the physical sciences.

7. Gary Brent Madison, *The Phenomenology of Merleau-Ponty* (Athens: Ohio University Press, 1981, 148).

8. Maurice Merleau-Ponty, *Phenomenology of Perception*, 430.

9. Leto II, to his mother, The Lady Jessica. *Children*, 104.

10. David Abrams, *The Spell of the Sensuous*, 209–10. The horizon metaphor links time to space. And indeed, whereas Herbert falls back on the rational predilection to spatialize time at certain moments in *Dune*, for example, "he would return to the vision of pure time, of time-become-space" (354). The task of a pure phenomenology would be to describe time as it appears and not in spatial metaphors.

11. Heidegger, *Being and Time*, translated by John Macquarrie and Edward Robinson (Oxford: Basil Blackwell, 1967). See also, Merleau-Ponty, *Primacy of Perception*, translated by James M. Edie (Evanston: Northwestern University Press, 1964).

12. Finding us always and already living remains the case even in the numerous examples of people "remembering" or "foreseeing" their own deaths and then dying exactly in that manner (see, e.g., Jung, *Man and His Symbols* [New York: Dell, 1968]). The memory, foresight, or dream image still occurs to a living consciousness.

13. Merleau-Ponty, *Phenomenology of Perception*, 216; see also Gary Brent Madison, *The Phenomenology of Merleau-Ponty*, 61.

14. *Phenomenology of Perception*, ibid., 347.

15. Madison, op. cit., 133; Merleau-Ponty, *Phenomenology of Perception*, ibid., 390.

16. The Preacher at Arrakeen: A Message to the Sisterhood. *Children*, 171.

17. Leto II. *Children*, 75.

18. Edmund Husserl, *On the Phenomenology of the Consciousness of Internal Time* (Dordrecht: Kluwer, 1991); the following discussion of Husserl's work on internal time consciousness owes much to Algis Mickunas of Ohio University for his lectures on phenomenology and David Thompson of Memorial University for his internet-published review.

19. Touponce, *Frank Herbert*, p. ii. Ecological consciousness recognizes the interconnection between all things, and the importance of understanding the context or background against which an action will be carried out.

20. O'Reilly, *Frank Herbert*, 1981.

21. See *Heretics*.

22. Brian Herbert, *Dreamer of Dune*.

23. Brian Herbert, *Dreamer of Dune*.

24. Leto II, to his mother, The Lady Jessica. *Children*, 105.

25. Please note that the use of the word "impression" is not a sense impression, as in Hume, or an illusory impression, as in Galileo. This "impression" is simply the intentional grasp of the note in its passing; the words "impression" and "presence" are used here synonymously.

26. Husserl, *On the Phenomenology of the Consciousness of Internal Time*.

27. Chani, wife of Muad'Dib. *Dune*, 441.

28. Paul Muad'Dib Atreides discusses prescience. *Messiah*, 52.

29. The "key-log" metaphor appears many times in *Heretics*.

30. *Children*, 345.

31. Madison, op. cit., 158.

32. Merleau-Ponty, *Phenomenology of Perception*, 407.

33. Merleau-Ponty, *Phenomenology of Perception*, 422.

34. Leto II to his mother, The Lady Jessica. *Children*, 104; one may argue that there is a great difference between one year and a thousand years. The difference is, however, quantitative and abstract. When I reflect on ten thousand years, my experience does not take ten thousand years. Indeed, for me, who has lived some forty standard years, ten thousand years appears in consciousness as an impossible protention. What is suggested here is, then, that the difference is of form not content; the structure of the consciousness of time remains protentional and retentional.

35. Majordomo Moneo Atreides. *God Emperor*, 36.

36. The Lady Jessica. *Children*, 29.

37. The Lady Jessica, while undergoing the Spice Agony. *Dune*, 348.

38. Jean Gebser, *The Ever-Present Origin*.

39. The Stolen Journals. *God Emperor*.

40. Jean Gebser calls the structure of consciousness that perceives and expresses its world as a spaceless and timeless presence the "magical" structure. This "magic" is not the deficient rabbit-out-of-a-hat type common today, but rather an experiential awareness of unity, an egoless group consciousness and an interweaving of human and nature that is still present today; it is most often seen in technology, in tele-vision's conquest of space and time, in the "isms" that unite and separate groups, in searches for unified theories, and in the incantations of advertisements and political promises. See *The Ever-Present Origin*.

41. *Dune*, 376.

42. The Stolen Journals. *God Emperor*, 5.

43. Paul after eating a spice-laden meal. *Dune*, 374.

44. The melody can still be heard because time does not collapse but rather shows multiple manifestations transparently, like the sound of music itself.

45. The Stolen Journals. *God Emperor*, 308.

46. The experience of Paul Atreides. *Dune*, 290.

47. The words of The Preacher at Arrakeen, After Harq al-Ad. *Children*, 377.

48. Herbert, *Listening to the Left Hand*.

Bibliography

Abram, D. (1997). *The spell of the sensuous: Perception and language in a more-than-human world.* New York: Vintage.

Agger, B. (1989). *Socio(onto)ology: A disciplinary reading.* Urbana: University of Illinois Press.

Allen, L.D. (1975). *Cliffs Notes on Herbert's Dune and other works.* Cliffs Notes.

Althusser, L. (1986). Ideology and ideological state apparatuses (notes toward an investigation). In J. Handhart (Ed.), *Video culture: A critical investigation* (pp. 56–95). New York: Gibbs M. Smith.

Aristotle. (2002). *Metaphysics* (2nd ed.) (J. Sachs, Trans.). Santa Fe, NM: Green Lion.

Barzun, J., & Graff, H. (1985). *The modern researcher* (p. 207). San Diego, CA: Harcourt Brace Jovanovich.

Bateson, G. (2000). *Steps to an ecology of mind.* Chicago: University of Chicago Press.

Berger, P., & Luckmann, T. (1967). *The social construction of reality: A treatise in the sociology of knowledge.* New York: Anchor.

Bleir, E.F. (Ed.). (1982). *Science fiction writers.* New York: Scribner.

Boise, S. J. (1966). *The art of awareness.* Dubuque, IA: Wm. C. Brown.

Boorstein, D. (1985). *The discoverers.* New York: Random House.

Bothamley, J. (1993). *Dictionary of theories* (p. 248). Detroit: Visible.

Brennan, K. (2006, February 1). "Star Wars Origins: Dune" (Jitterbug Fantasia <http://www.jitterbug.com/origins/dune.html>) 2/1/06.

Brentor, R. (Ed.). (1974). Science fiction and a world in crisis. In *Science fiction, today and tomorrow.* New York: Harper & Row.

Burrell, G., & Morgan, G. (1979). *Sociological paradigms and organizational analysis.* Exeter, NH: Heinemann.

Crusius, T.W. (1991). *A teacher's introduction to philosophical hermeneutics.* Urbana, IL: NCTE.

Deleuze, G., & Guattari, F. (1987). *A thousand plateaus: Capitalism and schizophrenia* (B. Massumi, Trans.). Minneapolis: University of Minnesota Press. (Original work published 1980)

Derrida, J. (1973). *Speech and phenomena: And other essays on Husserl's theory of signs.* Evanston: Northwestern University Press.

Derrida, J. (1976). *Of grammatology* (G. Spivak, Trans.). Baltimore: Johns Hopkins University Press.

During, S. (1991). New historicism. *Text and Performance Quarterly, 11*(3).

Eco, U. (1979). *A theory of semiotics.* Bloomington: Indiana University Press.

Einstein, A. (1920). *Out of my later years.* New York: Random House.

Fisher, D. (1970). *Historian's fallacies: Towards a logic of historical thought.* New York: Harper & Row.

Foucault, M. (1970). *The order of things.* New York: Pantheon.

Foucault, M. (1972). *The archaeology of knowledge.* New York: Pantheon.

Freire, P. (1970). *Pedagogy of the oppressed* (M. Bergman-Ramos, Trans.). New York: Continuum.

Gadamer, H. (1975). *Truth and method.* New York: Seabody.

Gebser, J. (1991). *The ever present origin* (N. Barstad with A. Mickunas, Trans.). Athens: Ohio University Press.

Giroux, H. (1992). *Border crossings: Cultural workers and the politics of education.* New York: Routledge.

Habermas, J. (1984 and 1987). *The theory of communicative action* (Vols. I & II). Boston: Beacon Press.

Habermas, J. (1986). *Knowledge and human interests.* Boston, MA: Beacon Press.

Habermas, J. (1987). *The philosophical discourse of modernity* Cambridge, MA: MIT Press.

Hawkes, T. (1977). *Structuralism and semiotics.* Berkeley: University of California Press.

Hawking, S. (1988). *A brief history of time.* New York: Bantam.

Heidegger, M. (1962). *Being and time* (J. Macquire & E. Robinson, Trans.). New York: Harper and Row.

Heidegger, M. (1977). The question concerning technology (W. Lovitt, Trans). In D. Krell (Ed.), *Martin Heidegger: Basic writings* (pp. 287–317). New York: Harper and Row.

Herbert, B. (1999). *The notebooks of Frank Herbert's Dune* New York: Perigree. (Original work published 1988)

Herbert, B. (2003). *Dreamer of Dune.* New York: Tor.

Herbert, B., & Anderson, K. (2002). *The Butlerian jihad.* New York: Tor.

Herbert, B., & Anderson, K. (2005). *The road to Dune.* New York: Tor.

Herbert, F. (1974). Science fiction and a world in crisis. In R. Brentor (Ed.), *Science fiction, today and tomorrow.* New York: Harper & Row.

Herbert, F. (1987). Listening to the left hand. In T. O'Reilly (Ed.), *Frank Herbert: The maker of Dune.* New York: Berkley Books.

Herbert, F. (1999a). *Dune.* New York: Ace/Berkley. (Original work published 1965)

Herbert, F. (1999b). *Dune messiah.* New York: Ace/Berkley. (Original work published 1969)

Herbert, F. (1999c). *Children of Dune.* New York: Ace/Berkley. (Original work published 1976)

Herbert, F. (1999d). *God Emperor of Dune.* New York: Ace/Berkley. (Original work published 1981)

Herbert, F. (1999e). *Heretics of Dune.* New York: Ace/Berkley. (Original work published 1984)

Herbert, F. (1999f). *Chapterhouse: Dune.* New York: Ace/Berkley. (Original work published 1985)

Hillman, J. (1993). *The thought of the heart and the soul of the world.* Dallas: Spring Publications.

hooks, b. (1990). *Yearning: Race, gender, and cultural politics.* Boston, MA: South End Press.

hooks, b. (1994). Eros, eroticism, and the pedagogical process. In H. Giroux & P. McLaren (Eds.), *Between borders: Pedagogy and the politics of cultural studies* (pp. 113–118). New York: Routledge.

Hourani, A. (1991). *A history of the Arab peoples.* Cambridge: The Belknap Press of Harvard University.

Husserl, E. (1960). *Cartesian meditations.* Dordrecht: Kluwer.

Husserl, E. (1962). *Ideas: General introduction to a pure phenomenology* (R. Gibson, Trans.). New York: Collier. (Original work published 1931)

Husserl, E. (1973). *Experience and judgment* (J. Churchill & K. Ameriks, Trans.). Evanston: Northwestern University Press.

Husserl, E. (1982). *Ideas pertaining to a pure phenomenology and to a phenomeno-logical philosophy: First book* (F. Kersten, Trans.). Boston: Kluwer Academic Publishers.

Husserl, E. (1989). *Ideas pertaining to a pure phenomenology and to a phenomeno-logical philosophy: Second book* (F. Kersten, Trans.). Boston: Kluwer Academic Publishers.

Husserl, E. (1991). *On the phenomenology of the consciousness of internal time.* Dordrecht: Kluwer.

Illich, I. (1973). *Tools for conviviality.* Berkeley: Heyday.

Ingersoll, D., & Matthews, R. (1991). *The philosophical roots of modern ideology: Liberalism, communism, fascism* (pp. 161–162). Englewood Cliffs: Prentice Hall.

Jaeger, W. (1945). *Paideia: The ideals of Greek culture.* New York: Oxford University Press.

Jameson, F. (1991). *Postmodernism or, the cultural logic of late capitalism.* Durham, NC: Duke University Press.

Jung, C.G. (1968). *Man and his symbols.* New York: Dell.

Kress, D.F. (1993). *Martin Heidegger: Basic writings.* San Francisco, CA: Harper.

Lanigan, R. (1988). *Phenomenology of communication: Merleau-Ponty's thematics in communicology and semiology.* Pittsburgh: Duquesne University Press.

Lanigan, R. (1992). *The human science of communicology: A phenomenology of discourse in Foucault and Merleau-Ponty.* Pittsburgh: Duquesne University Press.

Lather, P. (1991). *Getting smart: Feminist research and pedagogy with/in the postmodern.* New York: Routledge.

Lessing, T. (1919). Geschichte als Sinngebung des sinnlosen. Munich: Beck. (Reprinted in Gebser [1991] *The ever present origin* (N. Bartstad and A. Mickunas, Trans.). Athens: Ohio University Press). (Original work published 1949)

Levack, D.J., & Willard, M. (1988). *Dune master: A Frank Herbert bibliography.* Westport, CT: Meckler Press.

Lingis, A. (1983). *Excess: Eros and culture.* Albany: State University of New York Press.

Littlejohn, S., & Foss, K. (2004). *Theories of human communication.* Belmont, CA: Wadsworth.

Lozano, E., & Mickunas, A. (1992). Pedagogy as integral difference. In E. Kramer (Ed.), *Consciousness and culture: An introduction to the thought of Jean Gebser.* Westport CT: Greenwood Press.

Lutz, W. (1996). *The new doublespeak: Why no one knows what anyone's saying anymore.* New York: Harper Collins.

Lyotard, J. (1991). *The inhuman: Reflections on time* (G. Bennington & R. Bowlby, Trans.). Stanford: Stanford University Press.

Lyotard, J. (1992a). *The postmodern condition: A report on knowledge* (G. Bennington & B. Massumi, Trans.). Minneapolis: University of Minnesota Press.

Lyotard, J. (1992b). *The postmodern explained.* Minneapolis: University of Minnesota Press.

Madison, G. (1981). *The phenomenology of Merleau-Ponty.* Athens: Ohio University Press.

Márquez, G.G. (1970). *One hundred years of solitude.* New York: Harper & Row.

McLuhan, M. (1964). *Understanding media: The extensions of man.* New York: McGraw-Hill.

McLuhan, M., & Fiore, Q. (1967). *The medium is the message.* New York: Random House.

Merleau-Ponty, M. (1964a). *Primacy of perception* (J. M. Edie, Trans.). Evanston, IL: Northwestern University Press.

Merleau-Ponty, M. (1964b). *Signs* (R. McCleary, Trans.). Evanston: Northwestern University Press. (Original work published 1960)

Merleau-Ponty, M. (1968). *The visible and invisible* (A. Lingis, Trans.). Evanston, IL: Northwestern University Press.

Merleau-Ponty, M. (1973). *The prose of the world* (J. O'Neill, Trans.). Evanston: Northwestern University Press. (Original work published 1969)

Merleau-Ponty, M. (1989). *Phenomenology of perception* (Colin Smith, Trans.). London: Routledge. (Original work published 1962)

Merleau-Ponty, M. (1993). Eye and mind. In M.B. Smith (Trans.), G. Johnson (Ed.), *The Merleau-Ponty aesthetics reader* (pp. 121–149). Evanston: Northwestern University Press.

Merleau-Ponty, M. (2002). *Husserl at the limits of phenomenology including tests by Edmund Husserl* (L. Lawlor with B. Bergo, eds.). Evanston, IL: Northwestern University Press.

Mickunas, A. (1974, September–October). The primacy of movement. *Main Currents in Modern Thought, 31*(1).

Mickunas, A. (1975, January). Contexts of art interpretation. *Journal of Aesthetic Education, 9*(1).

Mickunas, A. (1976). Human action and historical time. *Research in Phenomenology, 6*(1), 55.

Mickunas, A. (1981, October). *The primacy of expression.* Paper presented at the Circle of Merleau-Ponty Scholars, Colgate University, Hamilton, New York.

Mickunas, A. (1986, March). *Nietzsche and rhetorical aesthetics.* Los Angeles: American Philosophical Association.

Mickunas, A. (1989). Moritz Geiger and aesthetics (E.F. Kaelin & C.O. Shrag, Eds.). *Analectica Husserliana, XXVI,* 43–57.

Mickunas, A. (1991). *The ways of understanding.* Unpublished manuscript.

Mickunas, A. (1991, November). *The cosmic traces.* Society for Phenomenology, University of Memphis, Memphis, TN.

Mickunas, A. (1997). Life-world and history. In B.C. Hopkins (Ed.), *Husserl in contemporary context.* The Netherlands: Kluwer Academic Publishers.

Mickunas, A. (1999). *The primacy of expression.* Unpublished manuscript.

Mickunas, A. (2006, June 10). *Prospects of Husserlian phenomenology.* http://newschool.edu/gf/phil/husserl/Future/Future_Mickunas.html>

Mortimer, J.A., Pirozzolo, F.J., & Mattetta, G.J. (1982). *The aging motor system.* New York: Praeger.

Nicholson, H.B. (2001). *Topilzin Quetzalcoatl: The once and future lord of the Toltecs.* Norman: University of Oklahoma Press.

Nietzsche, F., (1954). *Thus spoke Zarathustra.* New York: Penguin.

Odin, S. (1982). *Process of metaphysics and Hua-yen Buddhism.* Albany: State University of New York Press.

O'Neill, J. (1989). *The communicative body: Studies in communicative philosophy, politics and sociology.* Evanston, IL: Northwestern University Press.

O'Reilly, T. (1981). *Frank Herbert.* New York: Frederick Ungar.

O'Reilly, T. (Ed.). (1987). *Frank Herbert: The maker of Dune.* New York: Berkley Books.

Palumbo, D. (2002). *Chaos theory, Asimov's foundations and robots, and Herbert's Dune.* Westport, CT: Greenwood Press.

Polkinghorne, D. (1983). *Methodology for the human sciences.* Albany: SUNY Press.

Pusey, M. (1987). *Jurgen Habermas.* New York: Tavistock.

Rinzler, J.W. (2005). *The making of Star Wars Revenge of the Sith.* New York: Lucas Books/Del Ray.

Shor, I. (1992). *Empowering education.* Chicago: University of Chicago Press.

Sloterdijk, P. (1987). *Critique of cynical reason.* Minneapolis: University of Minnesota Press.

Smith, B., & Smith, D.W. (1995). *The Cambridge companion to Husserl.* Cambridge: Cambridge University Press.

Smith, M.B. (1993). Merleau-Ponty's aesthetics. In G. Johnson (Ed.), *The Merleau-Ponty aesthetics reader* (p. 203). Evanston: Northwestern University Press.

Spivak, G. (1988). Can the subaltern speak? In C. Nelson & L. Grossberg (Eds.), *Marxism and the interpretation of culture.* Urbana: University of Illinois Press.

Stewart D., & Mickunas, A. (1974). *Exploring phenomenology: A guide to the field and its literature.* Athens: Ohio University Press.

Suzuki, D.T. (1970). *The field of Zen.* New York:

Suzuki, D.T. (1968). *On Indian Mahayana Buddhism.* New York: Harper and Row.

Taussig, M. (1992). *The nervous system.* London: Routledge.

Touponce, W.F. (1988). *Frank Herbert.* Boston: Twayne.

Valdes, M.J. (Ed.). (1991). *A Ricouer reader: Reflection and imagination.* Toronto: University of Toronto Press.

Vico, G. (1968). *The new science* (T. Goddard Bergin & M. Harold Fisch, Trans., 3rd rev. ed.). Ithaca, NY: Cornell University Press.

Walter, N.I.M. (1950). *The sexual cycle of human warfare.* London: Miter Press.

Watts, A. (1966). *The book: On the taboo against knowing who you are.* New York: Vintage Books.

West, C. (1993). *The new cultural politics of difference: Race, identity and representation in education.* New York: Routledge.

Williams, R. (1983). *Keywords: A vocabulary of culture and society* (rev. ed.). New York: Oxford University Press.

Biographies

Kevin Williams

Kevin Williams was born on the same day as Frank Herbert, October 8, but in the year 1963. He is an Associate Professor of Communication and Chair of the Communication Department at Shepherd University, West Virginia. He lives with wife TC, their dog Diggity, and an assorted and sundry collection of "purebred" appalachian mountain cats. He can be reached by email at drkwilliams@mac.com and kwilliam@shepherd.edu. He can be found on the web at http://webpages.shepherd.edu/kwilliam

Danielle Corsetto

It all started with giraffes. Danielle Corsetto started drawing them when she was four and quickly moved on to talking dogs, bugs, horses, unicorns (because like most girls, she went through a "horse phase"), and finally, people. She created her first comic strip when she was eight and never stopped. She now draws and writes "The New Adventures of Bat Boy" for the Weekly World News and her own webcomic, "Girls With Slingshots," three times a week at www.girlswithslingshots.com. Danielle lives in beautiful Shepherdstown with her adopted goldfish, Goldy,  and her pet roommate, Kris. Despite the "classified ad" tone of this bio, she's not looking for a date, but she's flattered that you considered. Your non-date-related e-mails can reach her at dcorsetto@gmail.com.

Casey Forbes

Casey Forbes recently graduated from Shepherd University with a degree in English. He loves traveling and free time, but he decided to trade those luxuries for another degree. His experience in journalism, editing, and theater all point to a continuing career in English. He now attends graduate school to further enrich his love of art and literature.

Author Index

Subject Index

CPSIA information can be obtained
at www.ICGtesting.com
Printed in the USA
FFHW01n0036170718
47400212-50544FF